HER NIGHTLY EMBRACE

HER NIGHTLY EMBRACE

....

THE RAVI PI SERIES

....

ADI TANTIMEDH

LEOPOLDO & CO

—

ATRIA

New York   London   Toronto   Sydney   New Delhi

LEOPOLDO & CO

ATRIA

An Imprint of Simon & Schuster, Inc.
1230 Avenue of the Americas
New York, NY 10020

First Leopoldo & Co/Atria Paperback edition July 2017

LEOPOLDO & CO/ATRIA PAPERBACK and colophon are trademarks of Simon & Schuster, Inc.

For information about special discounts for bulk purchases, please contact Simon & Schuster Special Sales at 1-866-506-1949 or business@simonandschuster.com.

The Simon & Schuster Speakers Bureau can bring authors to your live event. For more information or to book an event contact the Simon & Schuster Speakers Bureau at 1-866-248-3049 or visit our website at www.simonspeakers.com.

Interior design by Amy Trombat

Manufactured in the United States of America

10 9 8 7 6 5 4 3 2 1

The Library of Congress has cataloged the hardcover edition as follows:

Names: Tantimedh, Adi, author.
Title: Her nightly embrace / Adi Tantimedh.
Description: First Leopoldo & Co/Atria Books hardcover edition. | New York : Atria Books, 2016. | Series: Ravi, P.I. ; book 1
Identifiers: LCCN 2016019628| ISBN 9781501130571 (hardback) | ISBN 9781501130588 (paperback) | ISBN 9781501130595 (ebook)
Subjects: LCSH: Private investigators--Fiction. | London (England)--Fiction. | BISAC: FICTION / Mystery & Detective / General. | FICTION / Media Tie-In. | GSAFD: Mystery fiction.
Classification: LCC PS3620.A6955 H47 2016 | DDC 813/.6--dc23
LC record available at https://lccn.loc.gov/2016019628

ISBN 978-1-5011-3057-1
ISBN 978-1-5011-3058-8 (pbk)
ISBN 978-1-5011-3059-5 (ebook)

Dedicated to the memory of my parents
Adisorn and Orasa Tantimedh

HER NIGHTLY EMBRACE

ONE

Before we start, there's something you should know.

I see gods.

Usually in the corner of my eye. They just pop up from time to time, deities from the Hindu pantheon.

I never talk to them. I don't want to.

They never talk to me, just watch in silent judgment. Occasionally they tut-tut and tweet about me to one another on their phones.

I'm not mentally ill. Honest.

Back when this started, I was switching from antipsychotics to mood stabilizers to antianxiety to antidepressant medications before I finally got it under control.

I haven't been seeing many gods lately. That must be a good sign.

"What am I doing with my life . . . ?"

I pushed the thought to the back of my mind as I knocked on the door to the luxury suite.

"Who is it?" The voice of the man in the room was a little high-pitched, nervous. He wasn't expecting anyone.

"Hotel security, sir," I said. "We have reports of a leak downstairs, and it might have come from your bathroom. We need to take a look."

"All right! Hold on!"

I heard a rustling of sheets and grunts as he pulled some clothes on. The man who opened the door was middle-aged, a little pudgy and balding, blinking in a bathrobe.

"Mr. Hollis?"

"Er, yes?"

That was the cue for Hector and Dave to barge in from behind me. They used their fridge-like bodies to push through the door and take Hollis by the arms and carry him into the room. I walked in and put the Do Not Disturb sign out before I shut the door.

"What's going on?" cried the blonde in the bed. She pulled the sheets up to cover herself. Dave and Hector deposited Hollis on the bed next to her. Her name was Bambi. Of course it was. She had, as Dave would say, *big bazongas*.

"Relax, honey," Dave said. "This won't take long."

It was just as well that Dave and Hector dressed like plainclothes cops. They used to be cops, so they still had that vibe. Like them, I was in a suit and tie, so we all maintained a veneer of authority and intimidation.

I snapped a few pictures of Hollis and Bambi with my phone and emailed them back to the agency in London.

We were in the Hilton International Hotel in Midtown Manhattan. I'd spent the last five days tailing Hollis and Bambi, taking pictures of them canoodling in restaurants, kissing in the back of cabs, groping each other at the top of the Empire State Building and the usual tourist spots. Ironically, following them let me do the tourist thing, which I'd never done before in New York.

Dave pulled out a little video camera to film Hollis and Bambi for good measure. He made sure he got a shot of the lines of cocaine on the nightstand and the clothes and underwear scattered on the floor, leaving no room for doubt as to what Hollis and Bambi had been up to.

"Stop! What are you doing?" cried Hollis as he tried to hide his face.

"You motherfuckers!" screamed Bambi. "Get out! Get the fuck out!"

"Bear with us, sweetheart. It'll just take a minute," Hector said as he picked up her clothes and handed them to her.

My phone rang. London. I answered.

"I have Roger here for you," Cheryl, our office manager, said.

"You still there with him, Ravi?" asked Roger, my boss.

"I have eyes on Mr. Hollis."

"Good. Stay on the line. You'll want to watch this." A chuckle came over the phone.

Oh, God. When Roger says that, it means I'm about to witness something horrible. Roger lives for this shit. I don't.

The smartphone on the bedside table rang. Hollis went pale when he saw the number, and answered with shaking hands.

"HOWARD! YOU SHIT! I CAN SEE YOU RIGHT NOW! YOU AND YOUR YANK FLOOZY! DID YOU THINK I WOULDN'T KNOW?"

Margaret Hollis must have been in Roger's office, looking at the photos I had emailed to his computer. It wasn't my idea to barge in on him like this, but she requested that we did to put the fear of Wife into him. Two years' worth of pent-up rage after he smooth-talked and manipulated her into thinking his having a bit on the side was all in her imagination. Now she had hard proof and wanted him to know that he was well and truly fucked. We didn't need speakerphone mode to hear her.

"YOU THINK YOU COULD LIE TO ME ABOUT WHAT YOU WERE UP TO ON THOSE TRIPS TO NEW YORK? CLIENT MEETINGS, MY ARSE! AND WITH MY MONEY! WELL, HOW MUCH DO YOU THINK YOUR BIMBO IS GOING TO LIKE YOU AFTER I STOP YOUR CREDIT CARDS AND FREEZE YOUR BANK ACCOUNT—EH? *EH*?"

"This is too intense for me," Bambi said, who hastily and rather messily pulled her blouse and miniskirt on.

"I'VE GOT YOU NOW, HOWARD! YOU'RE FINISHED, YOU HEAR ME? YOU'LL BE HEARING FROM MY LAWYER! YOU WON'T HAVE A POT TO PISS IN WHEN I'M DONE WITH YOU! ALL THE MONEY CAME FROM MY FATHER, ANYWAY! DID YOU TELL YOUR TART THAT?"

Bambi headed for the door. Hollis started after her, but Hector pushed him back onto the bed as Dave continued to film him.

"Bambi! Wait!" cried Hollis. "Darling! I'll sort it out!"

But she was gone.

"YOUR JOB THAT I GOT YOU IN THE COMPANY? GONE! YOUR SEAT ON THE BOARD? GONE! YOUR CREDIT CARDS? FROZEN! YOUR CLOTHES THAT I BOUGHT YOU? I'M HAVING A BONFIRE IN THE GARDEN TONIGHT!"

"Oh, God!" he cried, and made a lunge for the window. We were on the nineteenth floor. He was that desperate.

"Whoa! Easy there! Settle down!" Dave said.

Dave set the video camera down to help Hector wrestle Hollis away from the window and to the carpet. He made a wailing, keening sound like a dying animal that had been shot. I noticed that the camera was positioned on the bedside table to catch the entire struggle. Dave was a consummate professional, after all. The footage reminded me of BBC nature documentaries in which tigers brought down a hapless gazelle. I could almost imagine David Attenborough narrating.

I'd almost forgotten I was still holding my phone to my ear when Roger's delighted voice came back on.

"Enjoy the show?"

"As train wrecks go, I rate this one a seven," I said.

"Good result, Ravi," he said. "Come on home."

For Roger, it's not a good result unless someone's world ends up in ruins. I looked at Hollis and saw a fat little boy caught with his finger in the cookie jar—whimpering, crying, trying to make mummy feel bad and forgive him. This is what my life had come to.

New York City was such a cultural boiling pot that *all* the gods were here. Not just Hindu gods, but all of them—Chinese gods, Japanese gods, even Yahweh Himself pulling multiple duty for the Jews, the Catholics, the Greek Orthodox, the Lutherans, and what have you. Fortunately, the city was so crowded and everyone was so busy that we could happily ignore each other as we went about our business, so I didn't see any gods all week, and I didn't even have to take my mood stabilizers to make them go away.

Hector and Dave were nice enough to drive me to the airport. They were always happy to meet someone from the London office. I wasn't about to discourage their belief that London was more civilized and cool. They were still a bit punch-drunk from the hotel. We all were.

"So how long you been in the job, Ravi?" Hector asked.

"Six months."

"Seen a dead body yet?" Dave asked.

"Nope. Not planning to."

"Good for you, brother," Hector said. "Dave and me, we saw a ton of stiffs when we were cops. You never forget the smell."

"Smell's the worst," Dave said.

Hector Camacho and Dave Kosinski were like the American versions of Ken and Clive at the London office, ex-cops who had become PIs because they liked to fuck shit up. I suppose every branch of the firm has guys like them. Ken and Clive made me think of violent, muscle-bound versions of the Thompson Twins from the Tintin comics, if the Thompson Twins were a gay couple.

"Now, Ravi," Hector said. "No offense, but you don't got the cop vibe. What did you do before you became a private investigator like us?"

"I was a high school teacher."

Hector, driving, was so shocked that he nearly let go of the wheel to look at me quizzically. I would have hated to die in a crash in the Midtown Tunnel. *I went to New York and all I got was a lousy car accident.*

"You're the new blood in the company and you never had any law enforcement experience?" Dave said.

"Back in the London office, Ken and Clive are the only ex-cops. The rest of us come from different walks of life. Ken and Clive trained us."

"What the hell kind of pool is Roger hiring from these days?" cried Hector.

"Well, the Boy Scouts are still too young," I said. "And too ethical."

That at least got a laugh out of the guys.

"We're just bustin' your balls, brother," Dave said. "You're all right."

"How long did it take you to get your license?" Hector asked.

"I don't have one. You don't need a license to be a private investigator in the UK."

Hector had to struggle to stay in control of the wheel again.

"Are you shitting me? You mean to say any schmuck in England could hang out a shingle and call himself a private eye?"

"Pretty much, yeah. I was surprised, too, when I found out."

"Holy shit, Dave! What are we doing here in New York? We could've been living large in London the last couple years!"

"Yeah! Why didn't anyone tell us sooner?" laughed Dave.

"You know how much time and money it took us to get our licenses?" Hector said. "The hoops we had to jump through? Then how much more it took for us to get permits to carry guns?"

"Well, in the UK, we don't get to carry guns," I said.

"Oh yeah. There's the downside," Hector said.

"Always a downside," Dave sighed.

I was really glad we couldn't carry guns back home. I wouldn't want to be anywhere near Ken and Clive if they had guns.

My mother's words whenever I misbehaved as a child were echoing in my head as I sat in coach on the Virgin flight back to London.

"Child of Kali, sowing chaos and mayhem wherever you go . . ."

I was feeling a bit shit. Did Roger really think I would enjoy watching that poor bastard Hollis see his world come crashing down on him? Was he still trying to toughen me up, teach me something about myself that he thought I didn't already know? My problem wasn't that it shocked or appalled me. My problem was that it *didn't* shock or appall me.

I looked at the photos of Hollis and Bambi on my phone because I just needed to rub my face in my own moral decline.

"Vacation snaps?"

The woman sitting next to me had just the right gleam of mischief in her eyes to pull me out of myself.

"Not my holiday."

"Let me guess. Private eye."

Her name was Ariel Morganstern, and she was from Rhode Island. She had red hair, freckles, a cute overbite, and a tattoo of the goddess Kali on her arm. She wore tight jeans and a black baby-T. She told me she had saved up the money from her banking job, had quit, and was now backpacking around the world.

I envied her.

Having a partner and coconspirator on a boring flight made life bearable.

"Your first time in London, then?" I asked.

"First time in Europe," she said. "I'm so excited. Then it's off to India after that."

"You touring or doing the spiritual journey thing?"

"Spiritual—how'd you guess?"

"Your tattoo. Nobody picks Kali for the hell of it."

"Good eye. Guess that's why you're a detective. Most guys don't really see it. They're usually looking at my boobs."

"I kind of have a relationship with Kali, whether I like it or not," I said. "Word of advice: Don't swim in the Ganges. My relatives never did. If you want to visit ashrams and holy cities, go to Rishikesh."

"Gotcha. So do you live in India?"

"Londoner, born and bred. My parents emigrated from India. We still have a lot of family there."

"Say, what did you mean about 'a relationship with Kali'? That's kind of cryptic. Not everyone talks about the goddess of chaos, death, and rebirth."

The words came out of my mouth before I could stop them:

"I think I blow up people's lives."

She laughed.

"They're usually bad people, but still . . ."

"Do you help people?"

"I try, but I don't know . . ."

She looked at me and didn't seem turned off. Just as well, I didn't tell her that I had a tendency to see gods from time to time. And not in the figurative sense.

"Kali may be a goddess of death, but she's also a goddess of compassion," she said. "She liberates souls from the prison of their egos. Maybe you should remember that."

So that was why she had an elaborate tattoo of Kali on her forearm. Of course I would run into a god even here, after they'd been so quiet on this whole trip.

"I wish I could say that applies to what I do, but I don't think I'm setting anyone free."

What was I doing opening up to a complete stranger on a plane? Maybe it was because we both knew we wouldn't meet again after we get off in London. Maybe I needed to unburden myself of the weight of what I'd been doing since I had gotten the job at the agency.

Instead of recoiling in disgust, Ariel smiled, and it felt like a lifeline.

"I'm only in London for the weekend, then I'm off to Prague. Why don't we hang out before I go? I bet you can find something to help me with."

If this were a magical realist tale full of signs and portents, you might think Kali had sent an angel to reassure me, two nights at the Z Hotel in Piccadilly tracing the details of the mandala tattoos on her naked back and gently tugging on her nipple ring with my teeth, laughing away my existential angst. Skin on skin without malice or guile, solace and kindness, a brief escape but without redemption. Redemption was a myth, anyway. On Saturday, I showed her the sights and took her to my favorite cheap cafés in Soho. *Ariel.* Her name meant "Lion of God," but I saw her as a luminous, mischievous spirit, one that slipped in and out of my life like a dream. By Sunday night, she was gone, flying off as angels do when their work is done. In another life, she might have been a demon, but here she had the right mix of mercy and crazy to help me feel better about myself.

The feeling lasted till I went back to work on Monday and stepped into the next pile of insane shit that made up my life these days.

Do you still wonder why I hired you?" Roger asked.

I was not sufficiently over my jet lag for this kind of powwow in the boss's office.

"To appeal to clients from India and to South Asian clients, in general."

"Come off it. You're not the only Indian or Pakistani candidate we interviewed. Why do you think I picked you, a former schoolteacher, over the other ones?"

"Is this a trick question, boss?"

"Think about it. You're a smart lad. Well-read, well traveled. Head filled with books and Literature. Good people skills. Looks that are catnip to the ladies. You've probably read some Dashiell Hammett and Raymond Chandler, haven't you?"

"Yeah, but I never believed real-life detectives were like the books."

"Too right. We're a grubby, corrupt, disreputable lot, and you're a nice, middle-class lad with debts who's landed in our patch."

"Well, I'm not planning to work here forever."

Roger smiled at that. He liked to collect strays with skills. Brilliant fuckups with nowhere else to go. He'd opened the Golden Sentinels Private Investigations Agency with Cheryl Hughes as his office manager and Ken and Clive as his investigators back in the late 1980s in a tiny office near Fleet Street. Now he had expanded to this trendy space in Farringdon with immaculate décor and feng shui—and to offices across the world.

"Give up?" He was relishing this too much. "I hired you because you have no agenda."

"My agenda is to pay off my overdraft."

"No, that's your goal. You have no ulterior motive, you want to do your job well, and you're not using it as a stepping-stone to gain power or start a political career or start your own firm. That sets you apart from everyone else here, including me."

"And is that good or bad?"

"That's for you to decide, old son. I may not be the most observant Jew in the world, but even I know a mensch when I see one, and I reckon having one around here might be a good thing."

"For what, to be your conscience?"

"For a fresh perspective."

"I'm not sure I follow."

"You might have noticed that everyone here is an outsider. Ken and Clive were drummed out of the Met for being dodgy coppers. The rest of you lot are outcasts, misfits, and cock-ups. I would love to be welcomed into the Establishment. I've made friends with them, hidden their dirty laundry, provided them with services and information to help them get a leg up, but I know I'll never be fully accepted by them. Because I'm Jewish. Doesn't matter that my family's been here for generations, practically built Brick Lane back in the day. And you, Ravi, are also an outsider. You're just very good at hiding it."

"I'm not hiding anything."

"I know. You're an open book. But you haven't really read yourself, have you? You're not ordinary, my old son. Otherwise you would have found a normal job. I don't hire 'normal.' "

"So what's not normal about me?"

"You have the makings of a superb bringer of chaos. That's your special talent."

"You think that's a good thing for the firm?"

"Could be. I suggest you get used to it. Embrace it."

I had a mental flash of myself as an emissary of the goddess Kali, bringer of death and rebirth. Then I thought of Eris, the Greek goddess of chaos and discord. Discordia. This was not how people tended to think of themselves. The scary thing was that the idea didn't scare me. That couldn't be good. It was good for Roger, though. Chaos was his business model, his opportunity, his world. His love.

"Why are you bringing this up now?" I asked.

"Because you're about to move up a notch, Ravi. I'm making you the primary on a high-profile case we're getting today, and I want you on point."

"Thanks for the vote of confidence. Who's the client?"

"Technically, the client is the Tory Party. Mucho moolah. They're paying us from the party coffers, so don't be afraid to go all out. We're going to charge them top rate. Rupert Holcomb is in a spot of bother and needs our help."

Blimey. Our next prime minister, or so the papers would have had us believe. Rupert Holcomb, conservative MP for the London borough of Haddock West, one of the safest Tory seats in the universe. The party's latest Great White Hope. No scandals, no skeletons in his closet, no sex with farm animals (or at least, no photos of the deed), the very picture of a pleasant blandness that every party tried to find in their brightest stars these days. The one thing that gave his public image an edge was his relationship with the late supermodel and "It Girl" Louise Fowler. Everyone envied the lucky bastard for pulling her. By all accounts they were genuinely in love. Then she died from cancer, diagnosed too late. That added some pathos to his profile. He nursed her to the very end, and that won him a load of sympathy from female voters. All the market research proved it.

"So what does he need our help for?" I asked.

"I'll leave him to tell you about it. Now, I already pumped you up as one of our brightest young stars in the agency, so don't cock this up."

"Right. No pressure."

Just my job on the line, that was all.

Holcomb came into the office with his party whip, Hugh McLeish, and a couple of minders. It was McLeish who made the decision to hire us. He was obviously the real power here, grooming Holcomb and keeping him on the straight and narrow in preparation for declaring his candidacy for prime minister at the next general election. McLeish, hatchet man and inquisitor of the party, was the one who strong-armed Holcomb into coming in, and was here to hold his hand. We escorted them into the conference room. Cheryl served tea and sat down to take notes.

As soon as Holcomb sat down, the smooth, media-trained façade slipped. His body language changed. His shoulders sagged and he slumped in the chair. He looked small, haunted, and desperate.

I wondered what Holcomb's dilemma was. Someone blackmailing him? Compromising photos to track down? A missing person he needed to find? Background check on someone in his life to see if they were who they claimed to be? I reckoned it would fall into the usual range of problems a public figure like him would encounter, and it would be up to me to help him find the answer and keep it out of the papers. This would be another of those things that the general public would never hear about, if we did our job properly.

"My dead girlfriend is having sex with me in my sleep!"

. . . *Ah.*

Thanks a lot, Roger!

I stayed composed, allowing nothing stronger than mild surprise to show on my face.

"We already told Roger . . . Mr. Golden . . . ," stammered Holcomb.

"Yes." I put on my most reassuring smile. "But tell me, from the top. Take your time. You might recall certain details you missed the last time."

"It's Louise," the client said. "For the past month, she has been coming to my bed at night, and . . ."

He choked again.

"So your dead girlfriend has been coming to your bed at night."

I had to say it out loud just to see how it sounded. Nope, it didn't make me feel any less out of my depth.

"Yes, yes. It sounds mad, but it's true. She's been coming to me at night and—and, well, she has been, er, making love to me."

"I see," I said, struggling to maintain my poker face. "Could this be a recurring dream? I mean, wouldn't it be better to consult a psychiatrist? Or, if you believe it's . . . something else, an exorcist?"

"It's real, damn it!" he cried. "I know it's been happening while I'm asleep. It's . . . how do I put this . . . When you've been with someone long enough, you come to know their habits, their touch, their perfume . . ."

His face went tomato red as he stammered, and finally his ability to talk shut down. He probably would have been a lot less embarrassed if he were talking about getting mugged or blackmailed, but this was way out of his league.

And mine, too, but I wasn't about to admit that. It was my job to reassure him and tell him I was going to solve his problem. The best I could do here was pretend that I would.

"I can vaguely recall it happening, just on the edge of sleep! I never woke up! And there's—there's physical proof the morning after, when I wake up!"

"Physical proof."

"Yes, there's—the sheets are sticky when I wake up, and I can even smell her perfume, the brand that Louise always wore. It's always the same!"

"So how many times have these . . . incidents occurred so far?"

Holcomb looked to McLeish for support. McLeish only shot him a look like a serpent about to strike.

"Over five months now. They started two months after Louise's funeral."

"And how often do they occur?" I asked.

"On average once a week, sometimes twice. I never know when it might happen, some nights pass without incident, and I'm worrying myself sick wondering whether it might happen or not!"

"And you're always semiconscious when they happen?"

"You have to understand, my work is very tiring. I usually have to take medication in order to have a good night's sleep."

"What kind of medication?"

"Sleeping pills, over-the-counter stuff. Sometimes I need something stronger, like Valium."

"Anything else?"

Holcomb clammed up, embarrassed.

"Rupert has also taken Rohypnol on occasion," said McLeish.

"I know people call it a date-rape drug. It's prescribed by my doctor," Holcomb said, defensive. "I only use it for myself. It doesn't give me a headache like zolpidem does. I have all of them, and all prescribed by my doctor."

"No one's accusing you of anything, Mr. Holcomb," I said. "When was the last time you had an incident?"

"A week ago."

"Have you thought of hiring bodyguards? You know, to watch over your flat at night, make sure no one's breaking in?"

"My life isn't being threatened!" Holcomb said.

"But your sanity is," I said.

"Rupert's image depends on his accessibility and availability to the general public," McLeish said. "If the press find out that he has to have bodyguards with him, if they just get one photo, they can make him out to look snobbish, self-important, standoffish—at worst, insecure and paranoid."

I had to stop myself from agreeing too much that those last two qualities were already true.

"I need you to get to the bottom of this," Holcomb said. "I mean, it can't be true, can it? It can't be happening, and yet it is!"

"I don't think any of us in this room genuinely thinks it's a ghost," McLeish said. "So either someone has been playing tricks on Rupert, either to blackmail or humiliate him, or Rupert has been working too hard and having strange dreams. We want to resolve this quietly, but first we need to know exactly what's happening."

"Well, then," I said. "Leave it with me. I'd like a list of people you think might have it in for you, Mr. Holcomb, and we'll start from there. Before you go, Cheryl will draw up a contract, a client agreement, for use of our services. I'll contact you the moment I find anything."

Roger and I walked them out. We shook hands, made more reassuring sounds, and watched them leave. Then Roger winked at me and went back into his office. Cheryl went back to her desk like this was just another day at the office.

Seriously. *What the fuck?*

Walking back to my desk felt like a death march.

Granted, it was as pleasant a death march as you could get, with our open-space design where everyone was encouraged to share information and the latest designer ergonomic furniture. You'd think we were a tech start-up or PR firm rather than a detective agency.

Tailing adulterous spouses I could handle. Going through someone's trash to retrieve shredded documents and taping them back together I could handle. Distracting a target in a public place while Benjamin cloned his phone, I could handle. Interviewing people in search of lies and motive I could handle—Ken and Clive had trained me in that. But this? This was gonzo bullshit. Frankly, Holcomb needed psychiatric help more than a private investigator. I could tell from his demeanor he was clearly an addict. He should be in rehab. Instead his party was paying us—me—a ridiculous amount of money to track down a ghost. A sexy ghost. A ghost that fucked him in his sleep.

Of course it wasn't a ghost. It had to be someone fucking with him. (Pun intended.) I just had to find out who would have it in for him to come up with such a ridiculous scheme, simply to mess with his head. They would have to know how unstable he was to start with.

Time to start researching him while I waited for McLeish's office to email me the list of people I could interview. Research here often meant typing a search on the Internet. You'd be surprised how much of our work involves just looking up information online these days. Most of the time you could find most of the information you needed on someone that way. We often told prospective clients about that to give them a chance to save their money.

Everyone in the office was going to give me shit about this. Cheryl had quietly warned me that my number was up and Roger was going to throw me into the deep end of a fucked-up case. The rest of the gang had been there longer than I had and had all gone through that trial by fire. The ones that didn't get a result were let go, which opened up room for me.

Fortunately, the gang was busy. Even as I was looking up Holcomb's background, Olivia Wong and my evil brother-in-arms Benjamin Lee were at their desks double-teaming on an embezzlement case, tracking some missing finances to a shell company in the Isle of Wight using a bot Olivia had written that tracked their transactions. David Okri was out doing whatever it was Roger always had him out doing, which often involved wining and dining the rich and powerful. Mark Oldham was out recovering a stolen Frida Kahlo painting for the Mexican ambassador to London. Mark was quite brilliant when you got him to stop smoking weed for ten minutes. He seemed to breeze through every case handed to him as if it were just a game or distraction from his next joint and game of *FIFA* on the PlayStation when he got home.

"Take not my meager pleasures from me," he would say. "Lest I succumb to eternal despair."

Only Marcie Holder was idle, reading the old copy of *The Art of Being and Becoming* I'd lent her. Given how existential this job was, I assumed she was taking comfort in Sufi enlightenment as a respite from dealing with her long list of celebrity clients.

"I'm waiting for Ken and Clive to report in," she said. "Till then, I got nothing to do."

Marcie was our token American in the agency. She was one of those ex-pats who moved to London and liked it here so much she went semi-native, adopted many of our characteristics and ways but holding on to her American accent and identity. She originally had a cushy gig in PR, but some disastrous campaign whose details she still won't fill us in on cost her that job and she wound up here. All in all, she seemed to be one of those eternally cheerful people who always landed upwards as if that was their natural progress in life. Maybe it's an American thing.

Marcie handled celebrities. She brought along her contact list when Roger hired her, and her job was to protect the clients from scandals, clean up their dirty laundry. Every now and then the rest of us would partner up with her to help out. I can tell you that whatever notions of glamour we had about celebrities washed away very quickly once we were on a couple of Marcie's cases. I often came away from them with the urge to shower. Celebrities had way too much to hide, and for Marcie—and the agency—business was booming.

But there had to be more to her than this. Roger didn't hire cream puffs. If there was one thing that I had learned about my coworkers, it was that everyone here was a brilliant fuckup with nowhere else to go. And fuckups are dark, dark people. We're all good at smiling, wearing a smart suit we got from our clothing allowance and presenting a cool front, but the clients should never see how we get our results, or how we behave off-hours.

Marcie was on a stalking case. A singer had hired her to find and stop the guy who was casing her social media accounts, camping outside the clubs she went to, leaving decapitated Barbie dolls and sliced-up photos of her on her doorstep. Marcie and Olivia found the guy through his email and Facebook page within a day. Marcie sent Ken and Clive out to his address to give him a talking-to that morning.

"So what's our next PM like?"

"Frankly, I'm not impressed. If he's the best and brightest there is in the political landscape, we are in deep shit."

"In the flesh, he looks like whatever charisma he has was bought in a can from the Harvey Nichols Men's Care department," Olivia said.

"And now it's my job to pull a thorn from his paw," I muttered.

"That just makes him owe us. Or rather, owe Roger," Olivia said.

"If Roger has his way, everyone who's anyone would owe him." Marcie winked.

"Attention, everyone," Cheryl said. "Roger is making Mr. Holcomb an A-1 priority, so if you've finished your current caseload or are at a loose end, he expects you to give Ravi any backup with your expertise when needed."

"Shouldn't we just outsource this to the Ghostbusters?" Benjamin said.

"Ha-bloody-ha," I said. "Well, McLeish's people just emailed me some credentials, so I'm off to interview Holcomb's fellow politicians."

In the cab to Westminster, my mum called.

"Ravi, darling, I hate to trouble you when you're so busy, but Mrs. Dhewan is getting a bit aggressive."

"I warned you not to fuck with the Asian Housewife Mafia." I sighed.

Mrs. Dhewan was the neighborhood loan shark, middle class as they came, down to an ironclad set of rules to which she insisted everyone stick.

"They're my friends. It was just a few card games."

"A few card games? What about that loan for Sanjita's wedding? We're talking over twenty grand!"

"Yes, Ravi, shout it out loud so I don't forget."

"Mum—"

"Shout it from the rooftops so everyone knows, just in case I'm not embarrassed enough already."

"Have you told Dad yet?"

"Of course not. He'll just give me the same grief you're giving me, and God knows what he'll do."

"He'd just say you made your bed, now lie in it, and thank God you two don't have a joint bank account. You know I'm going to tell him, right?"

"Oh, darling, can you not? Can't we quietly sort this out?"

"By 'we' you mean me."

"I've started seeing a counselor."

"Good. The way addiction runs in our family, we don't need you becoming a full-on gambling addict. If Dad realizes that, he'll probably buy you a one-way plane ticket to Las Vegas and be done with it."

"You say that like it's a bad thing."

I sighed.

"Has Mrs. Dhewan started threatening you outright? Threatening notes? Flaming dog shit through the letterbox?"

"Not as such, but every conversation I've had with her has that little tinge, you know? She could kill my standing in the community with just a bit of nasty gossip. 'That Mrs. Singh, she's a gambling addict, terrible with money . . .'"

"All right, tell Mrs. Dhewan I'll go see her soon. No, better yet, tell her I'll take her to tea at Fortnum's."

"Oh, that will impress her."

"I'll see if I can work out a deal."

"Let's keep this between us for now," Mum said. "We don't want to worry your father, too."

"How is he? Did you finally get him to see the doctor?"

"It was like pulling teeth, Ravi. I had to tell the doctor how tired he'd been and it hurt to pee. The doctor has ordered tests."

"All right. Keep me posted."

My mother was normally quite rational. She was a teacher, after all. I suppose I became one to follow her footsteps and also to appease her and my dad when they kept asking what I was going to do with my life when I had my breakdown and dropped the religious studies. When you're Asian and middle class, you are expected to pick one of five white-collar careers: doctor, lawyer, engineer, architect, or banker. My father actually hoped I would pursue a PhD in religious studies and follow his footsteps as a religious scholar. Otherwise, my parents might have been happy with accountant, but I wasn't that into money. With my interest in literature, Dad and Mum might have settled for my becoming a published author, if only so that Mum could brag to her friends. Much as I liked to study stories and narrative, I wasn't really into writing fiction, so that was out. Getting my teaching qualifications and teaching secondary school was the compromise that suited me for a while; this allowed me to hide the craziness and dysfunctions at my core that I'd spent my years at university fully indulging. I did not see any gods during the years I was a teacher. Then I tried to protect a student from the teacher she was having sex with, handled it wrong, and ended up losing my job. That put me back to square one.

Not only did I have my own overdraft to pay off, but there was also the bill for my sister's fuck-off extravagant wedding. My parents just had to plan a big sodding traditional wedding for my sister so they could show off to friends and the family who flew in from India just how right they'd done by Little Sanjita. Dad was semiretired from academia, Mum was long retired from teaching, so as the oldest son, I couldn't not take up that burden. And now Mum's gambling debts, as well.

Do you see why I needed this job at the agency now? Why I couldn't afford to fail this case and get the sack? Digging up secrets, helping the rich and powerful with their dirty laundry, finding leverage against their enemies—a far cry from teaching secondary school in North London. A completely new life and career, the old one left behind like a burned bridge and somehow I didn't miss it as much as I thought I would. Two, three cases, and I could pay off all those debts with my bonuses. Now another twenty grand I had to pay off.

I just hoped I had enough of a soul left by the end of it. With luck, there might be some enlightenment, too. That would be nice.

I got out of the cab at Westminster—smart suit, notebook, briefcase, the picture of a serious junior political correspondent doing a profile on Rupert Holcomb. The secret to good social engineering was to look the part and walk the walk. Interview Holcomb's colleagues. McLeish had told them I was a sympathetic writer for a regional party paper and that they should afford me every courtesy. No one would ever assume you weren't what you claimed to be. By the end of the meeting, they wouldn't remember who you were, and you were home free.

Gentle softball questions about Rupert Holcomb's character. *What's he like? Anything weird about him? Who hates him?* His overall personality. His reputation among his peers. His haters called him "an empty suit," "bereft of any ideas of his own," "soulless." The usual stuff. Nothing that stood out at all. After the pedophile scandals, the years of media training and paranoia, it was typical that they would choose a candidate who was as bland as ever, as he expounded the usual party line about privatizing the entire country into oblivion, killing the welfare state and gutting the NHS, privatizing the educational system and everything you expect of a party that was dead set on turning Britain back into a Dickensian dystopia. Of course he didn't have the vision to think up those policies himself; they were obviously the work of the think tanks the party was into at the time. He was just the prompter monkey and thus was selected for his sheer dullness. I imagine his enemies in the party were just sucking sour grapes that he was picked to be poster boy over them.

At the end of the day, I could only come to one conclusion about Holcomb:

Christ, what a boring bastard.

He was too boring to have any truly interesting enemies. It was as if they couldn't be bothered to make the effort. Politicians are notoriously lacking in imagination, and there wasn't a single one of them I met who could possibly dream up a way to fuck Holcomb up with a plot involving a sexy ghost in his bedroom at night.

A whole day in the seat of government talking to everyone who mattered and I'd gotten precisely nowhere.

Pretty much like the government, really.

Since I could eliminate Holcomb's peers in Westminster from the suspect list, I had to consider the celebrity scandal angle. What if whoever was out to stitch up Holcomb was jealous that he had landed someone as fit as Louise and not them. An obsessed fan like one of Marcie's cases, perhaps? This seemed unlikely, though, since that kind of perp would be actively stalking Holcomb and sending him threatening notes. Alas, there were no threats against Holcomb, or we would have been hired to track those down. I had to start looking at Louise Fowler.

I hated interviewing grieving family members. It was almost impossible not to look like an opportunistic dickhead, especially if the deceased was famous.

A cursory Web search on Louise's career and tabloid exploits in the cab ride to her parents' house turned up a surprisingly mild record of antics and scandals. Her raciest photo shoots never veered beyond the tasteful side (but were still enough to be voted prime wank material for boys and men across the land). She had had a brief tryst with a Premier League footballer that ended when he couldn't take other blokes eyeing her and he got suspended for lamping some poor sod in a club over her. She had worked her way through an entire boy band, though they all ended it amicably and she stayed mates with the lot of them, even appearing in several of their music videos. Hints of mild drug dependency with stays in rehab. She hosted a few shows on fashion and lifestyle for satellite television, never starred in reality shows despite loads of offers. Lots of chatter expressing bewilderment when she began to go out with Holcomb and they announced their engagement.

Might as well get this bit over with.

Parents' house. Talk to them to get a picture of what Louise was like.

Nobody in.

Two minutes ringing the doorbell when her voice came up behind me.

"Hello? Can I help you?"

You could tell she was Louise's sister. Twenties. Graduate student in Literature. Similar lips and cheekbones, though without the smoothing-out from the plastic surgeon, same blond hair and sharp, intense blue eyes. Even in just jeans and a black jacket, she stopped the world.

"I'm looking for Mr. and Mrs. Fowler?"

"They're away on holiday. What's this about?"

"You're Julia, right? I'd like to talk to you about your sister."

"Oh, Christ, just piss off. We said we didn't want the press coming round."

"I'm not a journalist. I'm a private investigator."

I handed her my card. No lies, no cover story, no social engineering with her. Best to be honest here. She looked the type who could smell bullshit coming a mile off.

"I'm looking into whether someone might use your sister to hurt Rupert Holcomb and his reputation."

Fortunately for me, "private investigator" turned out to be a couple of rungs higher up in her estimation than "journalist."

"I suppose you'd better come in," she said.

Julia poured tea as we sat in the living room. She let me flip through a scrapbook of Louise's modeling photos. There was a progression of more punk, rock-and-roll fashions when she was young, moving to more upmarket designer labels as she became mainstream. There were framed photos of some of her magazine covers and shoots on the wall, including the swimsuit photos, all taking pride of place.

"Rupert has someone that hates him that much?"

"That's what I'm trying to find out."

"Unless he finally grew a personality, I can't imagine," she said.

"Did Louise have any ex-boyfriends or people who might have wanted to hurt her or her reputation?"

"No, she was on good terms with everybody. That's why people liked working with her. She was a real sweetheart."

"I can see why Holcomb fell for her. Then again, who wouldn't?"

"That's charisma for you. Lou had dollops of it."

"What do you think she saw in him?"

"The heart wants what it wants." She shrugged.

"There don't seem to be any photos of Louise as a kid here."

"The baby and childhood photos are in the master bedroom. Dad prefers to remember her before she declared war on him. That really kicked off when she first became a model. Sex, drugs, unsuitable boyfriends . . ."

"Yeah, I remember seeing those stories in the papers and *Popbitch*." Julia laughed.

I imagined Louise hovering behind Julia, watching intently as her sister answered my questions. Louise was dead but far from gone, her presence all over this house. Julia was still protecting Louise. Holcomb certainly believed this was a literal ghost story.

"We were dead surprised when she landed Rupert and calmed down. They met at some book launch party. He worshipped the ground she walked on. She had that effect on people."

"So why didn't she marry him? He certainly wanted to."

"She used to say that marriage was an institution used to control women. I think on a certain level she was afraid that, well, marrying him might hurt his career."

"Really? I would think marrying a supermodel would have done wonders for his career."

"All right, the truth is, she was already dying. Her cancer was at a late stage, and she didn't want to burden him by making him a widower."

"She really did love him."

"For all the good it did her," Julia said. "No, he made her happy. Can't ask more than that, can we?"

Once Julia believed I meant her and her family no harm, she warmed up and leaned in close as we spoke. Flirting seemed to be second nature to her.

"Glad you didn't think I was here to rob the place."

"What, a nice English boy like you?"

"Don't think anyone's called me an English boy before."

"Why not? We're all children of the Empire."

That smile, the type of smile that men in medieval times would slay dragons just to be blessed with.

"Well, thanks for your time," I said.

"No problem. I'm not a huge fan of Rupert's, but I don't want him to get hurt. It's already bad enough that he's such a . . . a . . ."

"Boring bastard?"

"Yes!" she laughed. "We are awful."

"That we are," I said.

As I walked away, I thought I felt her eyes still on me. I turned and saw her still at the door, waiting for me to look back at her.

She smiled, that smile again, and went inside.

THREE

The next morning, I got back to the office to log my notes. Ken and Clive were back from Marcie's errand.

"Sorted that stalker out, then?" I asked.

"He won't be stalking anyone for a very long time," said Ken, rubbing his bruised knuckles.

"Or using a computer," Clive said.

"Or eating solid food," Ken said.

"Shouldn't you put some ice on those knuckles?" I asked.

"Nah," Ken sneered. "He was like a fucking pillow."

Ken and Clive were brick shithouses. You definitely did not want them laying a hand on you. If you ever saw them coming after you, you'd run. But that would only piss them off and make them chase you, and their years as coppers meant they had a really good chance of catching you. And when they caught you, they would really want to lay their hands on you. You couldn't win if Ken and Clive ever set their sights on you. The lesson was never to give them a reason to come after you. I made it a point to live by that rule.

I walked over to Marcie's desk.

"What are you watching?" I asked.

"It's a Literary Terror flash mob."

On her computer, a video uploaded from a phone. About a dozen young men descended on a Central London bookshop and trashed the cardboard standee of Delia McCarthy, the talk show host. They proceeded to attack the table that held copies of Delia's latest lifestyle book, howling and singing as they ripped the pages up and tossed them into the air. Then just as suddenly, they ran out of the shop before the police arrived.

"Literary terror. Huh," I said.

"A troll threatened Delia on Twitter that this was going to happen. He also doxxed her last week and she had to move to a hotel," Marcie said.

"Have you asked Olivia to help tracking him?"

"She's still busy on her case. Dude, I could use a hand on this. You were a teacher: you know the literary world better than me."

"Once I get some traction on Holcomb, I'll see what I can do," I said.

As I typed my interview notes into my computer, David came running up like I'd eaten the last Jammie Dodger in the pantry.

"I can't believe Roger gave you the Holcomb case! You're not even a Tory voter!"

"And thank fuck for that," I said.

"It should have been me!"

"David, you're a lawyer. Investigations aren't your specialty."

"But I know the ins and outs of the party!" he protested.

Out of all of us, David was the one who was obviously using this job at the agency as a stepping-stone to a political career later down the line. He and I went way back to university. When I lost my teaching job, he was the one who hooked me up with Roger. His parents were from Nigeria and his family was well connected, so David was under pressure to go far. He had a law degree and was really more the agency's legal advisor than an investigator, but Roger liked to mix everyone's roles up. Roger knew David's parents and hired him for the access to certain people with power and money—Roger's two favorite things.

"Really, you don't want this one, mate," I said.

"Oh yeah? What is it? A leaked document? Compromising photos? Could be well tasty."

"Dead girlfriend having sex with him."

David did a double take.

"What?"

"Nocturnal emissions of the ghostly kind," Mark said woozily from his desk.

David tried to speak, but his brain short-circuited. He just walked back to his desk.

"Still should have given it to me," he muttered.

Roger, who must have overheard David and me, since his door was open, decided to come out and grace us with his presence. His Majesty wanted a progress report.

"I ran a theory that this might be some kind of honeytrap," I said. "Russians might do that kind of thing, but normally they'd just throw a woman at a guy, none of this sneaking in while he's unconscious stuff. The point is to have him hooked on the woman. So that's out."

"Too right," Roger said. "As convenient as it would be to have a future prime minister in your pocket, it's too early to go for Holcomb. He hasn't officially declared his candidacy yet, and the party can still decide not to run him if they decide he's too unsafe or unstable."

"So the best angle is still a campaign to smear him or drive him mad, as McLeish thinks," I said. "But if anyone wanted to discredit him, it'd be easier to set him up in public to say the wrong thing or fall over and look stupid, not in the privacy of his home at night where there are no witnesses.

"All solid theories," Roger said. "Where do they leave us?"

I could only shrug.

"Keep plugging," Roger said, and went back to his office.

Yeah. No pressure.

Olivia came over and plopped a small pile of printouts on my desk.

"Little prezzie, babes."

"What's all this?"

"Holcomb's medical records. My fortune-teller said I should give you a hand. Hitch my wagon to your star, as it were."

"Fortune-teller? You believe in that?"

"Not really. It's more a habit."

"How did you get all this?"

She shrugged, all coy. Whenever Olivia got coy, it meant she had just broken the law and gotten away with it. To the world, she looked like a respectable professional Chinese girl in librarian glasses, a Gucci dress, and designer heels, but when she was a teenager, she was one of the most notorious hackers in the world. She was so good that she never got caught, never bragged on forums, and always covered her tracks. Somehow, Roger sniffed her out—turned out he knew her parents, upper-middle-class bankers from Hong Kong who were early clients of his. He hired her when she graduated from LSE with the offer that he would let her use her bag of black-hat tricks to sniff out all kinds of financial and personal secrets that she might use on her way to becoming a power player in the business world.

"I was online looking into some bank records for my client. Thought I'd root around for you while I was at it."

We studied Holcomb's medical history together. No history of mental illness. Slight high blood pressure. High cholesterol. Some hypertension. Sleep apnea. He'd even had an MRI scan. No brain tumors. No neurological issues. Physically, he was normal.

"He had referrals to a Harley Street psychiatrist but never went," Olivia said.

"Typical," I said.

That's the sad thing about the British," Mark said. "We all fucking need therapy, but very few of us go."

"He doesn't strike me as mentally ill," I said. "Addicted to meds, but not mad."

"Aside from being a politician, you mean?" Mark said. "That probably means some serious pathologies right there."

"Take a look at his prescriptions," Olivia said with some glee.

"Bloody hell."

"He roofies himself to sleep?" Marcie said. "This gets better and better."

"Does this firm ever get normal people for clients?" I mused.

"The rich and powerful are not normal people," Mark said. "Normal people can't afford us."

I had a thought.

"Marcie, put a call out to your tabloid contacts, *Popbitch*. See if they're looking for dirt on Holcomb, or if anyone's offering to sell any."

"On it." She picked up her phone. "His star is on the rise. Now would be the time for a juicy scandal."

"Normally they'd be hiring *us* to dig up dirt," Mark said.

Cheryl walked over and looked at the printouts Olivia gave me.

"You done with that, dear?"

"Er, yeah."

"Good."

She snatched up the file, went over, and stuck it into the paper shredder.

"Don't want it hanging about to incriminate us, do we?" she said, and returned to her desk.

"I looked at Holcomb's financials," Olivia said. "Nothing out of the ordinary there."

If there were any financial irregularities, Olivia would have sniffed it out.

"I hope you remembered to erase your digital footprints, darling!" Cheryl said.

"Yes, Cheryl!" Olivia said, rolling her eyes.

"Always, Cheryl!"

"There's a good girl," Cheryl said, and walked back to her desk.

Olivia had a problem with Cheryl. Olivia had a problem with any woman who had authority over her, because as far as she was concerned, she was the one with authority, and the sooner the world knew that, the better.

"She's been with Roger since the beginning," whispered Mark. "Back when they were a little office off Fleet Street in the late eighties."

"They only had Ken and Clive in the old days," whispered Marcie. "And went from that rinky-dink little shithole to this place."

"So she knows where all the bodies are buried," Mark said.

"Wait, do you mean that literally?" Now even I couldn't help whispering.

"All the bodies," Mark and Marcie said in unison.

We glanced at Cheryl in awe and perhaps a little healthy fear.

She didn't look up.

Had she heard us?

She didn't let on.

"Do not. Ever. Piss her off," Marcie whispered.

"'Ere, mate, what are you doing on the stakeout front?" asked Benjamin, who had been conspicuously silent up till that point.

"I haven't thought about that yet."

"Got you sorted there." He grinned. "Just got the latest model surveillance gear. Gagging to try them out. How about we visit Maison Holcomb?"

Holcomb had given me permission to look over his flat in Pimlico for clues. The porter let us in, and Benjamin immediately started scoping out the best places to hide his new sound-activated webcams and microphones. Holcomb was away in Surrey canvassing and staying in the local Holiday Inn. I was still not inclined to treat this case as a ghost story but more as a locked-room mystery. Was this Phantom Louise only coming to fuck Holcomb in his flat, or was it following him around? If it was just in this flat, then it wasn't a haunting so much as someone who could only count on getting away with raping him here. Too many unknown factors in a strange hotel room, too many chances of getting caught.

I got a look at Holcomb's medicine cabinet. It was an addict's treasure chest, huge selection of prescription medications, all downers and sleep aids, Opiate City. My former students would have nicked all of this and sold it in school for a small fortune, and also kept a bit of it to use themselves.

Benjamin's cams and mikes were tiny, barely the size of a fingernail.

"The video uploads straight to our server at the office, so we can just review the footage on the computers," Benjamin said. "Bang! Bob's yer uncle. We stay on the case and get to keep our social lives."

Benjamin was our tech and surveillance expert, a snarky Chinese lad from Peckham. Oil and water in contrast with Olivia. He was hardware. She was software. GCHQ had tried to recruit him, but he preferred the private sector. "Can't be arsed to sign the Official Secrets Act," he said.

He was like James Bond's Q—if Q had the soul of a juvenile delinquent. He wasn't malicious, per se, but he loved mischief, especially the types of mischief you could get up to with the latest tech. And he loved his new, flashy tech, always upgrading, always ordering new gear with the expense account Cheryl allowed him because he always got results. I hate to admit it, but he was like my evil twin brother. Out of everyone at the agency, he was the one I had the most fun with, definitely a bad influence.

"Ken and Clive would call us soft for not spending all night freezing our bollocks off watching the flat from across the street," I said.

"Sod 'em! This is the twenty-first century!"

Benjamin hid another webcam up on the ceiling light.

"Clients want the old familiar stuff with newfangled bells and whistles," he said. "It's like buying a new car. Everyone likes a New Car Smell."

He opened his laptop to check the stream. There we were in 4K, standing in Holcomb's bedroom from the HDTV's point of view.

"We are the New Car Smell," he said.

Julia Fowler had been waiting over an hour in reception when Benjamin and I got back to the agency. Benjamin went back to helping Olivia with her embezzlement case. I escorted Julia into the conference room for privacy. She showed me an old video of Louise on her phone, dressed in a tight flowery dress and slow dancing and laughing with Holcomb at a birthday party.

"Louise became really girly. She loved dresses, frocks, high heels, all those trappings more than me. That was why she loved modeling. And I guess her brand of femininity was the type that men like Rupert fell hard for. And she just wanted to marry a nice bloke who treated her right."

"Why are you telling me this?"

"To show you that Louise and Rupert were the real deal. But she had a past."

"Go on."

"Dodgy boyfriend. Utter sleazebag. Photographer she lived with in Paris for a while. He has photos she was afraid would get out. He keeps them in a safe in his flat in Paris. Look, I know you're busy, but I need your help."

This could be my first lead. A shithead who might be out to mess with Holcomb for taking Louise away from him, perhaps?

I looked at Julia.

"Would you like to go to Paris with me?"

FOUR

Off to St. Pancras Station, taxi receipt to give to Cheryl. Two tickets on the company credit card, receipt for Cheryl for an expenses claim as part of the bill to the Tory Party later. And we were off.

You might think the three hours it took to get to Paris—three hours in a dark tunnel—were filled with awkward silences, but this wasn't the case.

"Sorry," said Julia.

"For what?"

"Using you like this."

"It's my job." I shrugged. "I want to know more about Louise and see if anyone from her past might be out to get Holcomb. You need backup. Win-win for us both."

God knows I was desperate for a bad guy in this case to focus on. One that preferably had a pulse.

"I Googled you," Julia said.

Here we go.

I shouldn't have been surprised. Julia must have vetted me before she decided I could be trusted. Anyone could look me up if they wanted, even if not all the facts were out there. They never are.

"Is there something you need to ask?"

"How did you find out that girl was sleeping with the teacher in the first place?"

"She was one of my students. She had trouble at home, and the bastard took advantage. The usual grooming, made her feel special, like he was looking out for her when no one else was. Thing is, she was smart, knew it was wrong deep down. I must have told all my students this kind of thing was wrong in passing, and she remembered it. After a few months, she came and told me what was happening with her. I told the principal and authorities immediately."

"Were you friends with that teacher?" she asked.

"Phil and I were friendly. Had the occasional drink. Never knew he was sleeping with a student. It's not something teachers generally spilled to each other."

"Would you have reported him if you were friends?"

"In a flash. I wouldn't have tried to have a friendly chat with him. That kind of thing is non-negotiable in my book."

"So how did it go from something as straightforward as reporting it to him trying to stitch you up?"

"I cocked up. Before Social Services came to take her away, she ran off. The police were called. They were looking for her. Then she turned up on my doorstep in the middle of the night. I let her sleep on my sofa before taking her to school the next day. When Phil saw me go to school with her, he accused me of being the one who was sleeping with her to muddy the waters. I ended up being investigated as his accomplice. Weeks of testimonies, had to get my own solicitor. That was when it hit the papers. The student insisted I wasn't part of it. In the end, her testimony saved me from getting arrested. Phil had his lawyer muddy the waters, as well. In the end, the student and her parents opted not to press charges, and they left the country. By then, I was tainted as much as Phil was, and the school used the excuse of budget cuts to sack me as well as Phil."

"To be accused of something monstrous," Julia said. "That changes you, doesn't it?"

"My mother was a teacher. It seemed like a good idea when I left university. I thought about going into publishing with my English degree, work towards becoming an editor, but in the end, I decided to go into teacher training, be of service. I reckoned the students would keep me on my toes. I was good at it."

"Are you bitter?"

"More angry than bitter. I felt like I failed my student. We didn't protect her properly. And she had to come out and protect me."

"What was it like, suddenly cast adrift?"

"Weird. I realized that I didn't really feel as if being a teacher defined me. I made some halfhearted attempts to find a new teaching position, but deep down, I knew I would never teach again. I was burnt-out."

"So the other guy, Phil—"

"He's still out there, but I don't think he'll land another teaching job, either."

"So how did you become a private investigator?"

"My friend David from uni. He'd been working a few years as the lawyer at Golden Sentinels. When he saw I'd been unemployed for six months and moping about, he talked me into going for an interview. Said it paid crazy-good money. Since I was in debt, I thought why not? I still wonder why they hired me."

She smiled. Like she knew something I didn't.

"Sorry," I said. "Banging on like that."

"It's fine. I had to ask."

She was still vetting me. I had no problems with that. I sensed her sister sitting there with us, beside her as she listened to my sob story, deciding that I could be trusted to help. Julia would protect Louise, even in death.

FIVE

Got off at the Gare du Nord, headed for the Metro. Got out at the 6th Arrondissement, the Saint Germain-des-Prés area. Louise's ex kept a flat he had inherited from his family here, the only way anyone could possibly have a place in this part of town. His name was Loïc Bazennec, probably the most French name ever. D-list fashion photographer who made a decent living on magazine shoots; he wanted to be Annie Leibovitz.

"Only more misogynist," Julia added.

His flat was in a backstreet on the way to Saint-Michel. The entrance to the building opened to a cobblestoned courtyard.

"Loïc isn't home this week. He's off for Fashion Week in Berlin," Julia said.

Social engineering is the art of subtly manipulating people into thinking that giving you what you want was the most sensible thing in the world. It's really a fancy way of saying "con job." The trick to social engineering is to always act with total confidence, like you're supposed to be there. That was what Julia and I did. We walked up to the front entrance of Loïc Bazannec's building like a couple coming home. Julia pressed the bell, and the door buzzed open for us.

Julia had a set of spare keys that Louise had held on to after she and Loïc had broken up. We climbed the stairs to his front door. I put on a pair of surgical gloves and gave Julia a pair so we didn't leave our fingerprints anywhere.

Swish flat. Old photos on the bookshelves of Louise with a lanky, jowly bloke that I presumed was Loïc.

"He was domineering. Abusive."

The walls of his flat were lined with oversize photos of nude models he had obviously taken great pride in shooting. He had a particular fixation on crotches and bums.

I hated this guy already.

Julia headed for the office area in the living room. She'd been here before, back when Louise was living with Loïc. How long had she been planning to do this? The safe was sitting under the desk. I recognized it as one of those common commercial models, barely larger than a shoe box, with a keypad and seven-pin tubular lock.

"Louise always meant to sneak back here to get those photos."

She entered a code on the keypad.

"Shit! He's changed the code."

"Let me have a go," I said.

When I was training for the job, Benjamin walked me through the gamut of safecracking: listening for the tumblers on combination locks, cutting another model open from the soft metal back, brute-force cracking the bigger models with a crowbar if you had the time. Then there were the cheap, crap ones with keypads.

Of course I carried a small lock-pick kit with me as part of the job. That didn't include a crowbar for brute-forcing a safe, though. The question, then, was which tactic to use.

I pulled out the safe from the desk, entered a random code to hear the beep of the error message, and then smacked the top of the safe with my palm.

Sure enough, the door flipped open. Design flaw in the spring.

Luckily for us, Loïc's mediocrity extended to his choice of safety appliances.

Julia pulled out a large manila envelope. Negatives and prints of Louise and some other women in handcuffs and leather straps and smeared in filth. They didn't all look consensual.

"His fetish was bondage and poo. He insisted his girls 'play' with him. Lou always regretted these."

She left the small wad of cash alone in the safe. I reached behind the safe door and pressed a little red button on the side near the hinge and heard a beep, resetting the passcode. Louise entered a new random code. Loïc would come back from Berlin to find he couldn't open his safe the next time he wanted to take out the photos for a wank. He probably didn't know how easy it was to open the safe, since if he knew how rubbish these safes were, he probably wouldn't have bought one. Julia was happy to let him stew.

I found nothing that would tie Loïc to Holcomb. Julia said Louise never told Holcomb about him, and they never met. We left the flat with the photos and walked over to the Pont des Arts. Louise took out a lighter and set the negatives and photos on fire, letting them flutter into the Seine. We watched the wind take them as they dwindled into embers before they hit the water. The lovers and tourists who passed us didn't bat an eyelash.

"I have to turn in a paper about *The Canterbury Tales* next week. It's stressing me out a bit."

"And you're not stressed about committing burglary?"

"I'll do anything to protect my sister," she said. "I'm going to write about 'The Miller's Tale.' Laughed my arse off at that one."

"The Miller's Tale." Story about a carpenter whose wife was cheating on him with a local scholar, and a second scholar also fancied her. When the second scholar pestered her for a kiss, she told him to close his eyes, then stuck her bum out the window. She and her lover had a good laugh when the second bloke kissed her arse instead of her mouth. The second scholar got pissed off and grabbed a hot poker to punish her, but it was her lover who stuck his arse out the window this time for a laugh, and he got the poker up his bum instead, screaming bloody murder and waking up the town.

"It's always the 'poker up the bum' story that everyone remembers," I said.

We laughed, trying to shake off the adrenaline rush from the breaking and entering we just pulled off.

Suddenly she kissed me, taking me by surprise.

"Thanks," she said.

"Just doing my job. I wanted to see if Loîc might have been the one out to get Roger. Now I can rule him out."

She kissed me again.

"When this is over, we should go out properly," she said.

As first dates went, this was pretty good. Nothing like a bit of breaking and entering for a bonding experience. I was probably crossing an ethical line here somewhere, but Julia wasn't a client, so I didn't feel any dings on my conscience.

In the corner of my eye, at the other side of the bridge, stood Kali. Goddess of death and rebirth, what was she doing here? Was I doing something that was about to change my life? I ignored her, a blur in the distance.

We took the Eurostar back to London. It was dark when we came out at St. Pancras. I put Julia in a cab, since she had to go home to write her paper. I headed home, still abuzz from our kiss, and passed out from exhaustion—exhaustion mixed with excitement.

SIX

What have you got?" I asked Benjamin.

"Only the most boring nature documentary ever."

We watched the cam footage that Benjamin had recorded overnight. Benjamin speeded up the video so we didn't have to endure in real time the scene of Holcomb coming into his bedroom the night before.

"Observe," said Benjamin, "*Torius parliamentus* in his natural habitat."

Holcomb changed into his pajamas, swallowed some pills that had to be the Rohypnol I had found in his medicine cabinet, and climbed into bed. When he switched off the lights, the footage went to infrared. He slept like a log. No one entered his bedroom throughout the night.

"I am distinctly disappointed in the lack of ghostly sexy times," said Benjamin.

"Did you get our clients' permission to put surveillance cameras in his flat?"

"Er, no," I said.

We didn't realize Roger had been standing behind us watching the footage all along. His face was a shade of beet red, like a blood vessel might pop any second, and his teeth were grinding as if he was trying very hard to keep his head from exploding. Benjamin and I couldn't answer. I let my gaze wander to Olivia talking to a pair of Buddhist monks in the boardroom. New clients who wanted her to secure their IT network from hackers.

"Tell me you're going to delete this footage and you've removed the cameras from that flat," Roger said.

"But didn't you say we should pull every trick in the book to crack this case?"

"This poor sod might be our next prime minister, and I don't want Special Branch knocking on our door if they find out we bugged his flat," said Roger. "You haven't answered me about the cameras."

"Err," muttered Benjamin.

"Imagine if this footage got out," Roger said slowly. "If we're lucky, only you two will go to fucking prison. If we're lucky, we won't get sued."

Benjamin was already scrambling to get his gear together to go back to Holcomb's flat to remove the cameras.

"Just you, Benjamin. Make sure you remove all the cameras and microphones. As for you, Ravi, get out there and earn your bloody wages."

I moved Holcomb's video file into the trash and deleted it. Olivia was laughing with the monks as they spoke rapid Mandarin while Cheryl served them all tea.

"Looks like you'll have to kick it old-school after all, eh?" smirked Clive from his desk.

Ken and Clive were enjoying watching the newbie squirm.

"Ain't no cuttin' corners when it comes to legwork," Ken said. "You're not gonna catch anyone red-handed sittin' behind a computer."

Ken and Clive were much less amused when Roger ordered them to go out with me to make sure there were no more cock-ups. He was putting the training wheels back on.

At least he let us take out the company BMW.

SEVEN

To Belgravia, off Eaton Square, within walking distance of Harrods on Knightsbridge side, to conduct a quick interview.

"Mind your manners," Clive said. "Don't say anything rude. Don't fucking judge. This is a classy manor, got it?"

"You're on thin ice as it is," Ken said. "Roger pulled a lot of strings to get you an audience here."

Clive rang the bell, and one of the most bored-looking beautiful women I've ever seen opened the door. She wore Chanel, her earrings and jewelry all gold and diamonds. She showed us into the living room.

The house was something straight out of *Country and Town House* magazine, the décor all velvet and *Laura Ashley*, and the proprietress, Madame Felicity, was immaculate in makeup and Gucci. She was the type of woman who used femininity as a weapon. The withering contempt of her gaze was the type to shrivel men's balls. She and Roger went way back. He'd never tell what kinds of favors they did for each other to earn this much trust, but that she was willing to talk to me spoke volumes.

"This isn't any old knocking shop, love," she said. "We get all sorts around here: celebrity chefs, sultans, sports stars, tycoons, politicos. They pay us as much for discretion as for the girls."

The girls here were all supermodel-levels of symmetry and sultriness. Not an ounce of fat on any of them, all slim waists and long legs, pert breasts that defied gravity and probably at least forty grand's worth of cosmetic surgery to achieve this level of flawlessness. Lips Botoxed to varying degrees of subtlety. Blondes, brunettes, the occasional redhead, chiseled noses and diamond cheekbones. The costs of the surgery would have been paid off after about ten clients. Some of the girls were so posh, you could practically name the finishing schools they went to. Others were paying off university fees and student loans. Ken and Clive told me not to ask about the occasional famous actress from Hollywood or Europe who did a bit of moonlighting here when acting work was thin on the ground and the bills were high. The men here looked like *GQ* covers. This was the sex equivalent of getting to test-drive a Ferrari or Lamborghini. Not for Ken, Clive or me, though, not with our salaries. For us, it was strictly "look, don't touch." Ken and Clive preferred rougher trade than the guys on offer here, and they were already a couple, anyway.

"We vet our clients as much as they depend on our discretion," Madame Felicity said. "Not everyone gets to come through the door, no matter how rich they are. We don't do underage stuff or pedos. Beyond that, anything goes between consenting adults."

"Did Rupert Holcomb come here?" I asked.

"Just the once," she said. "His minders from the party brought him here after his girlfriend passed away. His whip, McLeish, thought he just needed some relief. He looked like a little boy who had lost his mummy at the pier. Barely looked at my girls. Just spent an hour sitting on the sofa drinking a gin and tonic, then he muttered to his minders and they took him home."

"Fuck me, that's discipline," Clive said.

"I wouldn't call it discipline, mate," Ken said. "More like grief. He was still gettin' over his dead girlfriend."

"Do you get paparazzi or press hanging about outside? Could anyone have seen Holcomb leaving this place?"

She shook her head.

"Darling, this place is a bigger secret than GCHQ. If the press ever writes about us, it's Game Over. Besides, we have more than a few editors and publishers using our services. And would you care to guess the types of people who invested money in this place? At this location, hiding in plain sight?"

I didn't answer, but I did start to guess. The kind of money that could buy this place under a shell corporation, the paperwork for taxes, the sheer clout . . . We're talking a conglomerate of Establishment figures investing in Madame Felicity's business plan: a haven for secrets and sex. I wondered if Roger had a small stake in this place. It wouldn't surprise me if he did.

"You look a bit shell-shocked, old son," laughed Ken as we drove away from Belgravia.

He and Clive always had a good giggle at me getting another shred of innocence stripped away as the vastness of the world's sordid secrets opened up under my feet.

Only a call from Marcie saved me.

"Dude, we got a lead. Freelance bottom-feeder trying to sell dirt on Holcomb to the tabloids."

"What's his name?"

"Jonah Vankin. Used to be a stringer for the *News of the World* for their juicy scandals. He has a rep for creating them, throwing girls and drugs at celebs, then cashing in on the stories."

"You think he might be the type to hire a hooker to fuck Holcomb in the night and fit him up?"

"Politicians and spies may not have the imagination for that kind of high-concept scam," Marcie said. "But a tabloid twat might. Texting you his picture and details now. He hangs out at the Shoreditch most nights trying to get dirt, so he won't be home till late."

Sure enough, the picture of a grinning dickhead in a cheap jacket popped on my screen along with his address and number.

"Happy hunting," Marcie said, and hung up.

"I think we have our bad guy," I told Ken and Clive.

Relief all around.

EIGHT

Back to the office.

I asked Marcie to call Vankin. Better to have a cheery American chick call a toerag-on-the-make than a burley ex-copper or former schoolteacher. Didn't want to scare him off. Best to start with the path of least resistance.

Who could resist Marcie Holder in her cheeriest PR Woman voice with the promise of business and perks, especially when her default mode always sounded like she's flirting?

"This shit I got needs to get out there, darlin'!" Vankin said on the speakerphone. We were, of course, recording it for evidence. "The public needs to know!"

"Is it documents? Pictures?" Marcie asked innocently.

"Aw, man! Pictures! Future PM Holcomb *in flagrante delicto*! Sucking, fucking! Drugs! What have you! This is six figures' worth of scandal!"

"The trifecta of naughtiness," Marcie cooed. "We're interested."

"Christ," Ken muttered. "He sounds like a shopkeeper in Soho trying to sell us a dodgy porn DVD."

"So what area of six figures are you asking?" continued Marcie.

"This is top shit, babes! Could bring down the whole Conservative Party! Half a million ain't out of the question."

"Hold on, cowboy," Marcie said. "No publication pays half a mil without getting a taste first, no matter how much public interest is at stake here."

"Come on! I thought I was talking to someone serious here! It'll be well worth your while!"

I could feel him now: his cocky, coke-addled desperation, like an older version of some of my old students in North London. I used to catch them during break trying to sell baby powder saying it was gak, or orange tablets passing for Ecstasy, or a badly scratched-up Sony PSP they said fell off a lorry, and certainly looked it.

"Baby," Marcie said. "I represent a very serious conglomerate of interested parties. We're willing to talk."

"You gotta promise, yeah? This doesn't get bought up and then buried. This needs to be out there! And I get to write it up!"

"Believe me, you'll get your shot. We have ties not only with the papers, but outlets in the States like TMZ and Fox News."

"Good! I don't want some security people or private investigators trying to silence me. That's why I'm askin' half a mil, yeah? Danger money! I don't want Special Branch coming round my place, bumping me off, and making it look like I hanged myself while trying to have a wank!"

"What a charming image," Marcie said. "So what kind of pictures are these? Are they negatives and prints or is it all digital? We want to get an exclusive, not have you turn around and sell it to a bunch of other people."

"It's all on a drive. I give you my personal guarantee you will get all copies. My word is my bond!"

Clive snorted in contempt.

Marcie set up a meet. That night at the club in Shoreditch. Of course we weren't going to pay him a penny. While Ken and Clive went with me, Benjamin and Olivia would break into his flat to look over his computer. Hopefully, she could break whatever encryption he had on his drives to grab the photos.

"You owe me," Marcie said. "Help with my stalking case when you have a chance."

With that, she went back to reading her client Delia McCarthy's bestselling chick-lit novel, *Memoirs of a Bunny Boiler*.

"Is this research?" I asked.

"She's gonna ask me what I think of it when I talk to her," Marcie said. "I'm obligated to be able to quote it chapter and verse. Writers are needy like that."

NINE

Vankin insisted on meeting at the Shoreditch that night, his "place of power." This was not good. Too many variables, things that could go wrong. We couldn't control the space. Even on a slow night, this place was chockablock with Essex Girls, soap stars and, well, people like Vankin. That and the noise factor would make trying to talk to anyone a complete nightmare. We also didn't want Vankin to vanish too quickly, and there were too many nooks and crannies for him to slip away to if he decided to hop it. Knowing the layout of the place didn't help, since the crowds would be an added hindrance.

Ken, Clive, and I parked across the road and watched the queues form. At ten p.m., Vankin strolled up, cheap suit and hair gel, bypassed the queue of hopeful clubbers, shook the bouncer's hand, twenty quid folded in his palm, and was let in.

"Cunt's just the type to do a runner," Ken said. "Guilty conscience. You can smell it off him."

We were to meet him at ten thirty p.m. I looked at the crowd outside the club and decided I wasn't having any of that. We got a text from Benjamin: he and Olivia had gained entry into Vankin's flat and found his computer.

I waited till 10:35 p.m. and picked up our burner phone.

"Speak!" shouted Vankin over the din of crappy electrodance.

"I believe we have an appointment this evening."

"Where's the American bird I talked to? She sounded well fit."

"She's the facilitator. You're dealing with us."

"So where are you?"

"Outside," I said. "Where we can negotiate with some peace and quiet."

"Aw, no way, brah! We agreed to meet in here!"

"Mr. Vankin, we are taking you seriously enough to engage with you. We are, however, not willing to have to shout to be heard."

"Too fucking bad, brah! You come in or no deal!"

"Mr. Vankin, I have with me twenty thousand pounds in cash as a down payment for you in good faith. If you do not meet me outside in five minutes, I will be gone. You will never see me again, and I will make sure no outlet will hear your pitch, let alone make you another offer. Five minutes."

I hung up.

"Ooo-er!" Ken said.

"Please, sir, don't give me detention," Clive said.

"Don't spank me, sir," chuckled Ken. "I ain't done nothing wrong."

I rolled my eyes and stepped out of the car.

I had my speech all prepared. I was going to introduce myself as part of an international media conglomerate with political ties. Ken and Clive were here as muscle, of course. Of course we didn't have twenty grand on us. We just wanted Vankin to think we were either stupid or callously rich enough to throw that much money around for a dodgy set of naughty photos. The point was to keep Vankin talking long enough to suss out whether he was for real and for Benjamin and Olivia to go through his computer.

Vankin came out of the club, looked around, saw me, and started across the street. I put on an air of bored professionalism to set him at ease. Ken stepped out of the car.

I'd never felt the air change this much before I even said a word.

Vankin's eyes went wide with terror and he turned and scarpered like a hamster on fire.

"OY!"

I found out later that it was perfectly normal to see a guy getting chased down and beaten up in Hoxton late on a Thursday night. As it was, I only wanted to catch Vankin. Couldn't speak for Ken, though. One thing he and Clive taught me is that cops absolutely hate before forced to chase down a punter. It makes them really want to take it out on him later. That meant I had to get him before Ken did.

Vankin dashed down Shoreditch High Street and turned into Bateman's Row, then into Anning Street. Must have been all that cocaine in him that was making him run this fast. Ken was trailing behind me, cursing up a storm.

Vankin was nearly a hundred yards ahead of us when he turned around, confident that we wouldn't catch up by now.

"Come and have a go if you're hard enough, then!" he shouted, offering two middle fingers our way.

He totally missed Clive barrowing up behind him in the BMW and bouncing his scrawny stick figure off the bonnet.

Time slowed. Vankin in a graceful arc over the top of the car. Unpleasant crunch sound as he impacted on the tarmac.

"Jesus Christ! Was that really necessary?!"

"Stopped the fucker, didn't I?" Clive said.

"Eh, we've done worse." Ken shrugged.

2

TEN

No, he wasn't dead. Thank fuck.

He hadn't landed on his head. More like a hard belly flop. Yes, it hurt as much as you think. We called an ambulance anyway. Of course the police showed up to take a statement. And they turned out to be friends of Ken and Clive. It was pretty clear we weren't going to be arrested when they started laughing and clapping each other on the back as Ken and Clive told them it was a misunderstanding with Vankin snorting a bit too much gak while we were chatting, getting paranoid and running right into their car as they were driving up.

My karma was in the toilet for this, though. Among the onlookers, I could sense Lord Buddha, just out of focus, watching and judging me.

Vankin had a couple of broken ribs, a mild concussion, and a twisted ankle. As he was getting loaded into the ambulance, I tried to talk to him again.

"Why did you run, man? We just wanted to talk."

"Those two big fuckers with you," he moaned. "They had the smell of Special Branch."

"They're not. They hate Special Branch."

"That's what they all say. Or they could have been MI5!"

"You think the domestic services might want to bump you off."

"I know shit, brah. I am a primo depository of illicit intel."

"Leave it out, son," Clive said, rolling his eyes. "I've seen the list. You ain't on it."

Vankin's face fell like a little boy's who wasn't getting presents for Christmas.

"But I know shit!" he protested. "I know all kinds of shit!"

We let the ambulance take him away for the end of the most disillusioning night of his life.

"Is there really a list?" I asked Clive.

He just rolled his eyes and shrugged.

I phoned Benjamin to tell him Olivia could take her time with Vankin's computer. He wasn't coming home that night.

"No need," he said. "We're done."

"And?"

"You got me to give up my beauty sleep for this?" Olivia snatched up the phone. "It's all rubbish."

"Wait, what are you talking about?"

"First of all, Vankin's computer setup is strictly Amateur Hour. He doesn't have any security software installed, hasn't updated his OS for ages—he doesn't even have a sodding password for signing in! He's still running Windows Vista, for God's sake!"

"Did you find the photos?"

"If you can call them that. It's all piss-poor Photoshop!"

"Seriously?"

"He took a photo of Holcomb at a pub from the *Mail* and pasted a naked slapper next to him."

"Oh."

"And get this, there's one of Holcomb sucking a ten-inch cock in a gay threesome? He took the shot from Holcomb bobbing for apples at a village fair and pasted it into a spread from a gay porn magazine! It's full of bad cutting and pasting!"

"All right, I get the picture—"

"Not yet, but you will. I made you a copy of all of Mr. Vankin's stash. You know, in case you ever run out of cheap wank material."

"Thanks a lot."

Back to square one. No suspect. No resolution. And me one step closer to getting the sack for not solving Roger's Big Favor to the Tory Party.

Shit.

Shit. Shit. Shit!

ELEVEN

It's happened again!" screamed Holcomb.

Barely four hours of sleep before I got his call. And I didn't have the benefit of taking Rohypnol. Quick shower, my clean suit and tie, no time for coffee. Cab down to his flat. Arrived to hysterics.

Holcomb in his dressing gown, red faced, shaking.

I looked at the rumpled bed, the drying wet patches.

"Can you smell it? The sex? The perfume?"

He hadn't done this to himself. I'd been through his medicine cabinet and all the cupboards in the flat when I was last over with Benjamin. He didn't keep any women's perfume here.

"I didn't do this to myself! I don't sleepwalk! Someone is doing this to me!"

"Mr. Holcomb, I believe you. We will get to the bottom of this."

"When? You can't imagine the shame! The humiliation! The . . . not knowing! I can't endure this much longer!"

I looked at him. Started to really see him for the first time. Not the bland, empty suit on the telly or the papers, not the focus group–tested mannequin spouting platitudes and policies that were going to help the rich get richer and fuck up the young, the handicapped and the vulnerable, but the man. Or rather, the little boy who always did what everyone wanted, who didn't know anything better, who was desperate to be accepted. I'd assumed he was going to be party leader by name anyway, that he was just the front man pushing the policies the party committee had decided upon. They tended to pick not the most charismatic, but the most anodyne these days, the most market-tested, generic, faceless, inoffensive figure who could serve as a receptacle for sound bites and policy declarations. If the main parties could run androids, they probably would. But now I was seeing all the artifice stripped away and the victim underneath.

Oh, God, was I starting to feel sorry for him?

"Mr. Holcomb, you're not exactly cut out for this line of work are you?"

"Eh? What—what are you saying?"

"Do you really want to be prime minister?"

"Well, of course! Every MP dreams of that."

"I'm not so sure about that. Some of them just want to serve their constituents."

The confusion on his face was painful to behold.

"No, no," he muttered. "That was always the endgame. I was always going to be party leader, then PM. That was the trajectory. We had this all planned out. Do you see how all . . . all this can ruin those plans? Why won't you help me?"

"Mr. Holcomb, close your eyes."

"What—?"

"Just close your eyes and take a deep breath. There. And another. In. Out. In. Out."

The air in the room began to let up a bit.

"Better?"

"Yes, thank you."

"When you closed your eyes, what did you see in your mind?"

"A green field stretching far in the distance. England's green and pleasant land."

"How did you feel when you saw that?"

"Happy. I wish I could just sit in that field forever."

"No work, no worries, no stress. No meetings. No voters."

"Yes. I wish I could be here forever."

With that, his eyes snapped open. He tensed again, as if he'd been caught doing something shameful. I really wished someone would talk him into getting some therapy.

"What did you do to me?"

"I didn't do anything. Why? Do you think you did something wrong?"

"No, but—it's just—"

"Why would I judge you? Everyone needs that place you just found."

He relaxed, but only slightly.

"Can you hang on to that feeling?"

"I—I think so."

"Try to remember it. Do you have any appointments today?"

"Yes. A budget meeting, then canvassing in the afternoon."

"All right. Go about your day as you normally do. Can you manage that?"

I told Holcomb not to come home that night, that he should get a room at his club and sleep there. If he didn't get any nocturnal sexing there, we would at least know that it was a living person and not a ghost.

"All my life, I did what everyone told me I should do," Holcomb said as he left. "Louise, she was the only decision I made on my own. For myself."

Time to stop fucking about. I should have done this in the first place. I got back to the office to look up Louise's Facebook page and went through her friends list, cross-referenced their names with her interviews, and found another old boyfriend in Munich. His name was Gunter. Munich was a period of her life she didn't talk about, brushing it off in interviews as paying her dues, going where the work was, even if it wasn't high profile, before anyone heard of her, where she did rudimentary catalogue work.

I phoned Gunter up. He agreed to meet. He was nursing an expensive heroin addiction, so my call was serendipitous. He happened to be holding some old papers and records of hers. That I was asking for them meant they had to be worth some clobber, so he immediately demanded payment for them. I had to ask Cheryl for a thousand euros to pay him, but that was going to be part of the expenses, so she was kosher with it. Then a taxi to Luton Airport, an easyJet to Munich.

I met Gunter at the airport bar and handed him the money. He wanted to make small talk and have a beer, so I quizzed him about Louise as I read through the medical records he'd given me. They confirmed Louise's compromised immune system, the risks to her health that the treatments posed, her hormonal imbalance that exacerbated her condition that may have lead to her illness later. And Gunter was the boyfriend who was loyal enough to stick with her through this period. He even kept these records to protect her. Unfortunately, everyone had their price, and Gunter's was the increasingly expensive heroin addiction he needed to feed, so it was fortuitous that I happened to get in touch with him just when he needed to pay off his dealer and stock up on his stash.

"I loved her," he said. "But deep down I knew it wasn't to last. She was going to move on to great things and I would hold her back."

I questioned Gunter long enough to get all the answers I needed before I got on the next plane back to London.

Only seven hours had passed since I had flown out of London. It wasn't even late when I got back. There was actually a chance to wrap this case up.

TWELVE

She came at three in the morning, glided into his bedroom in the dark without a sound, muscle memory told her where everything was without needing to see. Her clothes slid off her like shed skin as she climbed into the bed and onto the man sleeping in it.

But this time, he wasn't asleep.

"We have to stop meeting like this," I said.

"Ravi?! What are you doing here?" Julia Fowler nearly threw herself off the bed in panic, but I grabbed her wrists and pulled her back before she toppled over and bashed her head on the carpet. I let her settle back on the bed.

"Don't run. I just want to talk."

In hindsight, Benjamin and I probably could have solved this case much sooner if we'd kept the cameras in place or, to go old-school, parked ourselves in the cupboard, and waited for her to show up, but I didn't really believe someone was actually coming in and fucking Holcomb in his sleep, so I concentrated on every other angle before coming back to this bloody obvious one. Chalk that up to experience, I suppose.

Eventually Julia stopped resisting and sat back on the bed. She pulled her shirt back on.

"Where's Rupert?" she asked.

"Sleeping at his club in town."

"How did you know it was me?"

"You and Louise used the same perfume. Remember when we were talking about 'The Miller's Tale,' the bit about the wife sneaking someone else's bum for the poor sod to kiss? That came back to me when I smelled your perfume in this room yesterday morning."

"After I—"

"Your last visit, yes. I also remembered there were no photos of Louise when she was little in your living room. I looked into Louise's medical history. No records going back more than three years, but there were plenty of records for Lewis Fowler, who had the same date of birth as Louise."

"How did you suss all this out?"

"I found an old boyfriend of Louise's in Germany from Facebook."

"Gunter." Julia's face darkened.

"He helped her get gender reassignment surgery there, away from the tabloids. The fights she had with your dad were about her being trans. Gunter kept her medical records from the clinic in Munich. I'm amazed he kept her secret that long."

"Gunter can actually be loyal, when he's not chasing his next high. Lou had the plastic surgery to sort out her face, her Adam's apple, but her health deteriorated. She couldn't go through with the genital reconstruction."

"She was going to go through with the complete transition? She passed the psychological assessment?"

"She wanted it badly. Needed it. Not all trans women do," Julia said. "Wow. Who would have thought Chaucer could be used for detective work. Too bad I can't write about that in my paper."

"So that was why Louise couldn't marry Rupert," I said. "She would have had to submit her birth certificate, and he would have found out."

"She loved him," Julia said. "I think the strain of putting off the marriage helped kill her in the end."

"But they had sex, didn't they? How could he not know she had a penis? She could hide her status in her job, but . . ."

"They always did it in the dark," Julia said. "So he never realized."

"Come on, how could he not notice?"

" Do you really want to know all the details?"

She picked up her phone and typed in a Google search, showed me the results. Some of them included pictures and diagrams. A lot more information than I needed.

"All right. I believe you."

"Eventually, she got too ill to have sex with him. That was when she had the idea that I could sneak in and take her place. She gave me the spare key when she knew they were coming back for sex. She planned which rooms he wouldn't be in, so he never saw me. Once they were in the dark, she would excuse herself, leave the bedroom, and let me in. I would do the rest."

"Here's what I don't get. I know you'd do anything for her, but why go this far? Why have sex with a man you don't even like?"

"I'm a sex addict."

"Ah."

"I've been diagnosed. No joke. You might think it's all fun and games, but it's not. When I was young, I was abused by my uncle, and it fucked me up right and proper. I don't have sex on impulse because I like it. It's because I hate myself. And I do it to stop hating myself, but I hate myself even more after I do it."

"I know. It's a compulsion."

"She was my best friend," Julia said. "She'd suffered so much, and I wanted her to be happy. And I didn't mind Rupert. It was convenient. I didn't have to talk to him afterwards. I didn't have to pick up some grubby sod from a club. It kept my addiction under control, and I even got to cut down on my therapy sessions."

"But you were still in your addiction. You shouldn't cut down on the sessions."

She looked at me, surprised.

"I've known a few addicts. Not sex addicts, but I get how it works."

She relaxed a bit.

"So why did you start doing it again after she died? You don't even like Holcomb."

"I could control myself for a while, but college started to get to me. Therapy wasn't helping. And I missed Louise. Doing it again felt like I was being close to her again, you know?"

"You could have talked to Rupert about it."

"You must be joking! You've seen how he is! He's beyond old-fashioned about sex! He's bloody clueless! I didn't want to have to deal with him being clingy and whinging. And if his handlers got wind of it, they might put pressure on me to marry him! Yuck! I knew Rupert took enough roofies to drop a rhino before he could sleep, so that worked in my favor. No muss, no fuss. I didn't think he'd notice in the morning."

"Well, he did. That's why he hired us to find out what was going on."

"I didn't think it was me you were after."

"Neither did I."

"I was going to stop. Really. I thought I was doing pretty well for the past week when I left him alone, just concentrated on my coursework, went to therapy."

"So why did you suddenly start up again last night?"

"Because of you, Ravi."

"Me?!"

"I like you, all right? I didn't expect that to happen. I didn't want to fuck you, because that would ruin it! I couldn't handle it, and I needed to get back to something familiar."

Christ. I'd become the case. That one ethical line I should never cross, and I'd ended up on the other end of it without even knowing.

"I didn't think Rupert would notice." Julia hugged herself. "I thought he would just wake up and vaguely think he had a wet dream, then get on with his day."

"He's been losing his rag over it. He thought he was going mad. He was going spare, enough to hire me to find out."

"Oh, God. I'm so sorry. I'm so, so sorry." She was like a little girl who'd discovered she'd done something really bad.

"You were just using him as a fuck doll. It didn't occur to you that this was a crime?"

"It's—I've been all fucked-up in my head. You were the first really good bloke I'd met for a long time. Then all those memories of Louise when we went to Paris together, all these mad feelings like I'm going to burst, just filling up and spilling over like I would explode if I didn't do anything about it. I was going to stop coming, but I couldn't help myself . . ."

She paused.

"Even now I still feel like Louise is sitting in the living room waiting for me to finish."

"I'm really glad she isn't," I muttered. That would have really freaked me out.

"So where does that leave us? I mean, I like you. Not just for a fuck. I really like you."

"Julia . . ."

"Are you going to tell him everything?"

"He hired me. He has a right to know. He thought he was going mad."

"I deserve that, I suppose."

We both knew what was at stake. Julia could be arrested and tried for assault. She and her family would be smeared all over the news—not to mention that Holcomb would be, too.

She put her arms around me, and we fell back on the bed.

"Can we just lie here like this for tonight? No sex."

"We can do that, yeah."

I was running on fumes, but we spent most of the night talking. We told each other our pasts and our traumas. We lay there until we fell asleep. Holcomb wouldn't be back in the morning. We would be long gone by then. This mess wasn't going away by any stretch of the imagination, though.

THIRTEEN

You hear all kinds of stories about private investigators overstepping their mark, especially if you're in the business. This is industry gossip. Some investigators talk about sticking to the law lest they get brought up on charges. Some of them have affairs with clients. Some of them take bribes to keep evidence from clients. Some of them get caught breaking the law for their clients and sent to jail, like the one who hacked phones for the tabloids. I say "them" when I really mean "us." Me. I was one of them. I'm no different, with the same moral and ethical temptations as the rest of them, no matter how much work I did back when I was pursuing my degree in religious studies. This was no abstract spiritual journey for pondering Enlightenment. This was a job where people's lives were at stake. In all likelihood, Julia would be arrested and charged. I didn't want to think about the impact on her family, especially if it hit the media. The impact on Holcomb and his career was beyond my imagination. But that wasn't my brief. Ethics demanded I did my job and disclosed my findings.

I reported everything to Roger and Cheryl at morning briefing. Nobody expected the answer to the Ghost Seducer case. Even Mark, who could be expected to reach the most gonzo flights of fancy, was impressed. Benjamin, typically, thought it was hilarious. Marcie was amused. Olivia was bemused. Ken and Clive just quietly shook their heads, as if something unpleasant about humanity had been reaffirmed to them yet again. Most interesting of all, Cheryl didn't seem to react as she just jotted this all down in the minutes. Roger, not surprisingly, was delighted. He did love a result.

Julia had decided to go home that morning, shower, and go to class as she normally went about her life, and wait for the bomb to drop. I said I would call her and tell her Holcomb's decision once I met with him and McLeish.

I could massage what I told Holcomb, hide Julia's identity, simply told him Louise hired a call girl to have sex with him in the dark. Should I do that? That would only throw up more questions: Now that Louise was dead, why would this woman continue to come and bonk him in the dead of night? I doubted Holcomb or McLeish would understand the impulses and pathology of addiction, let alone sex addiction. They would likely be out for blood. What good would that do anyone? Prison wasn't going to help Julia. What she needed was treatment. Or maybe prison was the rock bottom she needed to hit before she committed fully to treatment.

"None of this is your problem, old son," Roger said.

He called McLeish and told them we had solved the case. Shortly after, McLeish called back and said Holcomb insisted on coming in that afternoon to hear what I had found.

"What did you say to Holcomb when you last saw him?" asked Roger when he hung up.

"Why do you ask?"

"He trusts you, thinks you're a straight shooter who'll do right by him."

Now how could I betray him, after trying to ease his pain that morning? Because I couldn't let him suffer.

Roger could read it all on my face.

"What I said about having a *mensch* in my firm." He smiled.

FOURTEEN

I had no appetite for lunch, no Pret A Manger sandwich for me. I just sat at my desk brooding, but covered it up by typing up my notes and fact-checking on the Internet. Even though no one had brought it up or given me shit about it, everybody in the office was waiting to see how the meeting with Holcomb was going to play out.

At two o' clock, Holcomb arrived with McLeish and a man and woman who were either assistants or handlers. They weren't happy when I insisted I spoke only to Holcomb and McLeish. With the glass door closed, the boardroom was soundproof. I had Benjamin sweep it for listening devices half an hour before their arrival, per our usual protocol with sensitive cases.

Roger and Cheryl joined us, of course.

I told Holcomb everything. I started slow, walked him through Louise's history, emphasized that she was a woman trapped in a man's body who tried to correct that as much as she could, until she got too sick to complete her transition. I laid out how she had sex with him and saw his whole world drop away from his eyes. Things only got worse when I got to the part about Louise's surrogate. Of course, he asked who it was. I explained who and most of all, why.

I told him that Louise loved him.

Have you ever seen a man completely lose his shit? Trust me, you don't want to. This was a full-on wobbly. This was the Premier League of wobblies.

It was a gradual process, started with his lower lip trembling. I thought he might just burst into tears. If that was all that happened, it wouldn't have been so bad. No, next came an awful keening sound from his mouth, escalating into a banshee howl of despair. He leapt from his chair like a jackrabbit, grabbed the vase on the table, and threw it at the wall, where it exploded like a grenade. He threw himself on top of the table and began to writhe like a man on fire, clawing at his shirt and face. This was beyond rational, all reason and restraint falling away from him, leaving only impulse and unfocused emotion. Every regret, every disappointment, every loss had he ever suffered was working its way through him. He was all gesture without control now.

McLeish was taken aback, but gathered himself into a single expression of impatient disappointment. Roger had a look of mild fascination on his face, then nodded to Cheryl. Cheryl stayed perfectly calm, walked to the door, and asked Ken and Clive to come in and help hold him down. The two handlers rushed in, stopped, and looked on in horror.

"For God's sake," McLeish said. "Can't you do something? It's not as if he's contagious!"

The man made a halfhearted move to reach for Holcomb, then hastily withdrew. Nobody wanted to touch a writhing, raving man. Ken and Clive rolled their eyes and strolled over to the table. They grabbed Holcomb by the ankles and pulled him off, took his arms, and proceeded to hold him down.

The rest of the gang just watched from the door with a look of gleeful Schadenfreude on their faces. Benjamin was all set to film it on his phone if Cheryl hadn't come back from Roger's office and hissed at him to put it away. She had a first aid kit in her hands that Roger took, thanking her gingerly for bringing it.

Roger produced a syringe and loaded it up with sedative from a small vial in the kit.

"Christ, he ain't half-slippery," Ken muttered as he struggled with the squirming Holcomb.

David sidled up to me.

"Jesus, you broke him," he whispered. "What did you tell him?"

"The truth."

"Somehow," Marcie said, "I don't think it's setting him free."

"Hold him steady, lads," Roger said as he approached Holcomb with the syringe.

Ken and Clive had him bend over the table and, with one hand, yanked Holcomb's trousers down just enough to expose the top fleshy bit of his bum. With one deft move, Roger plunged the syringe into Holcomb and injected him with the sedative. I had a feeling this wasn't the first time Roger had done that here in the office. That he knew to keep a syringe and sedative in the first aid kit spoke volumes.

It took about a minute for the drugs to take effect, and Holcomb gradually stopped screaming and struggling. Ken and Clive carried him to the sofa in Roger's office while Roger conferred with McLeish.

"Do you have a private ambulance service you like to use?" Roger said.

"Whose is more discreet?" McLeish asked back. "Yours or mine?"

"Mine."

"We'll use yours."

Roger turned to Cheryl.

"Be a dear and give Charles a call, will you?"

The ambulance arrived in fifteen minutes. They knew not to use the siren, and they brought the gurney up via the building's service entrance.

As they strapped Holcomb in, I spoke to him.

"Remember that place? That green and pleasant land? Go there now, and stay there as long as you like."

Through his haze, Holcomb nodded, and the medics carted him off.

"Well," McLeish said. "That could have gone better."

"Did you know he was this . . . unstable?" I asked.

"We hoped he was made of sterner stuff. When we vetted him for the leadership position, we were just relieved that there was no pig-fucking in his background."

"Well," Roger said, "better to find out now than after you put him up at the next general election, eh?"

"Indeed," McLeish muttered. "Oh well, back to the drawing board. Next one we pick will be married. And to a real woman."

You transphobic prick. Thanks for reminding me why I'll never vote for you lot.

"God willing." Roger smiled.

McLeish shook Roger's hand.

"Thank you for your work," McLeish said. "They were right about you. Certainly earned your reputation."

"Best of the best, that's us," Roger said. "And absolute discretion."

"Do bill us for the damage today."

I could tell Cheryl was already adding up the broken vase and the other repairs from Holcomb's rampage, mentally laying out the invoice.

McLeish shook my hand, as well—respect for a job well done.

And with that, he and the handlers were gone.

My karma was going down the drain again.

I really hoped I would never land a case where a client thought he was getting fucked by his dead girlfriend again. But in this office, who could be sure?

FIFTEEN

Am I out of a job, then?" I asked as I closed the door to Roger's office.

"Why on earth would you think that?" he asked.

"Well, I— You saw what happened. I just blew up that man's life."

"That was going to happen with or without us."

He handed a glass of whiskey to me and clinked it with his own.

"What you got," continued Roger, "was a good result. We're the party's new best friend. And we can charge them extra. Bottoms up."

Roger was well happy. Another feather in his cap. Another notch on his list of important friends, a list from which he fully intended to call in favors when the time came.

The next few days were a holding pattern. Julia waited anxiously to see if there would be a police investigation. McLeish chose not to report anything to the authorities, with Holcomb's approval. The embarrassment not only to Holcomb but to the party for choosing someone who had been duped to that extent was just not worth it. Holcomb announced that he was stepping down from the party leadership race due to ill health and checked himself into the Priory in Roehampton. The official press statement was that he was suffering from stress and anxiety, which wasn't far from the truth. The stresses of his work as an MP and campaigning and all that. They mentioned grief and bereavement counseling, as well—that he hadn't had the proper time to mourn Louise—which was long overdue. As part of our service, we monitored the records and the press to make sure nothing of what I told Holcomb and McLeish was leaked. Discretion was what Roger charged for as much as investigations, and why he paid us so much. Eventually the press, who generally found Holcomb rather dull to start with, would lose interest in him and move on to the next politico who popped his head up in the publicity game.

Holcomb sent word that he would not be pressing charges and bore Julia no anger or ill will.

"I should go see him," Julia said.

"Is that such a good idea?" I asked.

"I need to make amends."

"He might not want to see you."

To my surprise, he agreed.

I took her over one afternoon and watched from a distance as they sat together in the garden. He looked smaller, diminished in his pajamas and slippers, but all the tension had drained from his body. This was the most relaxed I'd ever seen him. They spoke for a few hours, remembering Louise, and wept together. It looked rather therapeutic for them both. I didn't need to hear what they were saying to read the scene. She doubled over in shame and remorse for what she had done to him in his sleep. He was amazingly calm as he held her hand and forgave her. It might have been the drugs he was on. I didn't detect any rage or indignation coming off him. Maybe this was the real him, after all, underneath the awful policies he was espousing on the campaign trail. I had never been convinced that they were actual policies he thought up on his own, anyway. He really wasn't cut out to be a mouthpiece for the financial sector and the neoliberal lobbyists who had the party's ear. They'd just have to find the next candidate, probably one that was even more plastic, generic, and free from past and future scandal—double down on the blandness.

"Just because he forgives me doesn't let me off the hook," Julia said as we drove back into town.

"So what do you want to do?"

"For starters, stop raping sleeping MPs and stop having compulsive one-night stands that make me hate myself."

"At the very least. Yes."

"You've awfully calm about all this," she said. "How do you know about addiction, anyway?"

"Runs in my family. I had an uncle who died from alcoholism. I sussed out early on it wasn't the addiction, per se, but what triggered it. In his case, it was a broken heart after a lifetime of emotional pain."

"If you hadn't come along, I wouldn't have stopped, and it probably would have ended up going someplace really bad."

"I agree."

"So where does that leave us?"

I couldn't answer.

"Is this just a job for you?" she asked. "Are you doing all this out of some sense of professional and moral obligation?"

"I think it's more than that."

"Then it wasn't my imagination."

"Julia, I think it's obvious that I fancy you, and maybe you fancy me, but is there any future in an 'us'?"

"You saved me," she said. "You saved Rupert."

"So what are you saying? You want us to be official? You want us to be together?"

"Yes."

Against my better judgment, yes. Was it her chaos I was drawn to? Was it that she was clever? That she was unusually direct? That she was funny? Was I getting sucked into a vortex that might drown us both?

"You know, Julia, in my experience, you thinking I'm good for you may not last. In six months, a year, you might think I was holding you back, that I'm too clingy, too controlling."

"Are you controlling, Ravi?"

"I wouldn't be happy with you going off and bonking other people. That's not a relationship. That's just friends with benefits plus your addiction. I don't want to be your safe go-to shag."

"Then you shouldn't be," she said. "The addict shouldn't be the one to set the boundaries. The sane one is."

"What makes you think I'm the sane one?"

"Don't sell yourself short, Ravi."

"If I'm going to be your reason, your incentive to get better, eventually I'm going to become your ball and chain, and you're going to kick against it."

"God, listen to us," Julia laughed through tears. "We're painting with our dysfunctions here. What if I say I don't think of you just as a shag doll? What if I want the rest of you as well? I want your ambivalence about how fucked up this world is, I want your conscience that never stops nagging you. I want the eyes that you see me and this fucked-up world with, not just your cock and your hands. I want your reason and your kindness."

"Julia, you're crazy and you're clever, and you're ridiculously sexy in that English Rose kind of way that drives me round the bend. You're the very chaos that defines my life. This is a terrible idea that we'll both regret."

Both falling, both of us, hand in hand and round and round into a whirlpool of everything we want and everything we fear.

Looking back, I'm amazed that I didn't lose control of the car as we drove through the light rain up the M25, cruising in limbo on the London Orbital.

"This is a really terrible idea," I said, once again trying to convince myself more than her.

"I know, right?" She laughed as she wiped her tears and blew her nose into a tissue.

SIXTEEN

The day the payment for the case came in, Roger gave me a bonus as well as a bit of something for everyone else in the office who had helped out. The gang took me to the local tapas bar that evening for a celebratory drink.

"One of us!" they toasted. "One of us!"

My colleagues were the most cheerful sociopaths I'd ever met—and I used to teach *secondary school*.

"It just hit me," I said. "We're fucking dangerous."

"Wa-hey!" Benjamin said. "He finally gets it!"

"Respect!" David said.

"Ravi mate," Mark said. "We're all of us dangerous. Some people are just in denial about it."

"Too right," Clive said. "And some of us choose how to use that part of us when there's a call for it."

"Just don't lose your compass, old son," Ken said. "That's what sets us apart."

"Darling," Olivia said. "You're not a proper Golden Sentinels investigator until you leave one client's life a smoldering ruin."

"So I've been blooded now," I muttered. "Brilliant."

"What's that?" Benjamin asked over the din.

"I'm a bringer of chaos. A bloody bringer of chaos."

"To chaos!" the gang toasted.

My phone buzzed.

Julia was waiting outside.

I went out to her. The gang knew, of course, and they weren't going to judge her, but it would take time before she could hang out with us.

She put her arms around me as we walked.

"Are you all right?"

"My mother was right all along," I said. "I'm a child of Kali."

"I suppose." She kissed me. "That makes me a bride of Kali."

"I'll say it again. We're probably really bad for each other."

"Well, cosmic jokes are usually ironic."

That night, we celebrated said cosmic joke with a long night of lovemaking. It was the most appropriate move, after all.

And unlike her last partner, I was wide awake.

WAR OF THE SOCK PUPPETS

ONE

Sunday lunch at my parents', my weekly ritual of dread and delight. Julia was off to lunch with her parents. I'm sure they had their own unique brand of angst and dysfunction, not to mention the air of loss and grief still hanging over them. I don't think she'd even told them about her condition. It was still too early for us to introduce the other to our parents. We still weren't sure what our relationship was beyond the mutual decision to have one.

I brought a bag of my dirty laundry for Mum. Yes, I could afford to wash them myself or pay a service, but she insisted on it, since she had little enough to do with her time since she retired from teaching.

"How's work been?" she asked.

"Mad," I said, without going into any details.

"Your sister and Vivek are here already."

"Did Dad's test results come back?"

"They're positive. He has prostate cancer. Early stages."

I felt the bottom of my gut fall out. I was almost light-headed, but I kept it together.

My mother was quite relieved since I'd paid Mrs. Dhewan a visit the day before. She treated me to tea and desserts the way she used to when my mother brought me over as a kid for coffee and gossip. The ladies would sit behind us on the sofa chatting away while us kids played video games on the floor. Mrs. Dhewan was the picture of a Matriarch Who Must Be Obeyed Lest She Had Your Legs Broken, all smiles and feminine graciousness that hid her utter ruthlessness. She liked to play the Grande Dame in her gold and purple sari and gold rings. I presented the five hundred quid my mother owed her in an envelope. She didn't even need to open or count it.

"You are such a good son, Ravi."

"Can you not let her play cards with you and the aunties from now on, please?"

"She is cut off. She will have to settle for just tea and gossip."

"I think she'll survive."

Ironic that the neighborhood loan shark was nicer to me than my parents were.

Dad was on his sofa in the living room. I hugged him from behind. He patted my arm and broke it off.

"I worry about you," he said.

"No need."

"I'd like to die knowing my children are in a good place."

"Dad, you're not dying. Prostate cancer is treatable."

He just grunted. He was already melancholy enough most of the time without a cancer diagnosis.

We settled down and watched football in silence, but I was unmoored, in shock.

That was when I heard the humming.

It started out low, then got louder, until it threatened to drown out the football. Neither Dad nor Vivek seemed to hear it, and when I turned back to the TV, Lord Vishnu was standing next to it, quietly glancing at me with a look of mild bemusement. He was in a modern suit and tie, a lotus in one hand, a mace in another, his third hand on his hip, and a phone in his fourth hand. He started looking at his phone and tapping on it.

No. No, no, no, no.

I excused myself and stumbled out to the hallway.

"Mum? Do you still have any of my pills, the mood stabilizers I left here?"

"In the medicine cabinet in the bathroom, dear," she said from the kitchen.

I locked the door to the bathroom and found the plastic bottle in the cabinet over the sink. There were only four pills left, and they hadn't passed their expiration date yet, thank God.

I swallowed one and washed it down.

As I waited for it to kick in, I glanced in the mirror and saw Lord Vishnu behind my reflection, tapping away on his phone. I had the feeling he was tweeting about me. Probably under the hashtag "#ourownpersonalholyfool."

"Just leave me alone," I said.

I shut my eyes and took a breath.

When I opened my eyes, he was gone.

That was how the gods came back to me in a big way again since my breakdown. I would have to be careful from now on.

Lunch was pleasant enough for the first fifteen minutes or so, mainly because Dad kept silent.

"So, Ravi, how's life as a private eye, then?" asked Vivek Ghosh, my sister Sanjita's fiancé.

"Most of it is just Dumpster diving," I said. "I once followed a bloke to New York to photograph him cheating on his wife."

"No femme fatale coming to the office? No murders?" Vivek asked with a mildly salacious tone.

"That's just books and telly. If we end up with dead bodies, that's a big deal. Becomes a police matter."

"But the pay's good, yeah?" Sanji said. "I haven't heard you complain about your bills for months now."

"It's not bad. Paying off my overdraft and . . . the other thing."

Slight awkward silence. The "other thing" was Sanjita and Vivek's upcoming wedding. The two of them were suitably embarrassed about this. His parents and ours were annoyingly not.

"That's good of you, man," Vivek said. "You know Sanji and I would if we could—"

"Nonsense!" declared Mum. "Your parents aren't paying for your wedding. We can't have that!"

"But we didn't ask for such a big fucking epic wedding!" cried Sanjita.

"Language," Mum chided

"Vivek and I would be happy with a small reception with just the immediate family—"

"But the family wants to come!" Mum said. "All the way from Mumbai! We can't not have a big reception!"

We were in the cycle now. They'd had this argument for months without any change.

"Listen to your mother," Dad said.

"Is it worth it? Now Ravi is the one to pay off those bills!" Sanjita cried.

"Sanj, it's okay. Really," I said.

"It's not fair on him! After the other stuff he had to go through!"

"He's happy to shoulder the burden," Mum said, perhaps a bit too grandly.

Vivek and I exchanged looks. *Here we go again.*

"Always with the 'burden' and 'duty'!" said Sanji. "Vivek's parents were going to pay for the wedding but you had to just one-up them!"

"We're still on this?" I muttered. "Honestly?"

The inside of my mind was one long sigh and would remain so until I left the house.

"The fish is really good today, Mum," Vivek said, still valiantly playing the peacemaker, trying to defuse and deflect.

"Thank you, dear."

Dad, whom I kept in the corner of my eye, took a sip of water and sighed.

"Oh, Ravi, Ravi, Ravi . . ."

"Dad, Dad, Dad. What is it now?"

"To have fallen so far . . ."

I exchanged a look with Mum.

Here we go.

"So we're on that again, are we?" I said, trying to keep it light.

"Spying on adulterers. Looking at their dirty laundry. At the beck and call of the rich and powerful who can afford you."

"I'm making more money than when I was teaching."

"I raised my children to be good people. I had dreams my son would be a great soul, a mahatma. A holy man. Or at least gotten a professorship with tenure."

"That wasn't for me," I said. "Or teaching."

"And this job is?"

"What if this is all part of my journey? Have you thought about that? What if it's the part where I experience the pleasures and pains of the material life before I attain any spiritual insight?"

"A journey fraught with terrible deeds and terrible people."

I had to be careful not to raise my voice or get heated. The trick to talking to my father was to sound as reasoned and rational as possible, no matter what you were saying. Anger and aggression would have clouded any intent. And we didn't—couldn't bear to—talk about his cancer diagnosis.

"Doesn't understanding the core of these terrible people become part of treating them with compassion?"

"You're becoming like your uncle," muttered Dad.

"I'm not Uncle Pradeep. I'm not going to go crazy, lose all my money gambling and die of alcoholism."

Poor Uncle Pradeep. Never got over the woman who didn't love him back. I had to resist, again, the temptation to tell them that what I got up to in the job was a whole different brand of crazy than his.

"Dad and Mum are worried what their friends will think," Sanjita said, rolling her eyes.

"You and Mum tell your friends what I do?"

"They ask after you," said Mum, as if it was the most obvious thing in the world.

"You're embarrassed about my job, but not so embarrassed that you tell everyone in the neighborhood."

"They like to gossip. All those fishwives and harridans," Dad said.

"They all like to gossip," Sanjita said. "And judge."

"They're my friends!" protested Mum.

"A failed holy man turned private eye. Who would believe it?" Sanjita cracked, laughing.

Not helping, sis.

"You dig through people's rubbish bins," Dad said. "Listen in on their phone calls."

"You say that like it's a bad thing," Sanjita said.

Dad had learned by now never to rise to Sanji's bait.

"Actually, a lot of what we do is search for people on the Internet," I said. "A lot easier that way."

"Forget what you see on the telly, Vivek," Dad said. "Private detectives are seedy people doing seedy things."

Just what was up with him this weekend? It must have been too quiet and peaceful for his taste. Perhaps all this was just to deflect from having to think about cancer. Of course, I hadn't told him about Mum blowing five hundred quid on cards. That would have given him something real to get narked off about. But no, I kept my promise to Mum. And probably continued to enable her next Bad Impulsive Move.

"Oh, are you and Mum so embarrassed about having to tell your friends now?" Sanjita said, voice rising. "That's the thanks he gets for everything."

"Sanji," I muttered. "Really not helping."

"He's God's Suffering Man, and you won't even give him a break!"

"Everyone has to choose what to do once they've fallen, and he had to choose this," Dad said.

Oh, God, was he going to cry?

Wait for it . . .

No. Thank fuck. He was just moody today. Nothing had topped his meltdown the day I had announced that I was giving up Religious Studies. I hoped nothing would.

"So stop giving him shit about it!" shouted Sanjita.

"Sanji, dear," Mum said. "Can you please not swear so much? We don't need so much cursing at the dinner table."

"Your mother's right, young lady," Dad said.

"I'm not a fucking teenager!"

"So stop acting like one," Dad said.

My phone rang. *Saved.*

It was Marcie Holder.

"Sorry. It's work," I said, and got up from the table.

I went into the garden to take the call, really just an excuse to get away from the mayhem of the dinner table.

"Did I rescue you just in time?" asked Marcie.

"Do you know me that well already?"

"You're an open book, Ravi. You're also an unfinished book. That's what makes you interesting."

"Don't tell me you want to be the one who finishes writing it."

"Jeez, you make me sound all stalker-y!" Marcie laughed. "The only one who's going to write your story is you."

I hoped so, if the gods didn't show up and try to rewrite it on the fly.

"So what's up?"

"You said you'd help me with my stalking case. Well, while we were all enjoying our Sunday, it just kicked off. Another flash mob attacked the promotional display and standee of my client at a Waterstones in Picadilly this afternoon. Beat for beat a rerun of the last attack on Charing Cross Road."

"Was anyone hurt?"

"Nope, but a lot of frightened tourists, shocked customers, and mutilated books."

"Did the police catch any of the mob?"

"By the time the cops showed up, they had all vanished into Picadilly Circus and Regent Street."

"Surveillance cameras catch them?"

"You know how useful those are. Their faces were hidden and they just scattered all over the West End from Regent Street to Shaftesbury. If the cops are asking the public for help, it means they have no clue."

"So they already knew how to scatter," I said. "They planned it all the way to their getaway."

"Has this gotten interesting enough for you yet?" Marcie asked.

"I promised I'd help, Marcie. Let's talk first thing Monday."

"Have fun with the folks."

She hung up.

When I first joined the agency, I often wondered if Marcie fancied me for all the easy flirting. Eventually I realized that she just liked flirting with everyone.

"You are so full of shit," said Sanjita, joining me in the garden so she could light a cigarette.

"Why, I don't know what you mean," I said.

"Oh, private eye work is really boring," she said, imitating my breezy voice. "Just following cheating spouses and looking them up on the Internet."

"Hey, if I told Mum and Dad the really crazy shit I really got up to with my coworkers, they would freak the fuck out."

"Ooo-er."

"May they never find out," I said.

"I won't tell if you won't."

We glanced at Mum and Dad chatting with Vivek, Mum doting on him, Dad expounding something about being a good husband. Poor guy.

"He actually enjoys that," Sanji said.

"You know, you and Vivek could just elope. Get married at the Registry, then fuck off for the honeymoon before anyone knows it."

"Believe me, we thought about it, but once we get back, Mum and Dad will just insist on throwing a big fuck-off ceremony again. Back to Square One," she said. "Besides, you see Vivek's face whenever mum talks about the wedding preparations? He's actually well into it."

She took another drag on her ciggie.

"Hey, how bad is work now?" she asked.

"It's never dull, I'll tell you that," I said.

"You still seeing the gods?"

"Not so much, and I don't even need medication."

"That's a relief."

"Money's mad good, so I'm pretty much sorted, but I have to keep closing cases to pay off everything."

"No need to move back in with Mum and Dad, then?"

"Oh, God, don't even joke about that!"

TWO

First thing Monday morning, Marcie showed me all her notes and the security cam footage of the flash mob rampage at the Waterstones. Sure enough, someone had filmed the whole thing on their phone and had uploaded it to YouTube, so we looked at that footage, too. "Bookshop Flash Mob Attack" had gone viral. It also made the TV news and the papers.

"Vandalism, property damage," Ken mused as he glanced over at the video. "Runs the gamut of public order offenses if they're ever nicked."

"Don't these arseholes have anything better to do with their time?" Clive asked.

"And it's not as if any of them was going to go home and brag about it so their mums will turn them in," said Mark, emerging from his haze for a few seconds.

"An act of literary terrorism," Marcie said. "Coupled with some misogynist character assassination against my client."

"I just don't get all the hate," I said. "Why go batshit over a fluffy celebrity memoir?"

The book in question was Delia McCarthy's *Confessions of a Bunny Boiler*, which was a chick-lit mega-seller last year. Benjamin glanced at a few pages and thought it was a bunch of arse. Olivia thought it was amusing, which was as close to a compliment you were ever to going to get from her. Mark actually read the book from cover to over, but then it was probably easy, since he was stoned that weekend. Nobody asked Ken and Clive if they had read it.

Since she was Marcie's client, I didn't actually have to meet her. Marcie was the one to take point on any face-to-face and had already gathered all the information I needed. Sometimes it was a relief to just get on with the legwork without having to talk to the clients and hold their hand.

Delia McCarthy herself was far from the worst person who ever lived, contrary to what her attackers would have you believe. She wasn't some frothing right-winger spouting racist, anti-immigrant rhetoric. She hadn't gotten her start on a reality show. She started out as a journalist, a no-nonsense music fan from Glasgow with a snarky sense of humor. From there she became a tongue-in-cheek agony aunt for the people, got on the radio, got more and more gigs on Radio 1, then continued on to TV, hosting *Top of the Pops* in its last years, then a women's lifestyle show, then a talent show, and now a talk show, the TV personality's version of hard work and paying dues. She managed not to be tabloid fodder, being one of the early adopters of social media to galvanize and centralize her fan following, a mix of young women and young men who liked a funny, no-nonsense female voice. As an avowed feminist, she was well aware of the haters who had always been around since her music paper days. Delia, to her credit, was someone who owned up to her flaws. She admitted to anorexia in her teens, went through a few years of tabloid wildness that were mild by today's standards—a few drunken pictures from nights out in Soho, photos of the actors and football players she dated briefly—but overall didn't do anything too damaging that her enemies could use against her. "You just need to be a woman in public for misogynists to want to come after you," she wrote in a column for the *Sunday Times*.

And, of course, she was one of Marcie's clients in her PR days.

"It's not the book," Marcie said. "It's her whole social media presence. Her whole public persona that the trolls are attacking."

Ah, yes. I'd read through the printouts of Delia's tweets and Facebook posts. They were all perfectly innocuous ruminations about feminism and empowerment to her million-plus fans, most of them women and teenagers. I wouldn't exactly call her a proper role model, considering she wrote mostly about dating and finding the right bloke, but they offered mostly sensible advice about not losing their identities to some bloke. Ever since she started using her social media accounts as part of her agreement with the TV company and her publishers to promote her books and image, Delia had often received tweets and posts from men and the odd women calling her names. Looked like envy, since she was a TV personality with a glamorous life that made her and every celebrity a lightning rod for the envious, unstable, resentful, and unhappy. Then three months ago, the tone changed. The trolling became outright harassment, rape threats, death threats, attacking her books, her shows, her looks, her body parts.

"I'm gonna kick you in the womb!" . . . *"fukkin kill yrself"* . . . *"feminists are a waste of air"* . . . *"Raped first or killed first?"* . . . *"I'm going to piss up your cunt"* . . . *"kill yourself"* . . . and on and on for over a hundred pages.

At first she didn't take them seriously. She toiled long enough in TV to grow a tough shell. She certainly wasn't going to kill herself at the request of a bunch of saddos on the Internet. It was easy enough to just block them as they popped out of the woodwork. Even she had to admit that the people tweeting her photos of their cocks, of executions and animal cruelty, of her photos sliced up was a bit much. She reported it all and sent them to the police, of course.

Then she got doxxed.

One of the trolls managed to find out Delia's home address and posted it online. Three months ago, a man showed up on her doorstep and rang the bell. Her Filipino housekeeper answered the door but didn't take the chain off because he looked dodgy. He looked like a sad sack in faded denim and trainers and demanded to see Delia. Fortunately, she happened to be out at brunch. The housekeeper wouldn't let him in and shut the door. Delia came home late in the afternoon to find the cops waiting for her. They explained that the man had stood outside for the next two hours before her housekeeper called the police. When they showed up and arrested him, they found a kitchen knife in his jacket. He said he just wanted to see Delia. He pointed them to a tweet that posted her address, calling on everyone to show up and "get the bitch." That tweet had been taken down within an hour of its posting but it had already been screencapped and posted to a website devoted to hating Delia McCarthy. That was when Delia got herself some bodyguards and moved out of her house. That was also when she called up her old PR agent, Marcie Holder, for advice, only to find out that Marcie was now working for Golden Sentinels. Delia hired Marcie straightaway.

"Delia thinks there's a mastermind behind all this," Marcie said. "She wants us to track him down."

THREE

was still being tested. The subtext here was still "Don't fuck this up." I was still the new boy around here, even after eight months.

So far, there was no need for me to interview Delia McCarthy. Marcie had transcripts of her interviews already on file, as well as all the printouts of her articles, her books, and the offending posts and emails from her harassers. Marcie was the primary on this case, so it was her call. I was fine doing the grunt work.

"Hello, stranger."

I looked up—"Julia? What brings you here?"

She kissed me quickly in greeting, in full view of everyone.

"Got an interview with Cheryl and Roger."

"For what?"

"A job, of course."

"What?"

"Roger will see you now," Cheryl said, and with that, Julia walked into his office.

"Eyes on the job, Ravi," Marcie said.

I couldn't help stealing glances at Roger's office. Julia's interview seemed to be going well. Roger was all smiles, turning on the charm, no doubt bigging up the agency and the work we did, Cheryl gently but firmly bringing it down to earth with more practical information.

"Think he's going to hire her?" I asked.

"Blond, good-looking girl who could serve as eye candy and a honeytrap?" David said. "No-brainer for Roger."

That didn't make me feel better.

"So what does Delia want to do once we find out who's been organizing these attacks on her?" I asked.

"She hasn't decided yet," Marcie said.

"*Ours not to wonder why*. Got it."

So I sat down with the printouts and started going through the usernames of the abusers, marking out the ones that popped up most often. Delia's assistant had printed out the page that posted her address, so we had that to go on. And such was the trust Marcie generated in her clients that Delia also gave us the passwords to all of her social media accounts. That gave us a record of the harassment and its escalation in real time. The downside was that we had literally tens of thousands of posts to wade through.

I didn't have to read through all of them, of course. What I had to do was mark the names and handles of the abusers who popped up most frequently.

"I think some of these are the same people who set up multiple accounts to spam abuse at Delia. Sock puppets, they're called," I said. "There are the hit-and-run accounts. Those popped up once to post abuse, then got banned, then another came along with a similar username, posting similar insults. Then eventually most of them went away."

"Great. Now we can see if any of them are the ringleaders of the harassment campaign," Marcie said, pulling on her jacket.

"Where are you going?"

"To check in with Delia. Hold my client's hand, of course. That's why I need you to take point on this one. I'm on the phone if you need me."

Marcie's American-ness was always going to be on display, and she used that to her advantage. I had wondered for ages why she worked in public relations when I found out her background. She had studied international relations and journalism at Yale and could have been a journalist or worked for the government. She struck me as overqualified for PR. Maybe she just preferred the cushy life, not that PR was any less stressful. In fact, it was at the last company she worked for that she crashed and burned. The details were vague, but they were nevertheless now an urban legend in the history of disastrous PR campaigns:

It was one of those overbudgeted TV ads with a huge set and special effects involving fake snow and a temperamental reality TV star. The product was ice cream for a Christmas promo. The director was a hotshot rising star in the ad world well on his way to becoming the next Ridley Scott as soon as he got to direct a proper film. According to Marcie, the set was coked to the gills. And her client was bonking the director. The star, the director, half the crew, the production company, and Marcie had their hands full keeping the reps from the ice cream company from seeing what was really happening. Marcie obviously couldn't keep that up when the expensive special effects machines went wrong and dumped over a hundred pounds of pink goo that was supposed to pass for strawberry ice cream right over the star, the dancers, and the camera equipment. I forget what the bill was for that. Since the campaign had been Marcie's baby—she had pitched it—it had ended her career in public relations. She became known as the PR person who put her client in a bad spot with the most fucked outcome imaginable (short of someone getting killed). It was one fuckup, but it was too big to forgive.

"How did you come to pitch this campaign, anyway?" I asked. "You strike me as too smart for that."

"You had to be there," she said. "There was tons of dough in the ads industry at the time, and we were all coked to the gills, so all kinds of crazy, stupid ideas just sounded like the greatest thing ever at the time."

Just as she was wondering if she should pack up and head back to the States, Roger came a-calling. He offered her a position as the go-to gal that celebrities could bring their problems to. She already knew everyone in show business: actors, reality stars, sports stars, celebrity chefs, singers.

Marcie's celebrity clients gave Golden Sentinel a very nice turnaround, kept us in our expensive meals and wardrobe accounts that enabled us to look smart and upmarket.

"What I love about the British is," Marcie said, "they are a lot more ruthless and creative when it comes to destroying someone through satire.

It's a fate worse than death. Hundreds of years ago, the British perfected the art of it. When they decided they didn't like a public figure like a king or a politician, they would find the most vicious way to ridicule his worst traits. By the time they were through, they'll have destroyed his reputation and perception for all time, so we now only know that image of him. The real him is long gone. That is PR as a weapon, and I am a master of that weapon whenever somebody hires us to help save them from scandal. This is what this case is all about. We have to stop this guy from destroying my client's image."

With that, she was out the door.

FOUR

So Marcie's got you doing the dirty work, then?" Olivia asked. "She must be expecting some crazy shit to go down."

"Come on, we're just cross-referencing and compiling data," I said. "I don't even have to talk to the client or interview anyone. Just give the information we find to Marcie to give to the client."

"Easy-peasy, eh?"

"Easy-peasy."

Olivia chuckled.

"Oh, Ravi, why do you think Marcie picked you instead of Mark or Benjamin? There's an angle she's seeing that only you can bring to bear."

"Like what?"

"Like, oh, bloody great mess that's only going to get much more interesting and fun now that you're on it."

"Oh, come on!"

"No, you come on. Look at this, Ravi."

She held up the printouts. "She has you looking for a needle in a haystack. You don't know if it's just one needle. We're talking about a bunch of jumped-up armchair psychopaths who think they can hide behind the cloak of digital anonymity."

"Why didn't she ask you?"

"Because I would have told her to sod off and sort it out herself."

"Wouldn't Roger sack you for that?"

"I'm too valuable to sack. This firm's entire IT security is nothing without me."

"Olivia, I've been wondering . . ."

"Yes, darling?"

"Why are you here?"

"Paying my rent, of course."

"No, I mean, you have an IQ off the charts, you're from a respectable Hong Kong banking family. You have mad skills. You could be running your father's bank, or managing a hedge fund worth tens of millions of pounds, or be the CEO of your own company. What are you doing working at a private investigations firm?"

She took off her glasses and rubbed her eyes, weighing whether to tell me.

"Penance," she said.

"For what?"

"Do you remember that Pentagon hack from the 1990s?"

"Yes, before Anonymous became a thing. It was just hackers looking for evidence of UFOs, silly stuff like that."

"Well, they weren't that good. They didn't know how to breach the firewalls until someone on the usenet group they posted on told them how to do it. They were caught, but that 'someone' never was."

"Those guys who were arrested and extradited to the States never said they had help."

"Of course not. They weren't going to admit some teenager helped them crack that final hurdle to break into the Pentagon's computers."

"What's that got to do with all this?"

"It's background. I was in boarding school at the time. I was always good with numbers, figures, data, code. I wrote a bot that I introduced to the school's computer network that could change anyone's exam results. I sussed out how easy it was to peak at the emails coming in and out of No. 10 Downing Street before I finished my A Levels."

"All without getting caught."

"The best hackers are the ones you never heard about, who don't give interviews or brag about it on forums and message boards."

"So if you never got caught, why—?"

"I'm getting to that. First year I was at university, my dad implemented a new security system for his bank. They hired Oscar Jong, a bloke who was hyped up as an Internet security guru at the time. Those of us in the hacker scene knew he was a clueless twat with good PR. And my dad had hired him to shore up the online security of our family business."

"That must have been irritating."

"It seriously got on my tits. My dad and his board of directors were utterly clueless about the Internet. Their solution was to throw money at the problem. I couldn't very well call up my dad and tell him they hired a Muppet to protect over a hundred million pounds' worth of bank accounts. So I decided to do my own pentest."

"Pen—?"

"Penetration test. It's what every self-respecting institution hires experts to do: test the strength of their security systems. In one evening, I had the entire online infrastructure of my dad's bank under my control. I could have stolen all the money, and I mean literally all the money, out of the bank and transferred it to offshore accounts I could set up instantly if I felt like it. But no, I left all the accounts alone. I did, however, leave a message in the code to let Oscar Jong know just how thoroughly I had owned him. Then I used a proxy email account to write my father and his entire board of directors telling them how easily they had been hacked and how useless Jong was. I made it clear that I was not out to blackmail the bank or hold it ransom, that I was strictly white hat, that I was not going to make what I did public. I only wanted them to get their bloody act together, and Oscar Jong was an idiot and an incompetent. To prove that, I reset his passwords and locked him out of the system, and I challenged him to find his way back in. He never did. I'm the reason nobody hears of Oscar Jong anymore."

"So you ruined his career."

"He didn't deserve that career. Anyway, my father freaked the fuck out and wanted the hacker caught. He even hired his old friend Roger Golden to hunt the hacker down. Roger, my godfather."

"I didn't know he was your godfather."

"Now, Roger didn't know or care about computers other than when he used email and watched porn. He barely bothered to look into the hacker scene or go through Oscar Jong's enemies. He almost immediately sussed out it was me."

"How did he do that?"

"I know you think Roger is an East End chancer with a winning smile and a silver tongue. That's what he wants everyone to think. Underneath the expensive suit is a steel-trap mind that can read people like a book. He looked at the anonymous emails I'd sent to my dad and the bank and saw that it was personal. He deduced it was someone close to home, not a stranger. He'd known me all my life, even though I never told him I was good at computers or hacking, but he knew me well enough to see that I would be the type to hack the bank's website to prove its security was buggered. The one time I poked my head above the parapet and I got caught."

"So did he tell your dad?"

"It was a fraught meeting. Roger acted as go-between so that my dad didn't fly off the handle and go completely mental. He was already shocked that I was capable of doing it. We had to convince my dad that I was doing it on behalf of the family business. My dad at least saw the point, and sacked Oscar Jong. But it also put me on my dad's shitlist. Part of his problem was that a girl had bested him. Even though he had no problem with me growing up and having my own career, good old patriarchal sexism was still at play here. So Roger offered to take me under his wing. Once I earned my degrees, Roger offered me a job. I'm here for every time a bit of hacking is called for, because I can guarantee we'll never get caught."

Hacking was illegal and unethical, and to do it in private investigations were no exception, but the entire IT infrastructure of the firm was designed by Olivia. Our email was heavily encrypted, our Internet traffic was filtered through multiple proxies, and our firewalls and safeguards were all custom-built by her. Many clients assumed that Benjamin, as our resident tech nerd, was also the head of IT. It suited Olivia to hide behind that façade.

"So this is my exile. My dad has spread the word that I'm not ready for prime time in finance. Meanwhile, I toil away here and learn the secrets of the whole playing field. One day, I'll head my own company, on my own terms, and dear old Dad won't be able to do a thing about it. Now enough about me. Show me what you have."

"So why are you doing this for me?"

"Because I want to see what you do when you piece everything together. It'll be a giggle."

FIVE

With Olivia by my side, we logged into Delia McCarthy's social media accounts. I picked out the harassers who appeared most often on her timelines and asked Olivia to trace their IP addresses. Then we cross-referenced them to see how many of them shared the same IP address, which indicated that they were the same handful of people who had set up sock-puppet accounts to make it look like there were more trolls than there really were going after Delia. The IP addresses were with the usual providers: BT, Sky, TalkTalk, Vodafone, Virgin, and so on. Olivia easily "obtained" the real names and addresses behind those IP addresses.

I typed up the list, coupling the usernames with the IP addresses they posted from and the real names and addresses. There would be enough of a digital trail for Delia to submit as evidence when she decided to prosecute the worst trolls. This was a nice meat-and-potatoes job, easily wrapped up within a day by just going over data and finding the links, solved without my even needing to leave the office or meet the client.

I'd just finished emailing a copy of the list to Marcia when I heard Julia laughing with Roger and Cheryl in his office.

"All very impressive," Roger said as he walked Julia out of his office. "You can start tomorrow if you like."

"I'm sure we can find something for you to do almost immediately," Cheryl said.

"Thank you." Julia smiled. "This means a lot to me."

Roger winked at me.

"She's a keeper, this one," Roger said. "Hold on to her, Ravi."

What the fuck?

"Attention, children," Roger said. "I'd like to introduce a new addition to our little family. I'm sure you've already met Julia due to her relationship with our Ravi, but now she's formally joining us. She's a quick learner, sharp as a tack, and already well versed in the ins and outs of social engineering."

Oh, Christ.

David leaned over to me.

"Told ya," he whispered.

"I'll sort you out a desk and a computer, dear." Cheryl grabbed Benjamin to help her set up another workstation and terminal in our open space.

"Welcome to the Monkey House," Mark said with a salute.

While Benjamin set up Julia's office email and logins, she pulled up a chair and sat next to me.

"What are you doing?" I asked.

"Making myself useful, of course."

"But here? What about your studies?"

"I'm taking a sabbatical. Told my tutor I needed time off to sort myself out. My therapist said I could be of service as a way to offset my . . . condition."

"Julia, you know what we get up to around here. Why do you want to get mixed up in all of this?"

"I still remember what we did in Paris."

"Er—"

"It was a hell of a thrill. You were as high as I was afterwards."

"So you want more of it."

"While being of service, yes. And I get to be closer to you."

Olivia was amused. They all were.

I went into Roger's office and shut the door.

"You're here to talk about your girlfriend, I take it?"

"Is it such a good idea to hire her? She's totally green."

"So were you when we first took you in."

"Yes, but—"

"As you might have noticed," Roger said, "Julia is the very picture of an English Rose. You don't need me to tell you how rare it is to have someone pretty and intelligent who can blend in at almost any establishment and posh setting where they will grossly underestimate her and take her for granted, which makes her the perfect Trojan horse. Julia will be learning on the job with you, so do use her where appropriate. Consider her not just a colleague but a valuable investment in our arsenal of bright young things."

SIX

The cat, a striped orange moggie with an unflappable demeanor, even despite the ordeal she had gone through, meowed fitfully inside the cage as I carried it through Mrs. Dhewan's front door.

"Oh, Shashti! Did you miss Mummy?" Mrs. Dhewan cooed as she pulled the cat out of the cage and cuddled her.

I had given the cat a bath and fed her before I brought her back.

"You are a credit to your profession, Ravi."

"Thank you, Mrs. Dhewan."

"You do your parents proud. Now, who was it?"

"Nobody. You don't have to worry about them."

"That's not what I asked, Ravi. Out with it."

"It was the Sam and Trenesh Achari from two streets over."

"The Tamil boys? Those little devils. Were they going to torture my little Shashti?"

"They hid her in the toolshed and were all set to do it. I brought a couple of my colleagues with me, two ex-policemen. They put the fear of God into them. They're never going to torture anything again."

"Those Achari boys are mean little bastards," Mrs. Dhewan said. "I think I'm going to set some new rules around the neighborhood for our Tamil neighbors."

"Is it really necessary to exacerbate the ethnic tensions in the area?"

"Do not question how I keep the peace on my patch, Ravi."

"Understood."

Then it was off to dinner with my parents. My mother had confessed her situation to Dad and my taking on her debt. She seemed to time the drama for our weekly dinners for maximum effect.

"What have you done?" my father bellowed. "You've sold our son into indentured slavery to that—that woman!"

"Dad, calm down. It's fine."

"Fine? That woman is a criminal! What has she got you doing?"

"Why, my skills as a private investigator, of course. I helped rescue her lost cat the other day."

Sanjita suppressed a giggle. Vivek stuffed roti in his mouth.

"It was Mrs. Achari's boys. They wanted to hold it for ransom."

"Clueless teenagers. As if tension with the Tamils wasn't bad enough," Sanjita said.

"How do you know all that?" Vivek asked.

"Ravi debriefs me."

"So I kept a situation in Mrs. Dhewan's backyard from escalating," I said. "In return, she extended the period for paying her back."

Dad harrumphed.

"You see?" Mum said. "Nothing to worry about. Ravi knows what he's doing."

"That doesn't free him from the debt that you incurred," Dad said.

"Well, I did look up her and her family members online, found their social media group page, and discovered that Francis, Mrs. Dhewan's nephew, was trying to get a loan to buy a house."

"Did you do something illegal?" Dad asked, his back up.

"Not at all. A few months ago, my agency investigated a data breach at United Allied Bank and stopped a hacker from stealing money out of their accounts. United Allied were very grateful, so I called in a favor and helped Francis secure a loan. Mrs. Dhewan was so pleased that she agreed to charge me no interest in the repayment of the loan."

"Nice one," Sanjita said.

"You see," Mum said to Dad. "One step at a time."

Dad harrumphed.

The conversation inevitably turned to my job again. I told them about helping Delia McCarthy with her cyberbullying and harassment problem, how it was a fairly mundane and perfectly legal task of sorting through Internet posts and printouts to help her gather evidence to identify the culprits. Mum approved and even Dad didn't object. Vivek loved the story. Sanjita looked skeptical, like she was expecting the other shoe to drop. I insisted this was a perfectly straightforward case. I'd done my job, and that was that. I suppose I was still seeking my parents' approval, give me a reality check on my moral compass. Here I was telling them that I was still a good person and doing nothing wrong, that I was helping people so Mum and Dad wouldn't be disappointed or worried. All in all, I was in a pretty good place by the end of the evening.

Unfortunately, that changed two days later when Delia McCarthy decided to unleash hell.

SEVEN

On my way into Golden Sentinels, I made a call to my GP about getting a new prescription for pills. I didn't want to see gods, signs, and portents all the time. It was bad enough that my dad being sick was weighing on me, and that seemed to be what had triggered the new visions.

The first time this happened was when I told Dad and Mum I was giving up my degree in religious studies. I chalked it up to a breakdown. I would see gods on and off ever since. The last time was nearly a year ago when I lost my teaching job. Every time my life turned upside down, this happened. This job, my dad's illness, my mum's debts—stess, stress, stress. It all added up. The deeper I got into this job, the more fucked-up situations I was getting involved in, the more the gods were showing up. I should have known, but I was stuck well in now. I needed this job, I needed the money to pay off my own debts and the money Mum owed to Mrs. Dhewan. I'd actually put myself in a position where the gods would pop up in my life, and I was trapped now.

Marcie was making her presentation to our team. Delia McCarthy was an A-list client, so of course Cheryl gave her the floor. Roger and David were off to South Africa, something about setting up Golden Securities Limited, a South African branch of the firm, but with some fiddling with the paperwork so Roger wouldn't have to pay extra tax, even though in spirit it would be the South African branch of this firm the same way there was a New York branch, a Chicago branch, a

Mumbai branch, a Hong Kong branch, and a Los Angeles Branch. Marcie waited for Benjamin to finish his daily sweep of the office for bugs while everyone else read my report on the cyberbullying campaign against Delia McCarthy.

Olivia and I didn't need to because we were the ones who compiled it, after all.

"We identified a hundred and two individuals who were responsible for over ten thousand posts directed at Delia," I said. "Many of them created up to five sock-puppet accounts just to make it look like there were more of them ganging up on her. The worst offenders are the six we narrowed down. They actively organized and coordinated the flash mob, so we want to work out who they are. The other key target is a guy who started the whole thing off in the first place: George Rexton."

"The author?" Ken and Clive perked up.

"The very same."

George Rexton was a bestselling author of macho thrillers featuring manly ex-army mercenary Van Stark and his ongoing personal war against environmentalist terrorists, homosexual rich kids financing them, and damsels in distress who melted in his arms and onto his dick. The books sold around one hundred thousand copies each, despite hardly ever getting reviewed by the papers. He was a major earner for his publisher despite the lack of mainstream respect for him. Rexton liked to present himself as a hardscrabble, pulled-up-by-the-bootstraps, self-made author, and Delia McCarthy, with her higher public profile, red-carpet lifestyle, and higher book sales, got under his skin by her sheer existence.

"You can see that he started out arguing with Delia about feminism. That went on for months. He would belittle, defame, tease her. He even wrote about her on his blog. Just about all the hundred harassers followed him on Facebook and Twitter. We can tie it all to him."

Julia was reading the report keenly. Cheryl had already read it the night before, since she always reviewed copies along with David to watch for anything that might be incriminating, and the two of them had already apprised Roger of it before I arrived.

Marcie took over now.

"So I went over the intel Ravi and Olivia gathered with the client. She was very, very pleased, guys. She's now fully informed and armed for her next move. We are going, to quote our client, to 'get the motherfuckers.'"

Well, that was fair enough. We'd gathered enough evidence for Delia to present to the police. She was high profile, and the file was thick enough for them to take action. The UK did have adequate laws against harassment, cyberbullying, and hate speech, and there had been enough prosecutions of Internet trolls in the last few years to set a legal precedent. Unlike the United States, we'd sent Internet trolls to jail. It wasn't going to stop other unhappy and psychopathic dickheads from cyberbullying people, and not all of them would get caught, but it did send the message to society at large that this was not acceptable.

"We still don't know exactly who put together and incited the flash mob, though," I interjected. "It's one of the other five names on the Most Active list. That's what we need to find out."

"Did you know Delia McCarthy had a degree in psychology before she went into the media?" Marcie said. "We had a long talk over drinks. She walked me through the personality profiles of the types of people who would troll and harass her online. When they band together, they become a tribe with their own echo chamber, convinced there are no consequences to their actions because they can hide behind their keyboards and anonymity.

"It's mostly men, some of them are women. Really fucked-up women. They're antifeminist and misogynist. Some of them are just dumb teenagers with keyboards. Any female public figure is a target for them, and they chose Delia because she's on TV almost every day, so they get to ignore the problems of their own little lives and focus all their frustrations and hate on her. As a feminist, Delia has been thinking about this for a long time. She wants to take a stand, not lie back and passively get fucked."

Made sense. Delia McCarthy had been an advocate of women's rights since her music journo days, so she now had a bigger platform than ever to set an example. Good on her.

"So you all have the troll list. We're going to hunt them down and fuck them up."

Wait, what?

"This is a surgical strike," Marcie said.

"Surgical," Clive said. "We like that."

I couldn't help thinking that Ken and Clive were taking the meaning literally.

"Mark, Ravi, here's where you get to do as little work as possible. You have the minors list."

"Shall I put the fear of God into the nasty little kiddies, then?" Mark asked.

"Start out by texting their phones to let them know you're onto them and we know who they really are. You phone their homes and talk to their moms. Then contact their schools. Go ahead and release their posts with their names and fake handles attached."

"Like demonic telemarketers, we shall venture forth!" Mark declared.

"What about George Rexton?" I asked.

"Oh, Delia has something special planned for him," said Marcie. "Julia, you up for some undercover work, hon?"

"Hang on," I said. "Julia hasn't been properly trained on procedures yet."

"Chill, dude," Marcie said. "This will be low-maintenance. It's not like we're sending her to the Middle East. We just want eyes-on confirmation of his computer and domestic setup."

Julia shot me a look. She did not want me to rescue her.

Marcie called in a favor with a friend at Rexton's publisher to take Julia as an intern, where she would be assigned to help Rexton with getting his new novel ready. The aim here was to get close to Rexton. Julia was very game.

"I don't think this is a good idea," I said to her when we had a quiet moment.

"I'm just there to be a secretary and get information on him," she said. "It's not like he's a serial killer or a murder suspect."

This was a classic honeytrap op. Rexton was one of those dysfunctional, pompous writers who drank too much and had a roving eye for the ladies. He'd already been through three marriages, and much of his book earnings were spent on alimony. All of this was on record in the various interviews he had given to newspapers and magazines at the peak of his fame. His novels were steady sellers, and he was a regular fixture at literary festivals and readings. He was adept at using social media to promote his books, which pushed the sales despite the lack of mainstream reviews in the last few years. Julia, with her English Rose looks and long legs, was like crack cocaine to someone like him.

"I'm fitting a microphone to the button on your blouse and a camera to your pendant," Benjamin said. "When you get into his office, Olivia will send an email that downloads a virus to his computer."

"We're going to own his computer," Marcie said.

"You know," I said, "given how we're going to get the evidence of his fuckery, none of it will be admissible in court."

"Who says this is going to court?" Marcie said.

"Is this why you waited till David was out of town to launch this operation?" I said.

"He didn't need to hear this." She shrugged.

"So the only part of this case that's investigation is finding the people who organized the flash mob," I said. "The rest is, what, vigilantism?"

"That's a nice way of putting it," Marcie said, amused as ever.

"I don't mean to be the wet blanket here, but Delia McCarthy isn't really planning to go to the police with this, is she?"

"Only if she absolutely has to, but no, that's not part of her plan. She's a tough Glaswegian chick. They fight their own battles."

"So what exactly is her plan again?"

"What do you do when you go to war? You gather your army, plan your strategy, use every advantage you have at your disposal, which in Delia's case is her money and us, and attack your enemies until you destroy them utterly. Fairness has nothing to do with it. You totally want to have an unfair advantage over your enemy. Delia is a big fan of Sun Tzu's *The Art of War*."

"But isn't it a bit too soon to send Julia in undercover? She hasn't been trained in procedure, dos and don'ts."

"I can follow direction, Ravi."

"Aren't you being a bit protective about your girlfriend, mate?" asked Benjamin.

I hadn't told anyone at the office Julia was a sex addict. That was her secret, not mine to pass around. My fear was that she might be substituting thrill-seeking for sex, and there was the possibility that she might bonk Rexton. He was exactly the kind of horrible arsehole she would fuck in a moment of self-loathing and compulsion. It would be her way of trying to sabotage our relationship, to prove herself unworthy, and drive me away. I couldn't promise I would stay with her if she slept with someone else, no matter how much we were getting closer to each other.

"Are you going to talk me out of it?" Julia asked.

"Every cell in my body wants to."

"I'll be fine, Ravi."

I could feel chaos swirling and bubbling up from this case. At the far wall of the office, I could see Yama, the god of punishment, judgment, and death, leaning on one of the desks, watching us. He tapped his mace on his hand, looking like a headmaster ready to administer a thrashing. I hoped this wasn't a sign of where this case was going.

I went back to my desk and popped a pill.

EIGHT

My doctor's office hadn't called me back about my prescription, so I turned to Mark.

"No problem, mate." Of course he happened to have what I needed in his desk, which was a stash of all kinds of psychoactive medication. I gave him fifty quid for it. He didn't judge, handed me a fresh bottle of mood stabilizers.

Of course the gods were popping up to watch now. They had a front seat to my increasingly surreal and nasty reality show. After all, I wasn't just a soap opera of family illness and drama. With these recent cases, I was now swimming in waters most punters didn't get to see: the lifestyle of the rich, imperiled, and vengeful. Maybe the gods were always there, but it was in my moments of distress that they could manifest rather than stay in the shadows.

Benjamin gave Mark and me burner phones to call the people on the list. Even Olivia chipped in for a laugh. It went as well as you might expect.

"Hello, Mrs. Lewis, I'm calling about your son Matthew. Are you aware that he's been sending rape threats to Delia McCarthy? Yes, her on the television."

This usually resulted in profound embarrassment and apologies, a shamed teenager, and solemn promise not to do it again. It reminded me of my days as a teacher.

"Ms. McCarthy felt you might want to have a serious chat with your son," Mark purred in his most official-sounding voice. "Rather than bring in the authorities. We thought we'd spare you the grief, and you'd like to take care of it yourself."

"I have a little boy myself," Olivia said, though she did not have any children and wouldn't for years, if she could help it. "So I know how much of a handful they can be. . . ."

Between Mark, Olivia, and me, we crossed off the first thirty on the Teenage Shithead List by lunchtime.

We didn't always contact the mothers. We also texted the trolls themselves, addressing them by their real names and repeating what they had posted on Delia's timeline. This was often enough to have them pissing their pants, especially after we let them know we knew where they lived. These were usually fourteen- or sixteen-year-olds, so the threat of exposing them to their parents and the world at large was usually enough.

As for the adults, the truly obnoxious, the unrepentant and hateful, Olivia went hard-core. She had already gotten their basic information before, so it wasn't hard to send them viruses and worms that nuked their computers. All it took was a file attachment and a bit of social engineering, and she effectively owned their lives. Emails, photos, videos, credit cards, bank account information—Olivia saw it all. She held their computers hostage, froze their whole system, and put up a window on the screen that told them if they wanted control of their computers back, they had to upload a photo of themselves holding up a sign apologizing for threatening Delia McCarthy with their phones. She made them think it was the Russian Mafia that was fucking with them. Their fear was palpable even in their texts to Olivia's burner phone. It was quite gratifying. Once she saw proof they'd sent their apology photos, she released their computers. She found child porn on two of the computers, and anonymously forwarded the information to the police.

I had no problem being an instrument of retribution and karmic payback. For Mark, this was a nice diversion before his next spliff. Olivia took to playing Nemesis with particular relish.

It was probably just as well Delia was only well-known in the UK, so her harassment had all been from British scumbags. If she had been American, it would probably have encompassed the whole of the United States as well, racking up hundreds of trolls across two continents. Being confined to the UK kept the numbers relatively small. What still worried me was the rest of our campaign. Ken and Clive had been given a list of addresses—and had been allowed to run amok.

NINE

Ken and Clive worked closely with Marcie on their part of the campaign, or "op," as she liked to call it. Not all the names on their list were in London, so it involved driving up the motorways to reach them. The firm kept several cars for its investigators. The black BMWs were the official cars, as much to look impressive to clients as for their reliability. There was also a VW van for hauling things and people. The Ford and Vauxhall, exactly the same models that plainclothes police drove, were for jobs that we didn't want to be caught doing. The license numbers used were either those registered to a distant relative of Roger's who was long deceased or actual license numbers registered to cars in the Metropolitan Police Force. Yes, it was all highly illegal, but that never stopped Roger. The general MO of the firm was "whatever we can get away with."

Ken and Clive took the Vauxhall.

"So what's bothering you now?" asked Mark when we went up on the roof to have a spliff.

"Ken and Clive visiting those trolls to give them a 'talking-to,'" I said. "Should we worry about becoming accessories to what they might do to those people?"

"I wouldn't worry about it. Ken and Clive never lose control."

"Is that supposed to make me feel better?"

"You forget that Ken and Clive used to be pretty decent coppers."

"I never asked about their time in the force. They don't exactly invite questions."

"No, really, they used to be quite shit-hot as far as old-school, slightly sexist, slightly racist, but fair coppers went. They were bloody good detectives. They were thorough, diligent, never fitted up the wrong person."

By 'old-school,' it was probably safe to assume they used to beat up suspects to extract information and confessions. I have to admit I make Ken and Clive sound like a couple of meatheaded thugs, which was not true considering they were the ones who had trained me in investigative methods and procedures when Roger first hired me. They taught me what to look for when I entered a room, what kinds of behavior to look for in people, what to look for in what they said, how to read their body language, how to follow someone on foot or in a car without them cottoning on, how best to pick locks, what to say while undercover, the various techniques of face-to-face social engineering, how to carry myself to look absolutely convincing in any situation. They also taught me some basic fight and self-defense strategies, how and when to throw a proper punch—the type of punch that wasn't about showing off, but to put the other bloke down long enough for you to get your point across or get away.

"So what went wrong for them?" I asked. "It sounds like they actually liked being coppers."

"They just had to catch a case that did them in," Mark said. "It was a dead little boy. Orphan, so nobody really cared. Kid was supposed to be part of a charity foundation that took care of kids in trouble. This one had been sexually abused repeatedly, then killed and dumped. Investigation kept getting stalled. Witnesses were thin on the ground. Lots of stonewalling. Ken and Clive wouldn't let it go and eventually got a suspect: Lord Fowell-Treacle, Earl of Lowton."

"The one that went missing? I thought he did a runner, left the country because he was a suspect. I didn't know Ken and Clive were the officers in charge of the investigation."

"Ken and Clive reckoned he was part of a pedophile ring that included politicians, tycoons, and members of the Establishment."

"Is this the same one that's been in the news lately?"

"Probably. You think it's a big deal now, it was almost too unbearable to consider back in the nineties. And two lowly detective constables with a working theory and mountain of circumstantial evidence were not going to get far. The higher-ups started telling them they should drop it. Then Special Branch came in and asked for their notes and everything they had on it. The case was officially closed."

"So it was going to be covered up."

"They did cover it up. But Ken and Clive weren't about to let it go. They just bided their time."

"Where is this going?"

"This, my son, is where the tale enters the realm of pure speculation. It's all supposition because there are no actual witnesses."

I saw Lord Vishnu standing behind Mark, by the balcony, listening intently to this tale. Lord Vishnu was all about the balance between Good and Evil, so of course he would take an interest. I had a sinking feeling the outcome of this story was going to be mostly Evil.

"Let's say you had an aristocrat who had been getting away with his depraved, wicked ways for ages, protected by his privilege and the foot soldiers of the Establishment at his disposal. A Big Bad Wolf in real life. Without evidence or the possibility of arrest, conventional justice was just not going to happen. Until someone decided to take the law into their own hands. They knew he didn't travel around with bodyguards, so smug in his certainty that he was untouchable. Well, they were definitely going to touch him.

"They watched him for weeks, months even, till they knew his routines. They knew his comings and goings, when he went to dinner at his clubs, which brothels he went to."

"Were they trying to catch him with a kid?"

"It wasn't about that anymore. They knew he did it. They didn't feel the need to catch him at it. They waited for the right evening. The late night where he was alone in his car, driving out of London, on his way home to his estate, on the dark road where there were no CCTV cameras and it was near a forest. Imagine, if you will, the ending of a dark fairy tale."

Now Kali showed up, her skin all black, leaning on Lord Vishnu's shoulder, her tongue licking her lips in anticipation.

"Imagine our two gay huntsmen, pure of heart and full of hate, pulling over the evil lord on a lonely road in the dark of night, introducing themselves as policemen checking him for his alcohol levels. They got him to step out of his car to do a sobriety test. He'd had a couple of whiskies at his club. He would grumble as they led him away from the car and into the woods. There they would read him the charges against him, and after his protests, he would go from indignation to outrage to outright threats. The old 'Do you know who I am? I'll have your guts for garters!' They would let him shout his fill until he spent all his strength and energy. Eventually it would dawn on him that he would not be leaving those woods, ever. There would be no negotiation, no mercy no matter how much he pleaded. Our intrepid huntsmen were determined to put an end to the rampage of this Big Bad Wolf. They would make sure he would be done, and he would never, ever be found. His remains would be buried deep in a pit, so deep a random dog could never dig them up. They even went back for his car, drove it into the forest. They spent weeks picking out a spot, one for the wolf and one for his car. They buried his car, as well. You could say the earth had swallowed him up, and everyone went on with their lives none the wiser. The two huntsmen awoke from this dream and went back to their lives in the city as policemen."

"That's very pat, Mark, but—"

"Ah, would that it ended there. There was a huge hubbub over the disappearance of Lord Fowell-Treacle, of course. Big search, manhunts, detectives and investigators sent abroad chasing leads and rumors, the biggest vanishing in Britain since Lord Lucan. Our huntsmen didn't give a fuck, of course. Wasn't their case. They went back to be DCs, chasing crooks and murderers."

"Yeah, I remember the Fowell-Treacle Disappearance. I was still in university at the time."

"So being coppers, our huntsmen knew all about forensics and how not to produce incriminating evidence, how to hide their tracks. They'd seen the crims they went after try it to varying degrees of success. They knew how to do it better. As you know, that's what they taught us during training here in Golden Sentinels."

"So why didn't they stay in the Met?"

"Ah, well, what if their first was only that—their first? What if they got a taste for taking care of the murderers that would otherwise get away with it?"

"Is any of this true?"

"I told you, Ravi. All this is pure speculation. So to continue. The huntsmen start dabbling in this kind of cleaning every now and then. Never their own cases. They have alibis prepared beforehand. The flaw in their ongoing hobby is that they perhaps got a bit too good at it. The higher-ups start getting an inkling that they had extracurricular activities and start getting nervous. There was a common pattern to the disappearances. They were all pedophiles, some of them linked to the ring they started hearing about in the Fowell-Treacle case. That means the Establishment might start getting nervous about questions. Now the huntsmen's bosses had two suspects but no evidence. What to do? Why, the simplest solution would be to sack them, of course.

"How they did it was quite simple. Charge Ken and Clive with corruption and taking bribes. All it took was to plant some evidence in their lockers, cash and bags of cocaine from Evidence, and hey presto! You got two bent coppers on your manor! They called Ken and Clive in for a quiet chat. They could charge them and have a trial and send them to prison, or they could quietly resign, give up their pensions, join the world of us punters with no authority. Become someone else's problems. Since Ken and Clive were not interested in prison, they took the sacking. And just in time for Roger to hear about them through his various grapevines and come a-knocking. They were his first investigators after he and Cheryl set up Golden Sentinels and found there was so much work that they needed more than just him doing the legwork."

"Mark, how do you know all this, anyway?"

"Years ago, over drinks, of course. Most of it came from Roger. The rest from Ken and Clive. Of course, they weren't going to own up to it. You don't confess to anything if you can help it. They spoke of the night in the woods in the most removed and abstract language you can imagine. That way it became speculation and hearsay, useless as testimony in court."

I wondered if Ken and Clive were already lovers by then or if that had come later. Were they bound together by this or were they already attracted to each other, all under the noses of their colleagues, without ever coming out of the closet? No one would ever suspect Ken and Clive of being gay from looking at them. Besides, it was natural to assume Ken and Clive would smash their faces in if they called them poofs. That was how Ken and Clive liked it.

Over Mark's shoulder, I saw Lord Vishnu salute us and vanish. Kali laughed, danced a dervish, her many arms swinging as she spun and went on her way into the sky.

"So don't you worry about Ken and Clive dropping us into anything," Mark said. "We're well covered."

We finished off the spliff, and Mark ground it out with his foot before we went back down to our desks.

TEN

Sure enough, to nobody's surprise, Ken and Clive put at least two of the trolls on their list in the hospital.

They started small. The first one on their list was a university student who created the list that incited its members to gather as the flash mob that trashed Delia McCarthy's standee and display table at the Waterstones on Piccadilly. They knocked on his door late one night and flashed the rather convincing warrant cards Benjamin had whipped up for them on this occasion. They introduced themselves as Smith and Jones from the Internet Harassment Squad of the Metropolitan Police Force, which didn't really exist. They showed him printouts of the screencaps of the page where he invited people to gather and trash Delia's books at the shop. They showed him a page of code that traced his DNS ID and ISP address, through which they easily got his name and address from his IP provider. The kid's face went pale with each bit of evidence they presented. They knew just how to sound like authentic coppers. Then they smacked him about and smashed up his computer.

"We don't care if you have your term paper on it, or your music collection, or pictures of your girlfriend," they said. "Welcome to Real Life Consequences to your actions, you little shit."

The second troll was a pudgy thirty-five-year-old furniture mover in Bristol. Ken and Clive drove all the way out there to put the scares into him, too. They knocked on his door just before dinner. His wife and kids were there. He flat-out denied it. Then they showed him and his wife the printouts from his social media account with the path back to his IP address. He was shocked when his wife came clean and said it was actually she who had sent the abusive comments at Delia McCarthy. Then she collapsed before they laid a finger on her. Turned out she was suffering from stress and mental illness. Her husband called an ambulance. Ken and Clive didn't even soften. They just told her and her husband that if they see any more abuse coming from his account, they would be back to arrest them. That put the fear into them.

The third one was a twentysomething chartered accountant who was perfectly normal, other than he got a kick out of sending threats to Delia McCarthy. He thought it was a laugh. Ken and Clive beat the shit out of him outside his local pub, broke his fingers, and gave him the "we know who you are, what you did, and where you live" warning.

Marcie had insisted in knowing the details, and Ken and Clive actually agreed to tell her the details. She told them she didn't want them to be the only ones to shoulder the responsibility, and somehow, they trusted her. Whatever history they had with her before I joined the firm, I guess it went deep. If any of us ever got arrested or interrogated, we could be individually leaned on or gamed into giving up the story. We were now in Occam's razor territory.

"One of the worst, most vicious, ones was number four, the twat in the wheelchair," Clive said. "Stuff he was spouting at Ms. McCarthy, calling for her to be raped and chopped up, he was still sendin' abuse at her when we knocked on his door. And he was still a right shit, didn't change his personality when we rumbled him with the transcripts."

"You beat up a man in a wheelchair?"

"He was playing abuser, so we treated him like any other abuser," Ken said.

"We tipped him out of his wheelchair, took the battery out, took the wheels apart, let him try to put it back together," said Clive.

"Then we smashed his computer, too." Ken said.

"Jesus!"

"Relax. His caregiver would come over and find him the next morning."

Why was I the only one in the office who was appalled? Was everyone else that jaded?

As they told us each encounter, I could feel the karma in the room draining down the pipe. Their rule of thumb was, the more savage the troll, the more savage their punishment on him—for it was usually a him but for the rare exemption of mentally ill women. They sussed out the one who posted Delia's address and broke his ribs. I had the feeling Ken and Clive might have been content to just drive up and down the country beating the shit out of dickheads all the time.

By the end of the week, the message was getting through, if the fear and panic online was anything to go by. Some of Ken and Clive's victims posted on the message boards dedicated to slagging off Delia McCarthy that Rexton's barmy army congregated in. They talked about mysterious phone calls that threatened to expose them to their mums and school (that was us). Their computers getting mysteriously hacked (again, us). Their getting forced to upload humiliating photos of them holding up the confessional signs. All this created a sense of escalation that culminated in the first reports of two Men in Black showing up on their doorsteps and presenting them with evidence of their harassment, sounding like coppers, and laying the hurt on them. They tried looking up the Internet Security Division and found it didn't exist in any police force in the UK. That triggered the paranoid conspiracy theory talk, which was what we wanted.

"The government is coming for us!" "*FASCISM IS HERE!!!*" *"They're going to disappear us! Please get a screengrab of this page to prove we said it here first!"* *"shit im fukin scared now"* and so on.

Of course Olivia would proceed to hack into the message board and cause those posts to "mysteriously" disappear, which only fanned the fear and paranoia.

Then they started reporting Ken and Clive's beatings.

"How can they do this?" *"Broke my ribs hurts to breath."* *"fuckin hell they're really coming for us!"* *"No one is safe!"* *"I can't take this anymore."*

There was no way we would get them all—there were over four hundred of them out there. We just needed to get enough of them, the loudest ones, the ones the rest trusted most, and the fear would spread throughout the ranks.

And gradually, the members of the board began to drop away one by one. Olivia wrote a bot to track the hangers-on that would alert us if any of them did more than post the odd rant, and we would just go after them anew. All it would take was for Olivia to hack into their computers and own them from there.

Marcie was waging war on behalf of her client.

Delia McCarthy had unleashed hell.

And hell was us.

ELEVEN

Compared to all this other stuff going on, what Julia did with Rexton was positively tranquil.

As we were making calls in the office and Ken and Clive were gallivanting about the country terrorizing the trolls, Julia showed up on George Rexton's doorstep in West London. She told him his publisher had sent her to help him with any admin work or stuff like picking up his shirts while he finished his novel.

"I'm such a big fan," she said. "Anything you need, just let me know."

It took her two days to become indispensable to him.

It took him three days to become completely besotted with her.

"I just giggle a lot with him," Julia said. "He thinks I'm a bimbo, so he would never suspect me of anything."

Julia would drop in on Rexton once a day to check on him, and when he let her in, the tiny camera she was wearing on her broach would record the layout of his living room, including where his work desk and computer were. Olivia had already hacked into his computer and turned on its webcam so we could watch him all day. The feed was recorded on Olivia's servers here at Golden Sentinels.

I often wondered why writers wrote, and now I had a case study in George Rexton. He seemed to write to assert his ego, a sense of control over a world he considered a cesspit of socialists, foreigners, and homosexuals taking power away from him. Underneath it all, stronger than his other hatreds, was his issues with women. His bewilderment that women were beyond his grasp, beyond his understanding, refusing to do what he said. He cultivated the persona of a man's man, writing for men, men like him, or teenage boys who didn't know any better. That probably accounted for the six-figure sales his books earned regularly for his publisher.

When he wasn't looking, Julia hid several of Benjamin's webcams all over Rexton's house. They were the size of shirt buttons and fed the footage back to the servers at Golden Sentinels.

In bed that night, I watched the footage of Julia and Rexton on my phone—Benjamin had installed an app for streaming it.

"I hope I didn't lay it on too thick," Julia said.

"Nah. All you had to do was show up. You were just unattainable enough, yet seemingly within his grasp. Blokes like him are like greedy little boys who just had to lick that lolly."

"Right old lollypop bait, me." She laughed, cuddling me contentedly like a cat.

As Julia played her role to subtly hook Rexton in and wrap him around her little finger, I considered her ability to disappear and become another version of herself that people wanted, needed, or fantasized about. This was risky, thrill-seeking behavior. I didn't want this to trigger her sex addiction. She had thrown herself into different roles throughout her life, as a model daughter, a model student, a loving sister who would do anything to protect her transsexual sister. I saw that clear as day when she had no moral qualms about breaking into that flat in Paris with me to steal those photos of Louise. Was that tied to the abuse she had suffered early in life that she had never told her parents about? Did that damage the wiring of her psyche to create the Julia I now loved? She said she had been feeling empty and rudderless since Louise's death, and meeting me gave her a new sense of purpose, and that made her decide to come work for Roger. I didn't believe in destiny. I always thought it was a naff concept, but Julia's journey made me think it might have been Fate after all. Maybe it was the Asian in me. We had a tendency to think too much about Fate.

I realized that Julia was as much of a lost soul as the rest of us in

Roger's firm, only the newest addition to his menagerie of brilliant fuckups with nowhere to go.

In the corner of the bedroom, Bagalamukhi, the goddess of truth and deception, sat in my chair and observed us with a half smile whose meaning I couldn't read.

TWELVE

During their small talk, Julia "innocently" brought up Delia McCarthy, and that set Rexton off, as we hoped. He began ranting and raving about Delia being a "talentless cow who should stay in the kitchen and stop sticking it to us men."

"She's just taking our power away! As every woman in the media is out to do, and I'm going to do everything in my power to bring her down!"

"Bring her down?" Julia asked in her high-pitched dolly-bird persona voice. "How?"

"Oh, I have my people. Just you wait. I have legions of fans out there at my beck and call who will rise up into an army when I give the signal."

Bingo. Bang to rights. Of course, this could be dismissed in court as bluff and bluster, exaggerations of a drunken prat, but we weren't going to use this in a court of law. For us, this was further confirmation of Rexton's vendetta against Delia.

"Gosh," Julia said. "How exciting!"

Unsurprisingly, Rexton took Julia at face value because it was inconceivable to him that a woman could be smart enough to be playing him like a fiddle. If Julia knew anything, it was playing men without them even noticing.

"Have a drink with me," he pleaded. "Go on."

"Oh, but I can't," she giggled, and wriggled out of his grasp. Back at the office, I sat in dread that he might cross the line into assault.

"You really have to get on with your novel," Julia said.

"I can't write while you're here," he said. "You're driving me insane!"

"Then I ought to leave."

"No! Stay! I need you!"

Thus began the negotiations. She told him her job was to make sure he finished his novel on time. He was notoriously cagey and only handed in a complete manuscript. What was it worth to her to see him back at work? He wanted a fuck. She refused. He wanted her to show him her tits. She refused.

In the end, she gave him a hand job.

And our cameras recorded it.

THIRTEEN

You have to admit she drove a hard bargain," Olivia said. "She even got to wear rubber gloves before she wanked him off."

"I do not need to know my girlfriend is giving handies to a fat fucker who's halfway to going full-on rapist."

I hadn't watch the monitors when it happened.

The gods, however, took a keen interest, huddling behind Mark and Benjamin to watch the monitors keenly.

This went on for another three days. Julia would go to Rexton's flat after lunch. He would plead for sex. She would finally agree to pull on the rubber gloves and toss him off. Then he would zip up and begin typing at his computer while she went to strip off the gloves and leave. Every time I glanced at him through his computer's webcam, I felt an overwhelming urge to drive my fist into his increasingly punchable face.

"For fuck's sake! How much longer does this have to go on?"

"Let me check in with Delia," Marcie said.

All in all, I was building up quite the psychosexual profile of George Rexton, not that anyone at the office really cared. Marcie was happy to present my profile to Delia McCarthy.

I never met Delia face-to-face, so she stayed a somewhat abstract presence throughout this case. That was fine by me, since she was Marcie's client, and it was Marcie she trusted for advice, information, and hand-holding. They agreed that any information on this case should be presented to Delia in person rather than online because of the risk of her computer and accounts getting hacked, even with Olivia and Benjamin monitoring them. Marcie would go off and meet Delia, either at her production company offices, the TV studio, or for a drink. No one was going to suspect Marcie, since everyone remembered her from her days in PR and simply assumed she was catching up with her old friend and client Delia McCarthy. They were very adept at looking like two girlfriends doing lunch as Marcie presented her with all the dirt we had dug up in a thumb drive, including the footage from Rexton's house.

Delia got back to Marcie and said it was time to release the Kraken.

"The Kraken" was the virus Olivia had written up for this special occasion.

FOURTEEN

"Did you feel you were degrading yourself as part of your addiction or if you were taking control of a repulsive man?" I asked Julia when she came over to my flat at night.

Rudra, many-headed, god of rage, god of storms, was hovering over my shoulder, howling in my ear, waving his ax, driving my rage.

"Don't make this about you, Ravi," Julia said. "I didn't fuck him, because I knew how you would feel about it."

"That's just a technicality and you know it."

"I didn't get any of him on me."

"He could have attacked you."

"He didn't. I could read him. Are you disgusted? Do I disappoint you? What do you suppose this makes me? A slut? A whore?"

"I'm worried that this would trigger your sex addiction! You put yourself at risk! And for what? Are you doing this because things were getting too peaceful for you?"

Rudra's howling slowly stopped. Rudra stopped raging, calmed down, became warm, conciliatory.

"You acted like a professional," I said. "You did what was needed to be done for the cameras."

"Why are you dialing back? Come on! Have it out! Rage at me! Hate me!"

"I don't hate you!"

"Fuck me, then," she said.

We exhausted each other, spending all our pent-up aggression in makeup sex. Rudra meditated in the corner of the room and eventually left. It felt like he mediated the peace between us.

I told Julia about the gods.

"They show up in times of distress, and they're popping up for the first time in years."

She was amazingly calm about it.

"And all this time you had me thinking you were perfect," she said.

"I never said I was perfect. I just gave you the impression that I wasn't mentally unstable."

"You're mentally unstable?" she said in mock alarm. "I hadn't noticed."

"Well, neither of us is exactly the picture of sanity."

"Too right," she laughed. "Are any gods here with us right now? Were they watching us all this time?"

"Don't tell me that turns you on," I said.

"We all have our crosses to bear," she said. "Now I know yours. Thank you, love."

"For what?"

"For sharing your gods with me."

She kissed me, and we held each other like we never wanted to let go.

FIFTEEN

Rexton didn't know his computer had been at Olivia's mercy for days, and we could all watch him via its webcam. Julia had told us he was making progress on his novel, her presence in his life having given him the shot of energy he needed to write the rest of it, basing the sexy new love interest on her. Rexton always gave his hero a different love interest in each book, inspired by whichever new woman he had become infatuated with at the time. All three of his wives had appeared in his novels during the honeymoon period of the marriage before his drinking, roving eye, misogyny, and, well, him being him eventually drove them away. He would then go through a dark period of bitterness before the next object of desire came along. I'd skimmed through his books, all twelve of them to date, and found he seemed incapable of describing a woman in any terms beyond her hair, her tits, her hips, and her legs. I would guess the ones who refused to sleep with him in real life showed up as the ones who died bloodily. The love interest always ended up as damsels in distress for the hero to rescue, after which they happily shed their knickers and threw themselves at him like a lustful missile. Rexton's books were a veritable map of his mind. The nights in my flat where I waited for Julia to get back from cock-teasing Rexton became a book club for the gods. I could say I was reading his books to profile him, but I was really being masochistic and the gods would show up and read them with me, smiling and shaking their heads in amusement at the catalogues of human folly I had brought to their attention.

My pills were not keeping the gods at bay.

When she got home, Julia could sense something was up with me, but I just shrugged it off by saying I was worried about her spending time with a potentially violent arsehole like Rexton.

Olivia waited for Rexton to get further along with his novel before she recorded the video. It began with him typing away, taking the occasional swig of whiskey from a glass as he composed his magnum opus, mumbling dialogue and sentences to himself. The keylogger that had been installed let Olivia know he was on the final quarter of the novel. It was at the 4:27 mark when he paused to read the screen that Olivia unleashed her virus. You could see full-on the disbelief and confusion on his face as the words he had typed began to disappear from the screen in reverse order. Confusion turned to horror when the words didn't stop disappearing. The novel appeared to be self-erasing. Cue frantic tapping of the keys as he tried in vain to stop it. You could say the video was a portrait of the futility of man's struggle against death, that classic existential dilemma boiled down to a succinct ten minutes.

The video of Rexton losing his novel went viral in the most spectacular fashion. "Novelist Watches His Book Vanish" was posted via a proxy account linked to a disposable email address. This was Schadenfreude at its spiciest. In three days, the video had been viewed two million times. Then the copies and remixes began. Someone posted the video with *Yakety Sax* playing over it to enhance the slapstick vibe of it all. Gifs were created of Rexton's face howling in horror like Munch's *The Scream*. Other videos were posted with a viewer's commentary track over it. By the end of the week, the original video and its copies had amassed ten million views.

And this was only the first stage of the revenge Delia McCarthy had planned for George Rexton.

SIXTEEN

The next day, Rexton posted this on his blog:

> I can't go on. The loss of my latest novel, the best book
> I've ever written, and the humiliation of that video is
> too much for me. My life has been a long, bitter struggle
> against the forces that would control us. The bastards got
> me good this time. I'm not letting them take the rest of my
> dignity. Therefore, this is goodbye. Do not look for me. I
> am ending it all, on my terms, as befits a man.

"Oh no," cried Julia. "We went too far."

"Oh, that is utter bullshit," Marcie said. "He's not going to kill himself. He loves himself too much. This is a cry for attention."

"How can you be sure?" Julia asked.

"This asshole's written more than ten books. He can't pick himself up, talk to his publisher about getting a new deadline, and write it all over again? This is for his ego. Look at the comments. Only his fans bother to read his blog."

And us, actually, but only because this was work.

The comments were from fans begging him not to kill himself, to get help, full of dismay and disappointment that this most macho of authors should decide to top himself just because he had lost a manuscript. Some of them even said his books had saved their lives.

We looked at the video feed. Rexton was just sitting around sipping whiskey, not much different from when he wasn't writing. Julia was getting quite distraught, though.

"Where are you going?" I asked.

"I have to make sure," she said.

"That's what he wants. It's a manipulation, a cry for attention."

"How do you know? Look, it'll just look like one of my regular visits. If I find he's all right, I'll leave straightaway."

"Fuck that. I'm coming with you."

"Ravi!" She was getting exasperated.

"I'll drive."

Cheryl passed me the keys to the BMW.

SEVENTEEN

Kali rode with us, lounging majestically in the backseat while Julia and I continued to bicker in the front.

"I just feel responsible," Julia said.

"You're not. Rexton's gotta Rexton."

"I really don't need you to play knight in shining armor."

"How about just 'good boyfriend,' then?"

"I can handle him."

"He weighs at least fourteen stone more than you. If he gets coercive or violent, you're going to have a big fucking problem."

We arrived at Rexton's flat, and Julia let herself in with a spare key. Of course he'd given her a spare key. We found him slumped in his armchair in the living room. The place had an overwhelming stench of musk, stale booze, and spent cigarettes.

Behind me, I could feel Kali watching in anticipation. I didn't turn around to look at her.

"George? I just wanted to check on you. I saw your blog post."

"I hoped you'd come," he said, and got up to walk towards us. Then he saw me for the first time. "Who the hell is this?"

"I'm Ravi, from editorial. I'm here to tell you that we understand the situation. It's not your fault, and we can work something out with your novel. If you have any notes or handwritten drafts, we can help get them typed up—"

"They had to send a Paki to reassure me now?" he muttered.

He loomed over us, the darkness he was radiating was almost smothering. Anything could kick off now.

"Would, would you like me to wank you off?" Julia asked.

"Julia?! What is this? Are you suffering from some kind of Stockholm syndrome with this prick?"

"I don't feel we should leave him like this," she said.

"I want to fuck you," he muttered. "This would never have happened if you'd agreed to fuck at the beginning. The stars were aligned. That was supposed to happen. Now it's come to this. I'm buggered."

"Christ!" I cried. "Not that again! This is the most solipsistic, irrational bollocks I've ever heard!"

I was losing it, and I didn't care. I didn't care that the gods were watching, I didn't care that I was breaking Roger's Golden Rule: *Don't make it personal, don't insert yourself into the case.*

"It's none of your business," Rexton said. "This is between her and me."

"It is absolutely my business, arsehole! I'm her boyfriend!"

"You? I should have known. You lot, you come over here, take our jobs, sleep with our women—"

I'd stopped thinking at that point, I just reacted, reared back, and punched him straight in the face with all my weight behind it. I felt the *crack!* of his jaw against my fist, and he flew across the room, a lot farther than I expected. Ken and Clive were excellent boxing instructors, after all. Time slowed as Julia and I watched Rexton flip arse-over-tit across his table and crash through his TV set, landing on the carpet with his head through the screen.

Now I knew why Kali had showed up. She had known this was coming and just had to witness it.

Rexton lay there like a beached whale.

"Oh, dear," Julia said.

Kali filmed all this on her phone.

EIGHTEEN

Delia met with Rexton in the hospital weeks before her show and convinced him to agree to appear as a guest. There she presented him with all the evidence we had gathered, of him orchestrating the campaign against her, the flash mob organized by his fans, the attacks from his army of trolls.

Bang to rights.

He had been blissfully unaware of the counter-campaign we had waged on Delia's behalf, since he didn't frequent the message boards where they discussed what they did to her. He didn't know that they had been gradually dropping off with only a few impotent hangers-on left. He was still in the dark about how everything had come to pass. When he tried to file a complaint with his publishers, they told him that they never employed anyone named Julia even as an intern, and I didn't exist as a member of the editorial department.

The afternoon it aired, everyone at the office stopped to watch *Delia*, where she did her show on cyberbullying. Disgraced novelist George Rexton was her guest. His jaw was still wired shut, so he could only sit there and grunt whenever she asked him a question. She insisted on the show going ahead rather than wait for him to fully recover. He was, in her words, the embodiment of where cyberbullies could end up.

Roger and David were back from Cape Town. Cheryl had been updating them on the case via email, sparing no detail. Roger sat down and watched Delia's show with the rest of us to witness the fruits of our labors.

The papers had been running stories of Rexton's suicide note and his subsequent hospitalization. "Fall of a Novelist" was the common consensus. Marcie had leaked Rexton's history to some choice reporters, and they ran with it, writing profiles of a deeply dysfunctional and disturbed man. His publisher was forced to make a statement to distance themselves from him. Even Jonah Vankin, the tabloid journalist whom Clive had hit with the car months ago on the Holcomb Case, started a blog and got a decent number of hits for running tidbits about Rexton's behavior. He even wrote about the rumors of two men in black claiming to be from a nonexistent division of the police force showing up to beat up some of the commenters.

Olivia turned to Ken and Clive.

"Guess what, chaps, you're urban legends now!"

Ken and Clive grinned and gave her the thumbs-up.

Delia was the only one who had the whole scoop, since she had hired us to dig it all up, not to mention mold and create the current story. On the surface, her show appeared to be going for the redemptive tale of the author who behaved extremely badly and attacked her, but she forgave him and offered him a chance at penance. We all knew this was the capstone of her revenge. She ran the video of him panicking at the erasure of his novel from his computer, listed his sins to his face and the nation in meticulous, agonizing detail, all the while he couldn't swear or rant or answer back because his jaw was wired shut. This was her payback, to utterly humiliate him on national television and completely demolish him and his image forevermore. A man who wrote books of unreconstructed macho fantasies had been exposed as an impotent misogynist and fantasist, and his sales figures were plummeting by the day. As the architect of the counterattack against him, Delia had learned well from *The Art of War*, indeed. Indra, the god of war and thunder, showed up in the office, enjoying the final battle being waged on Delia's show. I tried not to look at him as he watched and applauded.

"You broke his jaw, did you?" Roger said.

"I didn't plan it. It just happened."

"Delia loved it," Marcie said. "The best punch line she could have paid for. It didn't even occur to her to ask for it."

"That's our Ravi." Roger beamed. "Always comes up with that extra touch."

I got a bonus. For punching a man. I gave that blood money to Mrs. Dhewan to cover another installment of my mother's debt. I gave it to her nephew Nandan, didn't stay to chat.

"Is it always like this at the firm?" Julia asked as we headed home one night after the office.

"More or less," I said. "Though usually with a lot less punching. Still want to work there?"

"Yes." She didn't even hesitate. "I feel like I'm learning something about the way the world works."

"That was how I got hooked myself."

"And I think I need to keep an eye on you," she said. "You're more fragile than I thought."

A week later, I took a day off while Julia was being trained in procedural methods by Ken, Clive, and Benjamin. It was my turn to sit with Dad while he got his treatment. Nothing to fill the void of the drip-drip-drip of the intravenous feed running into my father's arm except talk.

"You know how you used to tell me about mahatmas?" I said. "To be righteous and do good wherever possible? And I asked what if it wasn't possible to do good?"

"I said then try not to do any harm," he said.

"And what if it's a bit late for that?"

"If you get to that point, at least take responsibility for the harm you cause. Own it."

"You know," I said, "I think Mum and Sanjita fight over that damned wedding to cope with your condition. What better way to distract themselves from the fear and stress than to row over and over again about the nuptials."

"Ironic," Dad said. "Considering it's supposed to be a joyous occasion. Oh, you know the women in our family are highly strung. Let them have their drama. It's their way of expressing love. I just hope I live long enough to attend your sister's wedding."

"Honestly, Dad, you've always been a moody sod, but now you're getting downright morbid."

"Ha! Wait a few more months for the chemicals to pollute my liver. You'll see just how morbid a man can get."

"Not funny, Dad."

The silence again. And that need to fill it. With what, I dreaded to think.

"Have you begun seeing things again?" Dad asked.

"How did you know?"

"Your mother said you started taking your medication again."

Even on drugs, my father missed nothing.

"Perhaps we are a story the gods tell each other to make sense of the universe," he said.

"As long as they just watch, I'll try to live with it," I said.

"The pills aren't helping, are they?"

"If they did, the gods would go away."

"Let me offer another view. Perhaps you were always meant to see gods. It's the nature of shamans."

"Dad, you can't be serious."

"Why not?"

"Well—we're supposed to be rational and scientific. That's outright mysticism."

"Or it's a genetically inherited mental condition. You could continue to see it like that. Your uncle Pradeep had it, too."

"Isn't that what killed him?"

"Alcohol killed him. We should have understood better. He was self-medicating. He thought that seeing the gods had ruined his life. When you were a child, you saw them with him. That's why we were worried you would become like him."

"I don't remember that part of my childhood."

"Pradeep treated it like he was playing a game with you. You were too young to know the difference and too young to remember. Your mother and I never forgot."

"I thought I only started seeing the gods when I gave up the religious studies and had my breakdown."

"Oh, no. That was just the visions coming back for the first time since your childhood."

"So I'm not going mad so much as this is just how I am?"

"Well, are the gods telling you to murder people and do terrible things to their corpses?"

"No, thank God. They're very much in character as the gods we know. They're still figures of morality. Sometimes I also see little signs and portents for what's going to happen next. Maybe it's an expression of my intuition or anticipation of events. As for the gods, they mainly stand there observing . . . though they wear modern clothes and they have mobile phones. I think they're tweeting to each other about me."

My father laughed. I realized just how surreal it sounded to say that out loud and started laughing, too. It was good to have a laugh with my dad again.

"We're going to get through this, Dad."

"And we're going to help you get through this, too, Ravi," he said, patting my hand. "Now, what's on your mind?"

"I think I just had what psychiatrists call a 'breakthrough.' What you just told me just filled a gap I didn't know I had, and I understand something about my life that I hadn't before."

"Don't get ahead of yourself," said Dad. "You might just be losing your mind after all."

THE HIDEAWAY BRIDE

ONE

Once again: "Ravi, here's a client I'd like you to meet."

This was Mark's case, he who racked up more international travel than the rest of us. The clients were a Pakistani couple. Mr. and Mrs. Ibrahim. Punjabi. Mr. Ibrahim ran the Ibrahim Timber Company, with offices in London and Kabul. Multimillionaire. Of course he was. Roger only had rich clients.

"Our daughter has run away. We need you to find her and bring her back."

Obviously, Roger and Mark brought me into the room to reassure Mr. and Mrs. Ibrahim, as long as they weren't told I was not Pakistani. It irritated me when people assumed we were all the same. I couldn't even be bothered to explain that India and Pakistan were two different cultures. For one thing, Pakistanis are usually Muslims.

Anyway, Shazia was twenty-one years old. Just graduated university with a degree in mathematics. A studious, thoughtful, dutiful daughter.

"She is naïve to the ways of the world," Mr. Ibrahim said. "She has fallen in with a bad crowd."

"Did she take her passport with her?"

"It was missing when we searched her desk, so it's possible she has left the country."

"I hate to bring it up," I said, "but is it possible she might have gone to join a terrorist group?"

"We pray that hasn't happened," Mrs. Ibrahim said. "No, I know that hasn't happened. We warned her about Islamist propaganda, about being groomed."

"We need her back," Mr. Ibrahim said. "We've already arranged for her to get married. That is of utmost importance to our family."

And there it was. We had a deadline.

"Had Shazia met her intended husband?"

"Of course," Mr. Ibrahim said. "They were compatible. Most compatible."

"Is he aware she's run away?"

"We will have to tell him."

"I'd like to speak to him, as well, see if he might know where she's gone."

"We will have to tell him and his father that Shazia has run off because of pre-wedding jitters. And once she comes to her senses, everything will be on schedule."

Why did that sound like it wasn't true? I wondered.

Roger assured the Ibrahims we would do everything we could to find Shazia and bring her back for the wedding. Mr. Ibrahim seemed more anxious than his wife, and I had the feeling it was more about making the wedding date than about her safety or well-being. There was something about Mrs. Ibrahim's demeanor that made me wonder. She seemed oddly calm, beyond stoic. Roger laid on the charm and walked them out. Mark and I went back to our desks and set to work.

Dad was doing well. The gods had been quiet for the last three weeks, only lingering in the corner of my eye from time to time, just out of focus. I had reduced my dosage of the pills since things were peaceful. Julia was getting on-the-job training from everyone at the firm. Roger had her shadow Marcie, since he thought she would work best with Marcie's clients. Ken and Clive took her to the gym to teach her self-defense. Benjamin gave her the walk-through on the tech we used and the best social engineering sleights of hand. Olivia taught her computer security protocols and basic cheats and hacks. Olivia was actually better at teaching social engineering methods than Benjamin was. A posh finishing school accent was worth its weight in gold in the spying and private investigations business. Julia even shadowed me on a few of my cases, basic stuff like passing as a couple, or when I needed someone female to pose as a customer or potential client in a business. Julia was actually in demand whenever Mark, Ken, and Clive needed a pretty face to distract people.

My first year at Golden Sentinels was coming to as end, and all in all, I felt I was getting the hang of things.

"I really hope Shazia hasn't gone off to join a terrorist group," I said. "That'd take it out of our hands. We'll have to contact the police, MI6, and that lot."

"Nah," Mark said. "I have a good feeling about this one. I reckon our girl might be much more sensible than that. She probably did a runner for very good reasons."

"Like what, not wanting to get married?"

"Not wanting to marry this particular chap."

The chap in question was Samir Langhani, a couple of years older than Shazia. Son of Nabeel Langhani, one of the biggest arms dealers in Pakistan. He had been under investigation by the United Nations and Interpol for years, having sold arms to several rogue states, though there was no proof he sold to terrorist groups. Samir showed no signs of working for Daddy. He was known more for gallivanting around London and Europe as a playboy. Stories involving girls and wild parties were legendary.

"Sounds like dear old Dad put his foot down and insisted Samir finally settle down with nice girl from a good family," I said.

"With the added benefit of the families forming a financial power block," Olivia said. "Mr. Ibrahim stood to use some of Mr. Langhani's connections to secure some contracts for his international timber business, and Mr. Langhani might use Mr. Ibrahim to attain some degree of legitimacy."

"So not exactly a love match?" I said.

"How many arranged marriages are?" Benjamin asked.

"I grew up around marriages as business and financial transactions," Olivia said. "This is as old as commerce."

"It's all a bit medieval, isn't it?" Julia said. "Are you going to have to go through a matchmaker for an Indian wife, too?"

"Thankfully, no. I put my foot down with my folks. Besides, I've got you."

I was reminded then that my sister, Sanjita, had gone off and found Vivek on her own to head off the family trying to use a matchmaker to find her a husband. Well, more accurately, they'd been going out for years, so when Mum started bringing up marriage and some of the aunts starting threatening to stick their noses in, Sanji declared she would like to marry Vivek. Not exactly a tale of wild passion and romance, but there you go.

Mr. Ibrahim had frozen Shazia's credit cards and bank account when she ran off, so she had very limited financial options. He hoped this would drive her to come home, but so far, no dice.

My desk phone rang. The electronic ring sounded odd, unlike the usual ring we had.

"Never neglect your laundry," the voice on the other end declared. It was oddly melodic, almost sing-song.

"Sorry?"

"Always pay attention to the laundry, my son." I couldn't quite tell if it was a man or a woman. "Therein lies the important details."

"Who are you calling?" Marcie asked.

"What?" I said.

"You just picked up your phone."

"Oh, er, I had an idea, then decided against it."

I put down the phone.

Shit.

So the gods had started talking to me now. What was this all about? I think that was Kali. What did she care about my laundry? My mum did my washing for me every weekend.

Damn. Just when I thought the gods were leaving me alone. It was time to pop a pill.

TWO

Mark and I drove out to the Ibrahims' mansion in West Kensington to take a look at what Shazia's home life was like. The place was tastefully decorated with elephant sculptures carved out of wood and South Asian art.

Shazia's room, however, was a treasure trove of clues to her tastes and personality.

"Our girl's a geek," Mark declared, delighted. "I like her already."

Aside from her textbooks, her bookshelf was lined with science fiction and fantasy novels. She had a flat-screen TV and DVD player in her room, and her DVD collection consisted of box sets for *Doctor Who, Buffy the Vampire Slayer, Firefly,* and an assortment of anime. She was a huge *Sailor Moon* fan; both the manga and remastered DVDs occupied a place on her shelf that was practically an altar.

"How do you recognize all that stuff, anyway?" Mark asked.

"My students were into it, so I would hear about it all the time back when I was teaching."

I didn't think she'd gone to join any terrorists. A girl who loved escapist genre fantasies that celebrated freedom and tolerance would have an imagination that had been vaccinated against the narrow, restrictive, and repressed nihilism of jihadist ideology. Her parents would be relieved to hear that.

She'd taken her computer with her. If she kept a diary, she must have taken it with her, as well. Maybe she wrote it on her computer. It might be a lifeline to keeping in touch with friends she trusted. And perhaps she didn't want her parents to look at her computer and find out what she was really up to, including running off without warning. She had also taken her smartphone with her, probably so her parents couldn't see what was on it or use her contacts list, but she'd kept it switched off since she disappeared. Too bad, but we knew her email address, and Olivia could do something with that.

Back at the office, Olivia ran a search for Shazia's name and email address to see what kind of websites she might have visited. Mark and I did the obvious, of course, which was to find her social media profiles.

Shazia was a fairly typical twentysomething and not quite the reserved, strictly watched, repressed Muslim kid her parents had raised. She had a Twitter feed, a Facebook page, and an Instagram account. We may not have had her phone or computer, but Olivia easily unearthed her accounts and also the websites that she visited regularly over the last four, five years, as well as her online purchases, mainly geek fan stuff. She followed and was followed back not just by her family and cousins, but she also had friends outside of Asian and Muslim circles. She was part of a few anime fan groups and would meet them at conventions and get-togethers, always with her mother as chaperone to keep things on the up-and-up.

In less than three hours of tracking her online footprints, I had a profile ready.

If developmental psychology had been my field, I could have written a paper about how kids grew up using pop culture to explore and moderate their identities, and how comics and cartoons from Japan had been used by kids to navigate and come to terms with their gender identities and sexuality. That was what I noticed when I was teaching secondary school. Of course, at Golden Sentinels, Roger wasn't always interested in the hows or whys, merely the results.

"Shazia Ibrahim is a lesbian," I said. "That's a major reason for her doing a runner from her traditional arranged marriage."

"Are you positive?" Cheryl asked. "She could just be experimenting. She's still young enough to be fluid."

"Normally, I'd be more cautious about my conclusions, but it all adds up: She's a big fan of science fiction and fantasy books and shows that featured prominent gay and lesbian characters. She's a big fan of the *Sailor Moon* manga and anime, and that series has a big following among lesbian fans because two of the heroines in it are a couple. She's also a fan of *Rose of Versailles*, a historical manga set in pre-revolutionary France whose heroine is a cross-dresser who commands the palace guards and is admired by both men and women. Her blog likes to talk about anime and manga that feature lesbian characters. She's huge on *yuri*, which is manga about love stories between girls. When we looked at her Facebook and her Instagram account, the photos were of her with a lot of female friends, and several of them were lesbians and members of the LGBT community. She's a member of several LGBT fan groups for science fiction, fantasy, and anime. One woman is in more photos than the others, and often posing with her. Adelaide Robertson. My bet is Adelaide Robertson is her girlfriend. They're in love, and wherever Shazia's run off to, it's with Adelaide. Adelaide is probably paying the way for both of them."

"So what we have here is *The Case of the Runaway Lesbian Otaku*?" Benjamin said.

"Oh, *please!*" Olivia said. "A female *otaku* is called a *fujoshi*."

Off our blank looks, Olivia rolled her eyes.

"It's Japanese slang for 'dirty girl.' Female nerds."

Yup, Roger really did hire us for our specialized knowledge.

"Right, then," Olivia said. "I'll start checking for air tickets under both their names."

"Do we tell her parents she's gay?" I asked.

"I strongly advise," Roger said, "that we refrain from mentioning that to them."

THREE

We looked at Adelaide Robertson's social media footprints, as well, to find out who she was and what she was like. She was twenty-five, Australian, a few years older than Shazia, came from Melbourne. She was an academic specializing in Japanese literature. She met Shazia on a yuri fan site where they discussed the nuances of Japanese high school honorifics and etiquette. This went on for three years and they must have taken their conversations to email and private chats. They fell in love. You could tell just from the way they spoke to each other on the public forums as they discussed the latest manga and anime. We cross-referenced the other members of the message board they spoke to, determined which ones they were friends with. Found their Instagram accounts where we saw the same photos they took with Shazia at the anime conventions. Olivia dug up all their addresses. Half of them lived in campus dorms. Most of the others lived with their parents. They could have provided support to Shazia and Adelaide when they decided to run away. We decided to find Adelaide's address but found out that she had given up her flat and left a few days after Shazia's disappearance.

Olivia found two one-way air tickets bound for Tokyo issued to Adelaide Robertson and Shazia Ibrahim. I won't go into detail how Olivia got that information, since it involved hacking, which was, I shouldn't need to say this, illegal.

Mark and I presented our findings to Roger and Cheryl.

"I shall tell the Ibrahims of this," Roger said sagely, smug in his certainty that his boys and girls would have results. "What next?"

"It's been five days, and they haven't left Japan. We haven't found any plane tickets for leaving. Adelaide is there for a literature conference. Benjamin also did a search and found that this week was also Comiket, the biggest comic convention in Tokyo. Shazia and Adelaide are very likely to be there."

"Then we can probably find them there."

"Hold on, boss," Mark said. "Over half a million people go to Comiket. And in a space the size of several football stadiums. That's assuming Shazia isn't wearing a costume or a mask. Sure, a Pakistani and a white girl will stick out there, but it's still a tall order if you don't know where they're going to be. It's a massive hall."

"There's also the fact that Mark and I, being non-Japanese, will stick out on the streets of Tokyo outside of the convention, and if Shazia is on the lookout for people her parents might send to find her, she'll see us coming. And if she sees me, a fellow South Asian, coming near her where there are hardly any of us, it'll likely set off her alarm bells that her family have sent us after her. She'd be right."

"Are the Ibrahims willing to spare no expense on this, boss?"

"They said they were," Roger ventured, cautiously.

"Even so," Cheryl said. "I don't think we should throw good money after bad. We don't want to waste our time sending people over."

Mark leaned his head out Roger's door.

"Sorry, Benjamin!" he cried. "You're not going to Tokyo!"

"*Aw!*" Benjamin cried in disappointment. He was hoping to stop by Akihabara and stock up on tech toys, surveillance equipment, and *hentai* Blu-Rays.

"Call Golden Sentinels Tokyo," Roger said. "See if Takeshi Ito is available and have his people do the legwork."

Yes, Roger had set up an office in Tokyo. Technically, it was more like a franchise or subsidy deal. Takeshi Ito was already a PI over there, and he and Roger went way back. Roger with his silver tongue charmed Ito-san into agreeing to become a partner in the Golden Sentinels brand, which enabled Roger to have another office in his international network and for Ito-san to not have to deal with the tedious tax paperwork while also expanding into a full-on upscale firm.

"Right, then," Mark said. "Looks like I'll be either staying up late or waking up early to phone Tokyo."

Since Mark was the primary on this case, I could leave it to him and get on with the rest of my life.

FOUR

I found Lord Vishnu and Lord Shiva reenacting their fight from *The Mahabharata* outside the hospital. It was a show for my benefit. They didn't transform, merely charged at each other and wrestled, throwing each other across the car park.

Julia, of course, didn't see them. As long as I didn't react, she wouldn't know they were there.

They looked like two blokes from a council estate having a scrap, except they were, well, gods, blue skin and all. Vishnu in denim and jeans, Shiva in a bomber jacket and track pants. At least they didn't transform into their various avatars. They kept the fight totally street.

As I recall, in one version of this fight, Shiva lost on purpose. He did it so that he could absolve himself of burdens and responsibilities he had grown weary of. In return, he granted Vishnu boons for helping him save face.

Why this story? Why now?

My dad had told me this story when I was a kid. He had reminded me again when I was doing my religious studies.

I kept walking, did my best not to look at the gods, even if they were staging this fight for me. I really did not want to interact. First, Kali calling me about laundry, now this. I didn't know what was worse, getting cryptic messages and clues or being told outright what they were getting at.

Christ, I hoped this wasn't a sign that my dad was dead. I popped a pill as we walked into the hospital. Julia knew right then that I was seeing gods again.

"It's nothing," I said. "They're just being drama queens."

Dad was out of surgery but still heavily sedated.

I saw Buddha standing over Dad's sleeping form while we sat around him making bad jokes. Buddha was awfully chill, wearing denim, checking his phone as he watched over my dad. Mum took an instant liking to Julia and spent the evening grilling her to get the dirt on me. That took her attention away from Sanjita, so the two of them weren't bickering for once. We didn't talk about her wedding. We didn't need to. It was inevitable at this point, especially when I had the loan shark debt to prove it. I couldn't help comparing our situation with Shazia Ibrahim's. Vivek continued to ask me about my job and my dealings with the great and the good.

"I don't really see much great or good about the clients. They're mainly just rich," I said.

Buddha tapped away serenely on his phone. I didn't want to know what the gods tweeted about me.

FIVE

Mark was practically living in the office, receiving updates from Ito-san in Tokyo. His people had found the hotel Adelaide Robertson and Shazia Ibrahim had been staying at for her conference. They made a pilgrimage to Akihabara, went around the city doing the tourist thing, and most of all, they went to Comiket, where Adelaide and Shazia posed for photos with cosplayers dressed as their favorite characters. Ito-san's people even managed to film them on their phones and send the footage to our servers in London for review. They just looked like two people from the West doing the otaku tour. Ito-san's people even managed to get a list of the manga they bought, having gotten right next to them in line at the convention. Ito-san's people were geeks themselves, so they didn't have to pretend to be undercover. They even got friendly with Adelaide and Shazia and took photos with them.

"They seem like very nice girls," Ito-san and his people kept saying.

Mark told them to continue watching them, and not to confront them or talk to them about Shazia's parents wanting her back. We needed to know where they were going next after they left Tokyo.

Ito-san had his own IT guy, some kid named Kawashita, who created a private page on the popular otaku message board Baka-chan and managed to crowdsource their surveillance of Adelaide and Shazia to a few hundred eager forum members. For the next few days, members of

Baka-chan followed them and posted photos of the two of them as they went on another shopping trip for *doujin* manga in Akihabara, took a day trip to Roppongi, and enjoyed their holiday, totally oblivious to the hundreds of otaku discreetly filming and photographing them on their phones and posting their findings online for us to review.

"*Baka* means 'idiot' in Japanese," Olivia said, helpfully.

"Of course it does." Mark smiled.

Olivia kept tabs on Adelaide's credit cards and pinged a pair of tickets from Tokyo to Amsterdam. She had already hacked Adelaide's email and found correspondence with a Dutch landlord for a short lease on a flat there to begin at the start of the month. That date, just a few days away, coincided with Adelaide and Shazia's flight to Amsterdam.

"Cheryl," Mark said. "Can you book us some tickets to Amsterdam, please?"

Easy as that.

It wasn't very often that we got a heads-up on what our subjects were planning or where they were going, so we had an edge. Mark took me, Julia, Ken, and Clive to Amsterdam to wait for Adelaide and Shazia to show up in town.

So we found Shazia Ibrahim in rude health and even ruder sex. Or rather, Julia did. Shazia was living with Adelaide Robertson in a modest flat in Westerpark. Julia shadowed them for a bit, took turns with Ken and Clive. They all wore cams that Benjamin had given them so Mark and I could watch on our phones from our hotel room. We'd decided I shouldn't be the one to follow Adelaide and Shazia because she might think I was someone her parents had sent to come after her and run off.

"Alelaide has been showing Shazia the sights, especially the LGBT side. Shazia's taken to it like a fish to water. I overheard them discussing wedding plans," Julia said.

Ken and Clive posed as a gay couple on holiday, with Julia as their friend. It was funny, since Ken and Clive would never even express their relationship in public back home in the UK. They made a joke at the Sexmuseum. Shazia blushed and laughed, and started hanging out from there, holidaymakers making friends.

"God, they're really so normal," Julia said.

Back at our hotel, I could see Julia, Ken, and Clive were on the wrong foot. They'd been so used to tailing awful people that to come across a pair of women we usually thought of as "civilians" made them uneasy. We reported our progress to Roger, but Mark was unusually circumspect.

"How shall we go about this?" he asked.

"Her parents are longtime clients," Roger said. "So spare no expense. They want her back."

Mark drew up his plan, unusually quiet and without a quip or glee.

Ken and Clive were set to survey the area around Adelaide's flat for the best snatch points. We could easily score a van with untraceable license plates. Mark didn't have to bring any drugs; he already knew where to score the right ones locally that would keep her docile for the trip back to London.

"So we're a snatch squad now?" I said. "We're going to abduct a young woman and smuggle her out of the country and back to the UK. It's not the lawbreaking that I have a problem with here. It's that we're ruining this young woman's life. We're delivering her into a forced marriage. You don't have a problem with this?"

"It's the job," muttered Mark without much conviction.

"And how do we know Shazia won't end up the victim of an honor killing?" I said. "Once her unhappiness causes her to come out to her family? I don't know which would be worse, before or after she's forced to marry. It's not just a miserable life we'll be delivering her to, what if a family member or an in-law finds how different she is intolerable and decides to kill her for it? Do we really want to be directly responsible for that?"

I let that sink in. Nobody said anything for a long time.

"We ain't doin' it," Ken said, finally.

"Sorry?" Mark said.

"These two ain't a couple of criminals we would happily grab to extradite back to Blighty," Clive said. "This don't make us any better than human traffickers."

"I'll warn Shazia if you decide to go ahead with this," Julia said. "I will personally help them get away if I have to."

Bloody hell, we had a full-on mutiny here. I often wondered where they'd draw the line.

Mark looked at us for a long time. I waited for him to offer a clever comeback. Instead, he just offered a sad smile.

"Nice one," he said without irony.

Then he just got up and walked out of the room.

SIX

I found Mark by the canal, working away on his fifth spliff. That was quick.

"Mark, are you hiding?"

"Too right. I hit a wall on this one, mate."

"What do you mean?"

"Just like back when I was on the officer track in the Met. Flying high, golden boy. They pegged me for a future commissioner. Then you get to what they expect you to do to show you're one of them. Join the boys' club. Fuck over some civilians and climb over them, get rewarded. That's why I chucked my promising career and future. Now we're at a very similar impasse."

"You haven't done anything yet."

"That's coming. And I can't do it, mate. Why do you think I get myself marinated in Mary Jane all the time? It's the only thing that makes life in this veil of tears bearable."

"You really are a philosopher of despair," I said. "I would never have pegged you for a copper when I first met you."

"If we do our job here, we're going to fuck up that girl's life, Ravi. Her heart will be shattered, and we'll be the ones to watch the shards rain down on the floor before she ends up in a shithole of a marriage."

"We could just not approach her, tell Julia, Ken, and Clive we're going home. They don't like this any more than we do," I said.

"Then we don't have a result. It's a failure. Roger will sack us and hire someone else who has no problems doing the job."

Perhaps the worst part of this was that if we did decide to go ahead and snatch Shazia from her new home and her new life and somehow smuggle her across several borders back to London, I had no doubt we would be able to pull it off. In my short time with the agency, we'd dug up dirt on people, pulled dirty tricks that fucked up their lives, their careers, messed up their business deals, but those were people who were already in these wars of attrition the rich and powerful got up to with each other. Shazia wasn't part of this world. She was an innocent being used as a pawn, and we all knew it.

"Mark, do you want me to take over as lead? Take responsibility?"

"Why would you want to do that?"

"Take the load off you. There may be another angle to play that doesn't require blowing up Shazia Ibrahim's life."

"What have you got in mind?"

"Negotiate. Not with the Ibrahims, but with Samir Langhani, the prospective groom."

"Think you can pull it off?"

"I'll talk to him as one Asian to another. He's not in love with her. It's all a business transaction between their families. Maybe I can appeal to his better nature, work something out."

"Go on, then."

"I'm taking the first flight back to London. Tell everyone to stand by."

"This is why I need to be off my face all the time, mate," Mark said. "Just as well I never moved up to heroin."

SEVEN

Samir Langhani was staying at a five-star hotel in Mayfair, off Marble Arch. Penthouse suite, of course.

I had to phone and make an appointment to meet him to discuss his missing bride-to-be. He didn't seem particular anxious that she had run away because, surprise, surprise, he didn't really give a fuck. He was the type who didn't care about anything beyond his own pleasure. I'd met a few of those types of rich boys when I was growing up, and when my family had visited India.

He greeted me in an open hotel bathrobe that let his potbelly make a statement: he didn't need to work out at the gym. He didn't need to be good-looking. He was rich, so he could have any girl and as many as he wanted. That was punctuated by the two call girls lounging in their underwear on the sofa, sipping champagne. He'd been to the best schools here in the UK, went on the most expensive holidays, wore the most extravagant clothes, ate the richest food, and of course insisted on the most ostentatious hotel suites and the top girls.

"Had you met Shazia before?" I asked.

"Of course. We had a dinner here in London, with both our parents so everyone could meet and size each other up. Her father and my father already knew each other. It was pleasant enough."

"You know where she is, don't you?" he added.

Damn. He wasn't stupid. He would have been easier to game if he were stupid.

"We have some promising leads."

"So what are you really here for?" he asked.

"Do you like Shazia?"

"She's all right. A bit reserved. Seems to like a lot of that Japanese anime like a kid. That's what she comes off as. A little girl."

He was studying me for my reaction. I was in poker face mode.

"Why are you asking me all these questions?" he asked. "Are you vetting me? It's a bit late for that. The wedding's a done deal."

"I just want to see if there's anything about her you might know that we can use when we approach her about coming home."

"Like what?" He shrugged. "I found her rather reserved, a bit shy. Maybe that means she's a tiger in bed, but I haven't had the pleasure of finding out yet."

"How do you feel about marrying someone like that?"

"I don't see any problem. A wife is a wife. She'll do her duty at home. I can do what I like outside. I expect I'll be traveling a lot once I start doing more work for Pa, meeting people all over, here and there. I probably won't be at home very much."

"So you're planning on continuing the lifestyle to which you've become accustomed."

"Of course. You know as well as I do, in Asian society, that's as it ever was. This is an arrangement between our families. If Shazia wants to have her own life, she can. I'm not going to judge. We can stay out of each other's way and put up a front for family gatherings. I'm willing to negotiate."

I was imagining how Shazia would be in this sham of a life, sham of a marriage. Where would Adelaide be? At her own flat or kept in the same house? I didn't want to think about where this could all go. I knew then I couldn't discuss the possibility that Samir might call off the wedding. He could grass me out to his dad and her parents, and then where would we be? Me getting the sack for a start and Shazia grabbed and forced to come back for the wedding.

"And then there's the issue of children. Our families will expect that. I'm game," Samir said.

"She probably isn't."

"Well, she's going to have to be. We have a duty to fulfill, after all. I suppose she could just lie back and think of England."

EIGHT

Eventually Samir got bored with me and busied himself with the call girls. The gods were raging all around me as I returned to the office. Vishnu and Shiva were still fighting, and the entire pantheon was egging them on.

I didn't want to use the office phone to call Amsterdam, so I used my mobile.

"Julia, change of plans. Are you still friendly with Shazia and Adelaide?"

"I'm meeting them tomorrow for lunch."

"Good. See if you can talk them into getting married."

"Sorry, Ravi, did I hear that right?"

"Say whatever it takes. If they get married, have a license, it means Shazia can't marry Samir Langhani. It'll keep her safe."

"I take it your meeting with Samir didn't go well."

"Tell Ken and Clive to come home. We don't need them to grab her."

"So who do you want them to grab? Samir?"

I didn't answer.

"That won't work, Ravi."

"Just tell Ken and Clive. And help Shazia."

I hung up and found Marcie standing behind me.

"You going off the reservation here, dude?"

"I'm looking for a third option."

"Tell me."

"Samir is an abusive dickhead. He's in our world. Shazia isn't part of our world and doesn't deserve to be dragged into it. None of the team feels good about this."

"So you're going to, what, have Ken and Clive lean on him? He's rich, and his dad's rich. You can't scare him off. He'll just come after you with all his money, and if his dad has access to Pakistani Intelligence muscle, you're opening yourself up to a world of shit."

"Mark already fell apart. I won't, but if I have to get sacked to stop that wedding, I will."

"Whoa, whoa, let's not go there. Let's think. The job is to find her, right? You've done that."

"The Ibrahims also want her back, and she's not going to come back willingly. Unless there's no wedding she's being forced into."

"Okay, so the solution here is to kill any chance of a wedding. So let's think about this. If there was information leaked to the public that puts too much heat on Samir Langhani and his antics, that might sour Shazia's parents on the marriage."

"I like where this is heading."

"And then if his dad's business dealings, all of which were considered suspicious and already reported as such, were to be in the media that people actually paid attention to instead of just the business news, that could also make the family too hot to marry into."

"Can you do that?"

"Let me make a couple of calls. I still got some moves."

"Brilliant. Thanks, Marcie."

"That's what I'm here for."

NINE

I went back to Samir's hotel. My inclination was to tell him to fuck off to his face, none of that "breaking up by text" bollocks. Call me old-fashioned.

I came out of the lift and saw a couple of hotel staff wheeling a laundry trolley out of his room. He must have messed up a lot of sheets and towels judging from what he was about to do when I last left him. His sex toys were strewn on the bed, fresh after I left him.

I was about to knock on his door when I noticed it was slightly ajar. I pushed it open and went inside.

"Samir?"

His stereo was still blaring that Asian electro he liked so much, but there was no one in the suite. Empty glasses and booze bottles. Room service cart with empty plates. Bedsheets pulled off and all over the floor.

Kali's words from days before came flooding back to me.

"Always pay attention to the laundry, my son. . . . Therein lies the important details."

The laundry cart. Big enough to hide a sleeping body in. And two men to wheel it.

Shit.

Shit!

I ran for the lift in time to see the doors closing shut. No time to wait for another lift, but this was the ninth floor. I ran down the stairs, all eight stories. At least I was going down. Would they wheel him through the lobby or the service entrance in the back? Probably the back to avoid attention. They would still need to get to their vehicle in the car park. I didn't need to try to follow them, I just needed to get to the car park.

I cut through the lobby and ran to the car park in time to see the two bellhops loading Samir into the back of a van. As I ran after it, I finally wondered, *What do you think you're going to do?* I didn't have the company car with me. I had come on the Tube. No way was I going to catch up to a speeding van.

And I didn't.

I saw it go out into Marble Arch and disappear into Lancaster Gate.

TEN

The gods had gone quiet. Vishnu and Shiva's fight was over. Shiva threw the fight and Vishnu looked like the winner, both of them saved face. Now I understood how the fight was a reflection of this case. It was always going to end up with me in the end. The gods knew that before I did. The fight was a front, a distraction from what was really brewing away underneath. Another agenda was playing out. A desired outcome but through an unexpected route and secret moves. It was really chess, after all.

I got back to the office and told everyone what happened. They weren't upset about it at all. After all, he wasn't our client.

"Aw, man, Ravi," Marcie said. "I can't believe you tried to rescue the guy! Do you know how deep the shit you could have landed in?"

"Who grabbed him?"

"Sounds like an interested party."

"Marcie, stop being evasive."

"If I had to guess, it's probably the Americans."

"You mean the CIA."

"Well, it was probably a proxy, a contractor so they could have deniability."

"For what?"

"Sounds like extraordinary rendition," she said.

"Don't they do that to terror suspects?"

"And persons of interest."

"He didn't deserve it!"

"Are you sure?"

"He's not a terrorist!"

"We don't know that. He could be financing terrorists with his pocket money. God knows his daddy sells weapons to terrorists from time to time."

"Wait," I said. It finally dawned on me. "This is about the Americans wanting to get at his dad, isn't it?"

"That's probably it, yeah. They've been looking at him for a long time."

"So they kidnap his son?"

"Come on, you said yourself he was a dickhead, that he might have ended up being an abusive husband. Shazia has been saved from a nightmarish marriage she didn't want," Marcie said.

"You used me."

"I called some guys I know at the US Embassy."

"Including the CIA station chief, I bet. How long is Samir likely to be gone?"

"Well, with this kind of rendition, it's like disappearing down a hole, so it looks like he's gonna be gone long enough for there not to be a wedding. You saved Shazia. You can safely tell her parents where she is, and she can probably come home if she wants to. If she's already married Adelaide Robertson, they can't force her to marry some guy. She can decide to stay disappeared. The risk of an honor killing has been majorly reduced. They'll probably disown her, but she's got a new family now, right?"

"This isn't how I wanted it to go! We got a guy sent to Guantánamo!"

"Technically, it won't be Guantánamo. Chances are it'll be a black site somewhere in Romania or Poland or something."

"That's not the point!"

"Look, Ravi, he's not going to be tortured. They're just going to sit on him, treat him well, probably give him his cable TV and porn. They don't really want him. It's his dad they want."

"He's what, a hostage?"

"Collateral. They say to his dad, 'Dude, we got your kid. You want him back? Come work for us.'"

"So they're not going to arrest his dad?"

"No. He's better left in the wind as an asset. Think about all those people he sells arms to. They can keep tabs on them through him. They get to control the flow of information, know who gets what, and wait to grab the biggest fish. Realpolitik stuff. And when Samir marries? I think they'll want approval of the bride. It'll be someone useful to them, too, not some nice math major who likes anime. They'll be running that family like their own *Sims* video game."

"Marcie, how do you know this much about how the CIA works or what they want here?"

"Oh, you know, my friends over at the US Embassy. Everyone likes to gossip. It's not like any of this is classified."

"Marcie . . ."

"What? You got that look."

"Are you CIA?"

She looked at me for just a second too long, and then she burst out laughing. She laughed and laughed for a few seconds too long.

Oh shit.

Oh Christ.

Oh fuck.

What had I done?

What had I just been party to?

It felt worse when Marcie finally stopped laughing. She was still smiling.

"Walk with me, Ravi."

ELEVEN

We went up on the roof, as we often did to share a spliff with Mark.

"You were lucky I put the word out that you were a friendly," Marcie said. "They could have thought you were an accomplice and grabbed you, too. You'd be sitting in a cold cell in God knows where by now."

I was fighting a wave of nausea. The fresh air on the roof was not helping me.

"You okay, dude? Want me to get Mark up here to roll you a joint?"

"No. Just—just tell me the truth."

She sighed.

"It's not what you think," she said.

"I bloody hope not, because I'm thinking of some pretty bloody awful shit right now."

"Look, Golden Sentinels is not a CIA front, okay? You don't have to worry about that."

"There's a 'but' here," I said.

"Hey, ever since the seventies, the Company has been outsourcing a lot of work. All those movies, all that James Bond shit, none of it's true. The CIA runs operations, gathers intelligence—"

"Runs networks, topples governments."

"—and keeps governments in power. But sometimes, certain jobs they don't do themselves; they subcontract out. Gives them deniability. They can admit they didn't do something because it's true. Technically."

"And Golden Sentinels is on their payroll."

"As a preferred contractor, yes."

"For how long?"

"Since right before Roger 'hired' me."

"I always thought you were rather overqualified to be working here."

"Hey, in case you hadn't noticed, everyone here is overqualified. Except maybe Ken and Clive. They're old-school. They're the quintessential ex-cops turned private eyes."

"So your story about that commercial shoot that ended your career in PR, did that really happen?"

"Hell yeah."

"It was part of your cover, then? To make you look like you cocked up? Because you're too smart to be party to a career disaster like that."

"Aw, thanks for thinking that, dude," Marcie said. "But yeah, part of my legend, as we like to call it. Nobody would suspect a publicist who screwed up her career and ended up working here. Kinda broke my heart I had to fake being a fuckup. I liked doing PR."

"Hold on, if you're a spook, why do you come into work every day like an employee?"

"Ever heard of NOC? Nonofficial cover?" she asked.

"But don't NOC agents usually work for oil companies and travel? What are you doing hanging around a lowly private investigations firm?"

"It's my own pilot scheme. Intelligence officers run networks of assets. The more diverse that network, the better."

Then it dawned on me.

"You're Roger's handler."

"When the Company has a job for Golden Sentinels," she said, "they tell me about it, and I tell Roger."

"Roger," I said. "Always wheeling and dealing, looking for the main chance, the next big brass ring. He gets the attention of the intelligence services, but asks around and does a bit of thinking, decides he should do freelance work for the biggest fish of all: America. Nice big jobs for nice fat fees. That's how he expanded. Bigger office, latest tech, bright young things, the next generation of investigators."

"Yup, done pretty well for himself, our Roger," Marcie said. "So, what, you thinking about quitting?"

"I'm not going to be party to evil shit like today."

"Get over it, dude. Samir Langhani is not a good guy. His dad's an even bigger asshole. The CIA isn't going to arrest him. They want to flip him. Make him work for them."

"So they give him back his son, and in return he tells them who he sells weapons to so they can track those people. Thus, an intelligence network is born."

"You were always sharp, and getting sharper. Roger was right about you."

"You used me. I'm a patsy."

"No, you're an asset. Just like Roger's an asset. Everybody in the agency is an asset, and a damn good one."

"Is that supposed to make me feel better?"

"Okay, think about this. All those times you got on a plane to fly out on a case, to New York, to Chicago, to LA, you never had a problem with the TSA. You were never pulled out from the line, never stuck in a room and interrogated, never searched, did you ever wonder why? Because you're on a list. The opposite of a No-Fly List. It's a very special list. A Friends List. I made sure you were on it. Everyone here is on it."

"Does everyone in the firm know?"

"Sure they do."

"And nobody told me?"

"I guess we all assumed Roger, Cheryl, or one of the others might have told you? Eventually?"

Marcie paused and thought about this for a moment and just said, "Huh."

I'd heard enough for one day. I was out of words.

"Think about it," Marcie said. "We are good at this. We managed to tail this girl and her girlfriend halfway across the world, figure out what her deal is, and not fuck up her life. In fact, we saved her life without her ever knowing we were ever there. She and her parents will never know how big the bullet is that we helped them dodge. That was above and beyond what they hired us for. She's free to have the life she wants now. If her parents disown her, she has her own support network of LGBT geeks who will back her up. She can stay away from home because she has a family of choice now. You saved her life. You don't feel proud of that?"

I walked, headed for the stairs.

"Hey, Ravi. I'll see you tomorrow, right? Right?"

TWELVE

Marcie's PR magic did what she said it would do on the tin. Stories began popping up in the papers, first about Samir Langhani's exploits as a playboy dickhead all over London with cocaine and prostitutes, then about his father's arms dealing and the various investigations on him, and finally about Samir's mysterious disappearance from his hotel, skipping out on the bill, though they still had his credit card, so they charged him anyway. Then the stories started speculating that he might have been grabbed by the CIA. None of these stories would be running without the CIA's approval.

Julia was witness to Shazia and Adelaide's wedding in Amsterdam. Mark and Roger decided to finally tell the Ibrahims where Shazia was, omitting the details about everything else we had done, of course. I sat in to reassure them. We didn't tell them she was gay, only that she had already gotten married. Suffice to say, there was now no wedding to be had with any member of the Langhani family, who were going to be busy elsewhere for a long time. It was safe for Shazia to come back to the UK. She and Adelaide could live how they wanted now, with all the yuri manga and anime they could want.

The gods were taking a break, having spent the last few days putting on that performance from *The Mahabharata* for my benefit.

As far as everyone at the office was concerned, all was well that ended well. David was pleased we weren't going to be sued. Roger gave both Mark and me bonuses just because he was in a good mood.

There was just one more thing I had to do. I waited till we had clocked off and gone back to my flat before I told Julia we had to break up and, for her own safety, she had to quit working for the agency.

"Ravi," Julia said carefully. "You're actually freaking out right now. You're great at hiding it, but nothing you're saying makes any sense. We should talk about this when you're calmer."

"I am calm right now. I am also utterly rational."

"No you're not."

"Julia, I'm not negotiating or discussing here. I'm telling you what we have to do now. It was never a good idea to start with."

"We've been over that. What's changed?"

I told her about Marcie being CIA, about us being used to set up Samir Langhani getting grabbed and used as leverage against his father.

"And you're using that as an excuse to break up? We can get through this."

"There's no 'we' here. It's me she's trapped in her fucking web. Me and everyone in the firm. I thought Roger was the boss, but she's his handler. She can give him an order, and he'll happily do it because he'll get handsomely paid along with brownie points for it. She considers me an asset."

"That's good, isn't it?"

"As long as she's happy with me. She could send me to Guantánamo with one phone call!"

"You're overreacting."

"This is a real possibility!"

"So quit. I'll go with you."

"It won't matter if I quit. Marcie will still want to use me as an asset. She's taught me too much about tradecraft. She won't let her investment go."

"So you want to go through this alone?"

"Julia, this isn't some personal crisis with a bill or a problem client or a bump in our relationship. Our relationship is not the issue here."

"Really. That's the opposite impression you've been giving me for months."

"I'm telling you it's not safe to be with me."

"Well, that's my choice."

"No it's not. It takes the two of us, and I'm shutting this down now."

"Listen to yourself. You act as if this was a car you're getting rid of at a scrapyard."

"Julia, it's not because I don't want it. I do, but I can't have you in harm's way because of me."

"Did the gods tell you to break up with me? Is that it?"

"The gods don't tell me to do anything. And it's bad enough the gods talk to me. I don't know what they're leading me into. This is several layers of unpredictable shit I'm in! You can still get away from it all!"

"Oh, for God's sake, I'm not some princess you need to protect. You're not being noble here. You're just fucking scared!"

We got less and less calm the longer the night went on. Tears came. I had to put my foot down. I had to. I wasn't going to make excuses or lie. I wasn't going to say "It's not you, it's me." Actually, it *was* me. I was a potential death trap. I wasn't going to change my mind no matter how much she tried to talk me out of it. Julia had her pride. She wasn't going to beg, and I begged her not to. She clung on to me and I didn't want to let go of her, but in the end, that was how it had to be.

The rest of the night was a blur, but I still remember our tears and her pride, and my stupidity.

I just wasn't that brave.

THE LEAKY BANKER

ONE

Over three months and Julia had kept her word in not getting in touch. After an initial text from her asking if I was all right, there was silence. I texted her back to check that she was still going to therapy, then told her we should stop texting. I hoped she hadn't fallen off the wagon and gone on a tear fucking someone really horrible and catching a disease.

I'd stopped taking my pills. Fuck it. Call it an act of self-destruction or defiance. The gods were popping up all the time, more than ever, always in the corner of my eye, vying for my attention by just being there. I ignored them. I was still functioning. I wasn't psychotic, and they didn't demand my attention. My dad was still recovering after his surgery, but the days were rough for him. I was tempted to just curl up in bed in my flat and stay there forever, but then the gods would just pop up and stand around my bedroom all day, silently watching, silently judging, no fun at all. They weren't letting me wallow in my depression and self-pity. No, I had to go to work, be functional.

I suppose the job had settled into a groove for me. Just as well, since it helped take my mind off Julia. How much I missed her. The regret that gnawed away at me whenever I had a quiet moment.

Heartbreak sucks. It doesn't get any easier when you get older, doesn't get any less intense from when I was in my twenties, the hormonal misfires and dopamine level drops in the brain no better whether I was a spotty teen or a thirtysomething, like I was now. I reminded myself that there were bigger things out there than my heart that I made the choice to break, that there were things in the cosmos and the ether that swirled and whirled whether I had a breakup or not. The forces of karma and chaos carried on in spite of me even as I added to them. It would just be silly to go off the deep end and go on a bender or get into a fight in a pub or take drugs to dull the pain; there were still clients who needed me to solve their problems. At least there was still the adrenaline high of the job, I tried to convince myself.

So here I was, meeting a perp in a parking complex in Willesden on a gray afternoon, Bluetooth earpiece in so I could stay in touch with Benjamin and Olivia. I was even using "perp" because Marcie kept saying it like she was in a US cop show. The client was hers. Again. I still rolled my eyes at this cloak-and-dagger bollocks, the perp trying to be clever, insisting on meeting here so I could hand over the ransom to get back the heirloom he had stolen from my client.

I followed the thief's demands, drove the BMW to the top of a parking complex in Willesden to wait for him. I assumed he'd scoped out the place beforehand. Open-air roof, not many cars or people about in the afternoon. Frankly, it was a crap place for a meeting or exchange, too many ways to get trapped. Signs of someone trying to be clever who's really not.

The door to the stairwell opened and out he walked.

"You got da money?"

Bomber jacket, trainers, nervous eyes. He should have driven his car.

"Keep him talking," Olivia said on the Bluetooth. "Almost there."

"You don't have it on you," I said. "Why would I give you the money now?"

"I'll text you where it is."

"That's a crap exchange. Not buying it."

"You don't have over the dosh, I'm walking out of here," he insisted.

"I'm starting to see why he sacked you."

"Do what?"

"We looked you up, Will. Will Mosby. Some advice. When you rip off your boss, don't brag about it on Facebook. All we did was Google you."

He shuffled, eyes darting, trying to stay in control. I wondered if he might pull a knife on me.

"Just between us, I don't think that thing is worth 1.2 million, but you can't account for taste—"

"So fucking what? You're not getting it back unless I get da money!"

"You're not encouraging a lot of trust here, Will. You're already changing the terms."

"Stop fucking around! Just hand over the fucking money!"

"No."

"Fucking what?"

I was done playing. Olivia and Benjamin had been tracking the heirloom via its RFID chip and found a rusty old Golf GTI. The inside was a toxic dump, full of half-eaten food, McDonald's cartons, old trainers, porno mags, and shopping bags.

"Sure you don't want to join me in here?" Benjamin said, at which point Olivia told him in the poshest tone possible to fuck right off.

"Don't knock it till you've tried it," Benjamin said.

"I try anything once except incest, Morris dancing, and wading in rubbish with you."

"That's not the attitude you have in bed."

"Keep talking, darling," snarled Olivia. "And we will stop shagging altogether. You can go back to Japanese porn. We both know that's bloody boring compared to me."

Too much information . . .

"Huzzah!" cried Benjamin.

He'd found the heirloom in a Sainsbury bag.

"GPS. Sorry, Will. You're out of cards to play."

He opened his mouth to say something, but no words came. Instead, he ran for the door to the stairs.

Except the door swung open as he reached it, knocked him on his arse.

Ken and Clive came out the door. When Will texted me this location half an hour before the meet, we were able to look it up and suss the layout of the whole complex, including the corner under the stairs for Ken and Clive to stand in wait for him to show up, and time when to pop out.

"Fuck! Oh Fuck! Please don't kill me!"

"What? No, we don't kill people."

At least I didn't, anyway. Ken and Clive had that gleam in their eyes as they dragged him to his feet.

"Thank you. Oh, thank you."

He made to leave, but Clive kept his grip on his neck.

"We're still gonna have words," Ken said.

"Words your mum should have had with you about nicking things," Clive said.

"What are you going to do to him?" I asked.

"Don't you worry, mate. Go pick up the heirloom," said Ken.

"This toerag actually grassed himself up," Clive said. "Stupid really does find new ways to be stupid."

They were dragging Will towards the balcony, and I saw horns spouting from their foreheads and their eyes take on a yellowish hue. I pictured them dangling him over the edge and him screaming in terror. Yama was standing over them, not in a good mood, ready to pass judgment on poor Will.

"Let him go," I said.

This seemed to snap Ken and Clive out of it, and they looked at me, surprised.

"It's a lover's tiff. Client hired him as an assistant, had an affair with him, then dumped him. He stole something of value to get back at him."

"How did you—?"

"I could read it on your face, Will."

I turned to Ken and Clive.

"Look, what's the point putting him in hospital? It's over. He's lost. He's already shitting himself."

They looked at Will like panthers contemplating lunch. Karma was not a concern for them, considering they tipped theirs into the ground a long time ago. Finally, they made a decision, dropped him to the ground before me.

"Go on. Piss off."

Will scarpered.

For once, Ken and Clive chose not to fuck someone up. Progress, I suppose.

As we watched Will leg it out of there, Clive just had to put the boot in.

"Just 'cause you're heartbroken doesn't mean you have to rescue every twat who's been dumped, Ravi."

TWO

I picked up the heirloom from Benjamin and Olivia.

In case you were wondering, it was the fucking ugliest clown figurine I'd ever seen, the type of kitschy porcelain clown that made me think of serial killers. You might think it was worth a couple of quid in some souvenir shop in Blackpool or something, but the artist was famous, so it was worth 1.2 million quid at a Sotheby's auction, which was where the client had bought it. Marcie had read all about it years ago in *Artforum* and briefed me on it.

"Life's just one big cosmic joke, innit?" Benjamin said.

Somehow, even that didn't improve my mood.

I set the figurine in the seat next to me. God, it was ugly. Cosmic joke, indeed. I glimpsed Lord Vishnu in the backseat via the rearview mirror. He was busy with his phone, tweeting away, probably about me again. That bloody hashtag again.

#ourownpersonalholyfool

I drove to the club in Soho where Marcie and I were meeting the client. I'm not naming the client or the club. He's just not that interesting, and I don't need to get sued. The club was not one you'd find in *Time Out*'s Top 10. It was chintzy and garish, the kind of place that a tourist from Essex might think was the height of London glamour, exclusivity for wankers. Of course the client would hang out at this place. It was totally in keeping with his taste in expansive tat like this clown figurine.

Marcie was sitting at the bar when I walked in, my hand gripping the clown for dear life. It wouldn't do to lose or drop 1.2 million quid, no matter how repulsive it looked.

"And there it is." Marcie smiled. "Never thought I'd actually see this sucker up close."

"Don't tell me you actually like this thing."

"Dude, it's not about liking it. It's about being near the aura of an object that's acquired all that meaning. Crazy money. Art. Weird fetishized lust."

"What are you talking about?"

"Know why the client's wife hates it?"

"Other from good taste and common sense?"

"He uses it as a sex toy."

I was suddenly aware that I'd been gripping the clown very tightly for quite a long time.

"Sex—? The what now—?"

"He likes to stick it up his ass."

Marcie looked at my face and laughed.

"I don't think he'd cleaned it when it was stolen."

Marcie continued to have a good laugh as she watched me beg the bartender for antibacterial wipes to frantically rub down my hands with, then the clown from top to bottom.

"This is probably the cleanest it's been in years," she said.

I wish I could be as easily amused by life as she was.

"He's here," Marcie said.

I quickly dropped the wet wipes behind the bar counter as the client walked in. Fortysomething with an expensive suit, blandly pleasant air of your innocuous TV presenter. No, I still won't name him. He kissed Marcie on the cheek. He was her client, after all. His eyes lit up when I handed over the clown figurine, and he thanked us profusely like a mother reunited with her child. In this case it was a man and his dildo. I shouldn't judge people's relationships with their objects. This was just a very literal example of being attached to material goods, everything religion says we shouldn't be tied down by. But rich people really have weird relationships with their objects, the richer the weirder.

Marcie and I exchanged a look when he kissed the clown. I was really glad I had wiped it clean now.

THREE

"You need to get laid," Marcie said as I drove us back to the office.

"This again?" I moaned.

"Seriously, you're just moping around the office all the time. Everyone's been walking on eggshells around you."

"I'm getting the work done."

"But you're bringing the whole mood down, dude. Ken and Clive, when they get depressed, find a fight to pick, or go in a boxing ring to pummel the shit out of each other. Apparently, the makeup sex is amazing."

"Too much information, Marcie."

"Olivia does retail therapy and a spa day. Benjamin orders the latest tech. Mark has his weed. What do you have?"

"I have a full plate. That should be enough."

"Does this have anything to do with the CIA thing?"

"I'm not depressed about that. I'm depressed about breaking up with Julia."

"Why did you break up with Julia?"

"That's between her and me."

"Dude, I don't want to stick my nose in, but you've been on edge since that day. Every now and then you'd look off somewhere like you're seeing a ghost. Everybody's noticed it. What are you afraid of? You could quit. I would never sell you out. I would never make you do something you don't want to do."

"Without my knowing it."

"Come on! We're not the bad guys here."

"We're not the good guys, either. People hire us to be bad guys for them."

"Not all the time. They hire us to solve problems."

"And we're good at that. I know you take pride in that. It's actually good that you feel guilty about some of it. It means you still have a moral compass. We're not sociopaths."

"I'm not so sure about that."

"There you go. There's the Ravi I first laid eyes on when Roger first hired you. Admit it, we make a good team. I don't want to lose that."

Damn it. Marcie and I did make a good team. We had an easy rapport and she was happy to show me the ropes, explain how this world worked. Now I realized she was actively grooming me, turning me into a better operative. I was really glad we never slept together.

"So are we good?" Marcie asked.

"We're good," I lied.

She looked relieved.

"Shouldn't you call Cheryl to tell her this case is closed?" I said.

"What? Oh, yeah."

Marcie got on her phone to the office. A classical piano concerto wafted through the speakers, a melancholy waltz that I knew was going to be stuck in my head for the rest of the day. Cheryl was the only one in the office, holding down the fort. David and Roger were off playing golf with some money people from God knows where.

"Hey, Cheryl," Marcie said. "The clown is back in the client's hands. He's positively orgasmic. Even authorized a bonus. Said the payment should be in our account within an hour."

"Well done, you two," Cheryl said. "Good result. Ravi, did you actually talk Ken and Clive out of doing damage to Will Mosby? That's quite impressive."

"What was the point putting him in hospital?" I said. "He was already pissing himself."

"Well, don't make a habit of it, love. Ken and Clive are like beasts. Their bloodlust needs to be fed."

"I'll bear that in mind. What's that playing in the background?"

"Chopin's Waltz in A Minor. It's perfect when you're feeling wistful or when you have a broken heart."

Oh, that tune was definitely going to be stuck in my head all day now.

"See you shortly," Cheryl said. "Ta-ra."

She hung up. I turned on the car radio and tuned in to Radio 3. Sure enough, Waltz in A Minor came on.

"That's pretty," Marcie said. "Kinda sad, too."

"Perfect for wallowing," I said.

"Oh, man, we really need to get you laid."

"Look, I appreciate the offer, but I don't need help in that department. If I wanted to pull, I'd—"

My phone rang. What a relief. We saw it was David on the screen. I left it on the hands-free stand on the dashboard and put it on speaker.

"You still on the golf course, David?"

"Thirteenth hole. Boss is laughin' it up with his new friends."

We could hear Roger in the background with the businessmen David had included in this meeting. God knows what kind of venture Roger was getting them into here. No doubt copious martinis and G&Ts were being imbibed.

"Is everyone cosplaying as Detroit pimps?" asked Marcie.

"Ha-bloody-ha. Listen, Ravi, bit of an emergency. I have a new client for you. Mark's still in Mexico, and I can't leave Roger's side, so you need to go pick her up. Patching you through now. Go on, Sandra."

"Hello, are you there?" Panicked voice.

"This is Ravi Singh. I have my colleague Marcie Holder with me."

"My name is Sandra Rodriguez. I'm an investment banker for Holloway-Browner Banking. My life is in danger. I need you to come get me now!"

FOUR

We drove into the City and pulled up outside the Holloway-Browner building. It was one of the newer postmodernist glass monoliths in the City of London, and Holloway-Browner was one of the newer high-flying investment banks on the block, up there with Goldman Sachs and catching up to J.P. Morgan.

The Chopin was still looping in my head even after Marcie decided it was too sad for her taste and I'd switched the radio off.

As we waited, I glanced up through the windscreen and saw a ring of vultures circling in the air in front of the Holloway-Browner building. This had to be in my head. We didn't have vultures in London. What was this about? Some kind of sign or portent?

Just as I asked myself that question, I saw a man in a suit fall from the sky, through the center of the circle of vultures.

I thought this was another vision until he landed hard on the parked Volvo that was thirty yards in front of us. The impact blew out its windows, scattering the glass outwards as the roof of the car crumpled under the man's body.

"Whoa! Shit!" cried Marcie.

A woman screamed, and people started to run towards the dead man. A man in a suit got on his phone to dial 999.

A hand tapped on the window of our BMW. I saw a woman with panic on her face.

"Open up!"

I unlocked the back door and she jumped in.

"Sandra?"

"Go, go, go! If we don't get out of here, I'm next!"

"What's going on?"

"That man out there is my coworker Jack Higglesworth! Things have gone to shit! He didn't jump! He was thrown off the roof! Go! Now!"

We heard sirens in the distance, police and an ambulance. A crowd was forming around the crushed Volvo. The look on Marcie's face wasn't shock or concern, but excitement. She was going to enjoy the shit out of this.

As we drove away, Waltz in A Minor played out its last phrase in my head. Maybe it wouldn't be looping in my head for the rest of the day after all.

FIVE

Sandra Rodriguez insisted on stopping by her house to pick up some things. Fresh clothes, toiletries, pack a bag. She said she couldn't stay there as they knew where she lived, whoever "they" were.

"If this is a murder and your life is in danger," I said, "we should really go to the police."

"No! I can't have the police involved!" cried Sandra.

Marcie and I looked at each other. This didn't bode well. When a client didn't want the police to come and ensure their safety, it usually meant they were into something dodgy. Now we had to decide if we were going to be part of that, risk becoming criminally liable and getting charged as accessories.

"The police can't protect me," Sandra said. "This goes way above their paygrade. That's why I need specialists like you. Didn't David tell you?"

"How do you know David, again?"

"He's a mate. A bunch of us meet him for drinks from time to time. I got the sack from Holloway-Browner, and I was asking him for legal advice when things started getting weird. That's when I asked to hire your agency."

Marcie and I exchanged a look. Something about Sandra's telling felt off, like she was hiding something, controlling the telling to make herself look the victim to illicit sympathy. She just radiated duplicity. We'd been doing this long enough now to be able to smell it.

We arrived at Sandra's terrace house in St. John's Wood, a fixer-upper that wasn't cheap that Sandra had clearly bought as a symbol of her having made it in London.

"Just wait here," she said. "I won't be long."

Oh, we were her chauffeurs now. Of course.

As we waited for her, Marcie laughed.

"Well," I said. "She's special."

"Oh, she's a mean girl," Marcie said. "I like her."

Marcie had that same odd look on her face since Jack Higglesworth had splattered on top of that Volvo. She was surprised by that turn of events, but not horrified or shocked, just amused, as if a new vista of entertainment had opened up before her.

"Her idea of 'won't be long' is kind of different," I said, glancing at the time.

"High-maintenance gals need to pack a lot of shit when they're going away," Marcie said. "Dresses and clothes for every occasion, the makeup she's gonna need . . ."

Just then, a burgundy Tesla Model S electric car drove up and stopped in the middle of the street, not even bothering to find a parking spot because there weren't any open. An angry bloke in a suit and expensive wide-boy haircut stepped out and stormed over to Sandra's door.

I called Sandra on her mobile phone.

"There's an angry banker heading to your door."

"Oh, God! It's my ex! We didn't end it well!"

"Sandra! I know you're here! Let me in!" he screamed.

On the surface, this looked like a domestic: angry ex pounding on her door and shouting the whole street down. I'd told Sandra to go into the bedroom or bathroom and lock the door. Marcie stayed with her on the phone while I got out of the car.

"You sure you don't want to call the police?" I asked.

"No police, damn it! Get me away from him!"

I sighed and got out of the car.

"Open the fucking door!" Darren, his name was. "I'm not leaving till you give it back to me!"

"Fuck off!" she shouted from behind the door.

Great. She didn't lock herself away somewhere safe. This said something about the client's lack of common sense, but I tried not to judge.

"Is there a problem?" I said, trying to be as mild as possible.

"Who the fuck are you?"

He turned, expensive haircut, expensive designer casual clothes for a Sunday, and signs of expensive gak consumption that explained the loud twitchiness. Yeah, definitely a banker. Junior banker.

"She wants you to leave, or at least calm down."

"What? You in on it, as well? Shit, Sandra, what have you gone and done now!"

"I haven't done anything!" she shouted from behind the door.

"It's none of your fucking business!" he said, turning back to me.

"She called me and made it my business. What's it gonna be? This isn't helping."

"I'll show you what fucking helps!"

I knew he would swing at me. He had been telegraphing it from the start. I sidestepped the punch and brought my fingers up from under his arm, jabbed the space under his Adam's apple. He made a choking sound and went down. I took his wrist and pulled his arm back and up, forcing him to his knees.

"Aaargh!" he choked. "You're bending it all wrong!"

"I'm bending it just right. Now settle down."

He tried to swing around and punch with his other arm, but that only twisted the arm I held even farther. I put my free hand on the back of his neck and kept him bent over as I marched him away from the door, away from the house.

"Sandra is under our protection. I'm going to let you go now. Don't be stupid."

As I let him go, he stood up, seemed to calm, then reared up to lunge at me again, only for Marcie to stick a stun gun in his back.

He twitched and went down like a sack of potatoes.

"Stay down, dude," she said.

I rang the bell and told Sandra it was safe. She opened the door and let me in.

"I can't stay here. He's not the problem. There's worse that'll come after me. I'll explain once you get me out of here."

Marcie helped her pack a bag, and she brought her laptop. I watched over Darren, but he was spent after the stun gun.

As we helped Sandra out to our car, he stumbled to his Tesla.

"You can have her," he spat back. "Manic pixie murder bitch."

"That's creative," Marcie said.

"It's his latest nickname for me," Sandra said. "Bastard. Just get me out of here."

SIX

We took Sandra back to Golden Sentinels to get her story. She said this was about more than violent ex-boyfriends, painted herself as a whistle-blower. We sat her in the conference room and had Benjamin record her on video so that we had a record of her and what she had to say, in case anything bad were to happen.

"It's about having as many safeguards as possible," I told her. "You can never be paranoid enough."

That made her even more nervous, so of course I didn't say "In case you get killed." She was already highly strung enough.

"My name is Sandra Rodriguez. I'm an investment banker at Holloway-Browner international. My life is in danger."

She paused to let that sink in. Awareness of the dramatic effect her words had.

"Over the last five years," she continued. "My colleagues and I were Masters of the Universe. We lied to clients to make them think we charged them the lowest fees, snatched deals from rival banks, set up accounts within accounts, got up to all kinds of borderline and outright illegal shit for the God of Money."

Cheryl was taking notes. Marcie was there to provide Sandra with any emotional support, and play Good Cop should we need that. Ken and Clive were kicking back at their desks while Olivia sat at her workstation going through Sandra's laptop.

"Live hard, play hard. My lot, we made the biggest deals. We were the cream of the crop. The boss loved us. We were the über deal makers.

"We were arseholes and proud of it. No one could do what we did. We were moving tens, hundreds of millions every day. Bet big, win big. Lose big, fob it off to the clients."

I remembered Olivia telling me stories like this from back when she was in banking.

"If you failed to make your numbers, you were culled like a sick sheep at the farm. The team could tell who the weak link was, and we would let him know by leaving a black bin bag on his desk when he showed up in the morning. The black bag was meant to be like a body bag, to show him that he was a dead man walking. When our boss called him in for a chat in his office, that was when he was up for the chop."

"Sounds like a bit of a cult," I said.

"Does, doesn't it?" laughed Sandra bitterly. "Of course, when it comes to bite you in the arse, it's not funny anymore. And I certainly wasn't expecting people to start getting killed for it."

"Let's go back to that," I prompted.

"Jack didn't jump. He was murdered. He was part of the corporate finance team I was in. He was one of the weak links, got a bin bag on his desk two weeks ago. I think he found some anomalies, large sums going in and out of three accounts, all unnamed, just numbered. He was called in to talk to our boss, Stuart Powys. He said he was going to ask him about those accounts even we knew he was going to get the Talk. He never came back to his desk. Next thing we knew, he 'jumped' off the roof. That was when I knew I was next."

"Does anyone else know about those transactions?" I asked.

"My boyfriend—ex-boyfriend—Darren Cowley, whom you met earlier. He's a trader."

She stopped and looked at all of us.

"You don't believe me, do you? Darren coming after me. That was about this."

"I've seen enough to know you're scared," I said. "That's enough for me."

SEVEN

We gave Sandra a cup of tea and left her to collect herself in the boardroom.

"Did you come across this type of case back when you were coppers?" I asked Ken and Clive.

"All the time, mate," snorted Ken with contempt at the very thought.

"Never solved any of 'em," Clive said. "Witnesses clammed up, evidence got lost, orders from on high, things fizzled out."

"Especially when there was a 'sir' or 'lord' involved," Ken said.

"What do you reckon?" I asked. "Bankers set up dodgy accounts, then have to be bumped off so they don't talk?"

"Wouldn't be the first time," Olivia said.

"It's my first," I said. "And my first suspicious death. I just want to know what I'm in for."

"Well, her computer's clean. No viruses, no malware, no physical keylogger," Benjamin said.

We had Sandra's permission to go through her files. She was all ready to let everything hang out.

"They sacked me two weeks ago for raising a stink about not getting a raise. After all the years I put into that fucking place," she said, coming out of the boardroom.

When I told her that nothing would escape Olivia's forensic financial analysis skills, she looked a bit nervous, but gave permission anyway.

"Ms. Rodriguez! Sorry I couldn't handle your case personally, but as you've seen, Ravi is the best man we have!"

Now Roger made his appearance. He and David had gotten to the eighteenth hole with the new "friends." They were indeed dressed like pimps from Detroit, those crazy sweaters and baggy trousers. Marcie stifled her urge to giggle.

He bounded up and shook Sandra's hand, projecting his full charisma as he reassured her that we would keep her safe and get her what she wanted.

Why was he sucking up to her, anyway? He usually saved that for sheiks, tycoons, and politicians.

As he buttered up Sandra with as much of his oily salesman charm as he could muster, I set to work. Phoned Ken and Clive's contact at the police, promised him a hundred quid for a peek at Jack Higglesworth's file. I typed up an invoice for the hundred quid as part of the invoice for expenses we were going to rack up on this case. Cheryl had already run Sandra's credit card. It was one of the gold ones, with no spending limit.

"Who is she, anyway?" I asked David.

"Investment banker," he said. "Friend of some of my friends in the City. I run into her every now and then."

"Why's Roger so interested in her?"

"I dunno, something she knows or people she knows." He shrugged. "When she called me for help, Roger said we'd take her on."

EIGHT

Roger offered Sandra the safe house, "at a discount rate." I didn't even know there was a "discount rate."

The safe house was a bungalow between Victoria and Pimlico that Roger bought as a fixer-upper back in 1989 well below market price, probably knocked off by a favor he did someone. It looked like a pleasant, anodyne corporate residence but for the soundproofed walls, bars on the windows, and reinforced door with a state-of-the-art keycard lock that couldn't be picked. It was on the end of a quiet street with a view of anyone who could be coming or going. It was used to hide clients from paparazzi or hit men before a court appearance. Roger had the place swept regularly for cameras and listening devices just as he did the office. Marcie told me it had been used at least once a year, but not always for clients. It had also been used by various employees for entertaining. Mark and Benjamin were the prime suspects, but they always cleaned up and covered their tracks.

"There's tea, coffee, snacks. Takeout menus. If you need anything, Ken or Clive can pick it up for you."

"Looks all right," Sandra said as she looked around the living room and the open-plan kitchen. "Don't I get a keycard?"

"You don't need one. Either Ken or Clive will be with you all the time."

She seemed spaced-out.

"What did Darren want from you when he was banging on your door?"

"Sorry?"

"He was shouting 'give it back.' "

"Was he?"

"What was it he wanted?"

"I don't know."

"Sandra, I can't help you if you lie to me. You hired us, remember?"

She hesitated, weighing whether she should tell.

"Darren copied the details of the transactions onto a thumb drive. I told him to do it, and I took it."

"Do you have it?"

"Yes."

"Can I have it, please?"

Like pulling teeth.

This was moving faster than she had thought. She was flying by the seat of her pants and trying to find an angle. Here's the thing: all clients lie. They tell the story that benefits them best. It's about controlling the narrative before someone else does. It's about picking the theme and the message that puts them in the best light. And they hire us to help write it for them. Sandra had a mind to write it by herself, which was never a good idea. She was keeping things from us because she didn't trust anyone. I just hoped that wasn't going to bite us in the arse later on.

Sandra fished a SanDisk thumb drive out of her purse and handed it over.

"Oh, Darren encrypted it. I don't know the password."

"Ah."

"That was why we broke up. He started getting cold feet about grabbing those files. He must have known I would take it, so he put in a password out of spite."

"Leave it with me. We'll take care of it."

"Cheers."

"Anything else?"

"Yes, there's just one thing you could get for me?"

"Go on, love," Ken said.

"I could really do with some coke. I can give you the number of my dealer."

I had to stop myself from rolling my eyes.

"Yeah, I'll pick it up for ya," Clive said.

Great. Just what we needed. Borderline personality disorder *and* gak. That combination always went well.

NINE

I dropped the thumb drive off with Olivia back at the office. She didn't look happy about the password situation, but I was already late for Ken and Clive's contact at the police station.

I met the desk sergeant at the back of the station, away from the eyes of his colleagues. I handed him the hundred quid in ten-pound notes in an envelope, and he gave me Jack Higglesworth's file. It wasn't very thick, didn't take long to read through at all. No history of mental illness, no unusual behavior the day he jumped off the roof of Holloway-Browner and turned a parked Volvo into a J. G. Ballard sculpture ten floors below. The other bankers didn't report anything strange. No mention of interviewing Higglesworth's family.

"You finished?" Sergeant Riley asked. "I need to get that back on the DCI's desk before he notices it's missing."

I handed it back. He couldn't get away from me fast enough. Private investigators carried a certain stink around coppers, even the ones who took our cash whenever we needed a favor, never mind that many of them become one of us when they stop being coppers.

I'm glad I was never a copper.

So I continued to do my due diligence. Time to interview Jack Higglesworth's widow. I drove back to Central London, found the narrow terraced house in an upscale street. She worked as an interior decorator. I imagined the two of them split the mortgage on the house. She was glad to have someone other than the cops to talk to, someone who would actually listen to her.

"They told me it was suicide. Are you saying it wasn't?"

"I don't know yet. I just want to hear what you think."

"I told them he just wasn't the type. But they'd already made up their minds. He was terrified of heights. I couldn't get him up on the roof to make repairs after the last storm, let alone go to the top of his office. Why would he jump off the roof of his office?"

She was still numb from grief and shock. I glanced at their son sitting next to her on the sofa. Thirteen years old, hoodie, expensive sneakers, totally zoned out on his smartphone, texting his friends.

"How are you holding up, mate?" I asked.

"Whatevs." He shrugged.

The gods were swirling behind me. They were well into this.

TEN

Next morning: Sandra's ex-boss. I doubted he was going to talk to a private investigator, so I posed as an insurance investigator to ask about Jack Higglesworth's death. Got the business card ready. The number was one of Golden Sentinels' alternate phones where Cheryl would answer to confirm I was legitimate. Basic social engineering again. They didn't generally call, but it was best to be safe.

I'd phoned and made an appointment beforehand. As I walked past the traders at their computers, I saw none other than Darren Cowley at his desk, chatting away on his phone. We locked eyes for an instance. Shock in his. Then he quickly turned away and pretended to look at his computer.

I didn't have to wait long for Powys before he saw me in his office. Clearly, they didn't want me hanging around in the office long.

"I just have a few questions regarding Mr. Higglesworth's life insurance policy."

"Poor Jack. I feel sorry for his wife. Anything I can do to help."

Stuart Powys. Head of corporate finance. Red suspenders, expensive tie, and an even more expensive haircut. Slight paunch, slightly reddish face indicating a fondness for steaks and booze. Facing his early fifties with some reluctance. A man accustomed to his lifestyle. His handshake was firm, squeezed slightly too hard. An attempt to assert alpha male rules. Fine, I would give that to him.

I sat and took out a notepad. Best to look as innocuously officious as ever, not a threat. Bean counter. I even put on glasses for the show.

"Now, how many years did Mr. Higglesworth work for you?"

"Just under seven."

"I see. And during that time, did he exhibit any aberrant behavior that might have been a cause for concern?"

"No, not at all. His volumes were down. He wasn't making the numbers like the others on the team."

I remembered the videos of his hazing on Sandra's computer. . . .

"I suppose that might have caused a great deal of stress, but surely not suicide."

I looked at Powys evenly. There. A slight twitchiness. An impatience. He couldn't be shot of me soon enough.

"Do you have any idea why he might have been driven to take his life?"

"None whatsoever. It was a complete shock. I'd just had a talk with him about bucking up, doing better, then he walked out. The next thing we knew, he'd gone up on the roof and jumped off."

"You don't think he might have stumbled upon something he wasn't supposed to know."

"No."

"No what?"

"What?"

"That was rather quick. What are you denying?"

"Nothing."

Again, the answer that came too quickly.

How to tell when someone's lying: when they give rehearsed answers to questions before you'd finished asking them. Hand involuntarily going up to cover their mouth to conceal a falsehood, like he was doing now.

He was also flickering in and out of focus like a bad photograph. As if lying made him not quite real. I had to blink a few times, as the vision was getting annoying.

He took his hand off his mouth, rather self-consciously. Under the glass top of his desk, he shuffled his feet.

"Let me finish my question, Mr. Powys. Do you think Mr. Higglesworth might have stumbled across something that would make someone kill him and make it look like a suicide?"

Powys's face grew redder than ever.

"You don't think his death might have something to do with, I don't know, a deal he was working on, an account he was looking after?"

"What are you suggesting?" He was almost spluttering. "Are those questions an insurance investigator asks? I never—"

"You'd be surprised," I said evenly.

I put on the most neutral, professional smile I could muster, just the right side of shit-eating.

"Just covering the bases, sir."

ELEVEN

I asked to go up on the roof of the building to see where Jack Higglesworth had fallen from. Twenty floors up, with a full view of the City of London. Powys got a security guard to accompany me. It was the kind of rooftop where you could hold presentations and cocktail parties, so of course there were safety railings. It also was the type of rooftop where a suicidal man could easily climb over the railings and jump off.

Or be bodily lifted, struggling and wailing, by a couple of guys and thrown off. Up in the air, the vultures continued to circle. No one saw them but me, and I wasn't going to bring them up. I looked at the railings again and saw two Rakshasas, eyes red and bloodshot, their demon skins rippling with muscle, snarling and sneering as they grabbed Jack Higglesworth and threw him screaming off the roof.

Was this my mind seeing his killers as demons? Is this how unhinged I'd become? Was I just speculating, or was this the gods telling me that Jack Higglesworth was indeed murdered and I might be in over my head again?

"You all right there, sir?" the security guard asked.

"Yeah, just making a note," I said.

I left the Holloway-Browner building before they got tired of me and got into the car. Dialed Darren's mobile.

"Who's this?" he answered quickly.

"Darren. We hadn't been formally introduced. We met at Sandra's."

"What the fuck do you want?" His voice hushed; he didn't want anyone at the office hearing. "She got you doing her dirty work now?"

"We should talk."

"About what?"

"The thumb drive. Is that what Jack died over?"

"I can't talk here."

"If you're both in danger, it's what's going to save you. We need the password."

"What do I get in return, eh? She's already landed me in the shit."

"Then we really have to talk."

"All right, all right. Meet me at my flat after work."

TWELVE

I returned to Golden Sentinels to log my notes.

"Think it's a murder case?" Marcie asked.

"Leaning that way, but nothing concrete yet."

Everyone was huddled around Sandra's laptop.

"Ms. Rodriguez is a very prolific videographer," Olivia said.

On the computer: video of an orgy between the bankers. Mass of sweaty bodies rubbing against each other. Glimpses of Jack Higglesworth and Darren Cowley among them.

"Oo-er!" Benjamin was very interested.

"Ehh." Marcie shrugged. "I've seen better."

"Are we going to find you in here, David?" Olivia asked.

"Please! I would have better lighting and editing."

Another video: Darren, Gavin, and the bankers on the street at night, taunting a homeless man with wads of cash. And not for the first time on video, either.

"Bastards like abusing the homeless way too much," Benjamin said.

"All about asserting power," Marcie said.

"Is there anything tasty we could use beyond showing us these bankers are dickheads?" David asked.

Olivia opened some other files on the computer.

"Emails. This should be interesting to sort through."

"Again, might be considered property of the bank," David said. "We want to tread carefully here."

"If what she says is true, Sandra Rodriguez could become very famous for all the wrong reasons," Marcie said.

"That might be what she wants," I said. "And not good for us."

THIRTEEN

Darren Cowley's flat was one of those new modern units in Canary Wharf. He was on the tenth floor with a view of the city that was presumably one of the justifications for the amount of rent they charged. I arrived at six p.m. as we arranged and pushed the buzzer.

No answer.

I pushed it a few more times. Didn't hear any sound on the intercom to suggest anyone came to their front door. I dialed Darren's mobile but only got the answerphone.

I waited for more than half an hour. Nobody came in or out of the building. I tried him on his phone again to no avail, same with his buzzer.

It was coming to an hour when my phone rang. On screen was a photo of a tattoo of the goddess Kali on a woman's arm.

"Remember me?" Ariel Morganstern asked.

Ariel, whom I had met earlier in the year on a flight from New York. With whom I had a perfectly enjoyable Sunday in the period before the gods came back to hassle me.

"How could I forget you, Kali Girl?"

FOURTEEN

Ariel had just come into town from India. We had dinner at a Thai restaurant near her hotel in Covent Garden. It felt like we were back in that weekend we first met months ago and no time had passed. God, it felt good to laugh again, pretend I wasn't dealing with a murder case, that I didn't have to worry about my dad, that I wasn't heartbroken and thinking about Julia. The gods weren't there in the restaurant. Actually, Kali was there, watching, in the form of Ariel's tattoo. I could never totally escape the gods, especially not Kali.

"Still having your existential crisis?" she asked.

"Worse than ever."

I told her about the case with that ugly porcelain clown.

"So you ended up polishing a clown?"

"I hope that hasn't become a metaphor for what my life has become."

"Hey, sometimes an ass-clown is just an ass-clown."

"So what are you doing back in London?"

"Just passing through again. I actually went back to the States for a little job, you know, shore up the bank account, then it's back to India again."

"Again? You're not done?"

"Come on, you know better than anyone a spiritual quest is gonna take more than a couple of months trekking through India visiting ashrams. I didn't get to be there long last time before work needed me back. No, this time I'm gonna be there longer, go deeper."

"Go deeper? How?"

"Oh, you know, study more, meditate more, find some guidance, check out more ashrams."

"You haven't bathed in the Ganges, have you?"

"Nope. You told me not to on the plane, remember?"

"I do. I really don't recommend it. A lot of Westerners think it's the done thing and terribly spiritual, but the water's toxic. It'd be a great way to get hepatitis."

"Good to know."

Then she looked up at me with what we were both waiting for.

"Want to get out of here?" she asked.

Before I could say yes, my phone rang.

"I'm in Darren Cowley's flat," Benjamin said. "You'll want to get down here."

FIFTEEN

I called Ariel a cab to take her back to her hotel.

"Sorry about this."

"Don't worry about it," she said. "Work emergency. I get it."

I tapped my phone and buzzed hers. She opened my message.

"Voucher for a full treatment at the Thai House Spa in Covent Garden," I said. "Near your hotel. Help with your jet lag."

"And you just happened to have it stored on your phone?" She laughed.

"Perks of the job. We helped them out once."

"Are you bribing me?" She raised an eyebrow.

"Is it working?"

"Ask me tomorrow night." She smiled and winked.

I shut the door and sent her off, then ran to the BMW and drove out to Darren Cowley's flat.

Benjamin buzzed me in.

There are a few things I would happily go to the end of my life not seeing, and a half-naked dead man hanging from the ceiling with a full erection is very close to the top of my list.

"Fuck."

When I had clocked off four hours ago to go on my date with Ariel, Benjamin had volunteered to watch Darren Cowley's flat in my place, since he had nothing better to do: Olivia was going out drinking with her girlfriends from college and his online friends were too busy with babies and family stuff to play *Call of Duty* with him.

After the first hour, Darren was still a no-show. Benjamin got bored and, being Benjamin, decided to come inside to take a look. He managed to bypass the buzzers in the building's front door, and picking the lock to Darren's flat was even easier for him. That was when he found what was left of Darren Cowley.

"I think they'll call it autoerotic asphyxiation," Benjamin declared as he handed me a pair of rubber surgical gloves so we wouldn't leave any of our prints around the place.

"He must have already been dead when I got here," I said.

"See the booze and the drugs on the coffee table? The sliced oranges, the peels? No suicide note. This will read, 'Got high, got randy, decided to extreme-wank, went wrong.'"

"Hell of a coincidence," I said.

"What, he got so stressed out he would accidentally top himself?"

I looked at Darren, much as I didn't want to. There was a slice of orange in his mouth, apparently for biting down so the sour taste would jolt him from blacking out while the noose was tightening. There was the kicked-over chair near Darren's legs. His wrists were tied in front of his chest, seemingly part of the ritual to feel "helpless."

"He hasn't started stinkin' up the place yet." Benjamin sniffed. "So it's only been a few hours."

I was amazed at how calm and blasé Benjamin was. Then again, I realized I was, too. Granted, Benjamin had warned me about this before I got here. He was mischievous, our Benjamin, but without malice. But still.

"Something bothering you?" he asked.

"I'm bothered that I'm not shitting myself or freaking out over this. I might have recoiled and vomited, but I haven't. How are you so calm?"

"Ehh." Benjamin shrugged. "You work for Roger long enough, a stiff will pop up from time to time."

We started to look around. It was an expensive flat, full of the latest furnishings Darren must have paid for with his bonuses and salary before spending the rest of his disposable income on the recreational drugs we saw him and his colleagues indulging in on Sandra's videos.

Darren's computer was gone, along with any accessories like a hard drive. On the desk, we could see little dust patterns around the clean gap where his laptop used to be.

I heard coarse, guttural laughter echo through the living room and saw a trio of Rakshasas, the same ones I saw on the rooftop of Holloway-Browner, eyes glowing, demonic as ever, grabbing Darren as he struggled and begged, hauling him up on the chair and getting a noose around his neck.

Why the hell was I seeing demons from Hindu mythology? Why was I seeing human murderers represented as demons?

"Hang on," I said. "If he tied his own wrists up, how the fuck could he tie a knot that tight by himself, even in front of his chest?"

"Used his teeth, maybe?" Benjamin said.

"Not a knot this complicated or this tight. Someone did this to him. They could have just hung him without this 'autoerotic' bollocks. They tried to be clever and got sloppy."

"Why the hassle? Why not just fake a suicide? They could have forced him to write a note to say he was depressed or totally stressed out and couldn't take it anymore."

"Distraction," I said. "If everyone thinks he died by accident because he was a perv, there'd be fewer questions asked. At least until an inquest susses out what we just did. Buys the killers time. By the time there's an inquest, they could be long gone."

"Crafty bastards. I almost admire that."

What fucked me off was the sheer malice behind it, the shame and humiliation that Darren's family was going to go through.

Benjamin and I searched the flat, looking through the cupboards, the kitchen, the fridge, not convinced we were going to find anything.

"If they were professionals," Benjamin asked, "they would have looked where we looked."

"Well, there was nothing to find. Sandra already took the thumb drive. But if they interrogated Darren, they'll know she has it now."

We got out of there, left the door to the flat slightly ajar so that a neighbor might be concerned enough to take a look inside. Just to be safe, as we drove off, Benjamin took out one of the cheap burner phones he always carried around for emergencies like this to call 999. He even put on a fake posh accent.

"Hullo, police? I think something awful's happened to my neighbor. His name's Darren. Darren Cowley. Yes. His door's ajar, and a few hours ago, there were some strange sounds coming from his flat. I didn't dare go in. Yes. Prospect Tower. Yes. Flat 10C. Yes. Please hurry. Ta-ra."

He switched off the phone, took out the SIM card, and tossed it out the window. Then he tossed the phone out the window as well. He didn't take off his rubber gloves so there would be no prints on it.

I hoped we weren't too conspicuous in the surveillance cameras on the streets that night.

SIXTEEN

We reconvened at the office the next morning to sort out what to do next. Darren was already on the news. The police had gone to his flat and found the body. I'd called Ken and Clive and told them the news, but it was best to let Sandra sleep. The gods were gathered at the back watching us. I continued to do my best to ignore them.

"Two bodies now," Roger said. "This is getting well tasty."

"Any more and the police start sniffing around," David said. "We're going to need to be clear where we are legally if they find out we're involved."

"Now, if we do this right, the filth will never get a whiff of us at all," Roger said.

"Any luck on unlocking that drive?" I asked.

"You wanted me to brute-force an encrypted drive." She sniffed. "Yeah, sure, let's cure cancer. That would take less time."

"So how long is this going to take?"

"Anywhere between a few hours and NEVER." She pouted.

"Christ."

"Look," Olivia said. "The weak link in an encrypted drive is usually a weak password, but this one's turned out to be pretty strong."

"Can't you feed it through a password sorter or, or write a program or a bot to crack it?"

"Most sorters go through combinations of numbers and single words.

We were hoping Darren was crap at passwords, but it looks like he actually got a clue and decided on a combination of words or a phrase as the password; no bot can truly predict that, and we're buggered."

"Well, perhaps Ms. Rodriguez knows the password and is just holding it close to her chest," Roger said.

"Let's hope so," I said.

My phone rang. I didn't recognize the number.

"Mr. Chandra Singh?" Slight nasal whine in the voice.

"Speaking."

"Paul Mullins, *Morning Post*. Sandra Rodriguez gave me your number. We need to talk."

SEVENTEEN

Just what I needed, a journo from one of the tabloids.

I met him at a pub not far from the office, a watering hole for a lot of journalists and one of the last holdouts from the old Fleet Street days.

Paul Mullins was only in his late thirties, but the booze and fags made him look older than that. The closest he ever got to exercise would have been the times he ran for the Tube, which I suspect he avoided doing as much as possible.

He'd already ordered a vodka tonic, so I didn't have to get him one. I wasn't expecting there to be another round.

"Ravi, yeah?"

"What's this about?"

"We got a little prezzie in the post from your client Sandra Rodriguez today. It was postmarked two days ago. She said you would act as our liaison."

The day we first met. She must have sent it from work after David gave her my number and before we picked her up outside Holloway-Browner. Shit.

He held up a thumb drive, a duplicate of the one we already had in the office. She must have made a copy.

"What's this?" I said, stalling.

"You don't know? That's how you're going to play this?"

I looked blank.

Mullins laughed.

"Oh, nice one. All right. I get it, mate. I do. Your client wants a deal. But we can't do that until we know what's on this drive. And she neglected to tell us the password."

"It needs a password? What's supposed to be on it?"

A flash of irritation crossed Mullins's face, but he played it cool. Or as cool as a resentful alcoholic was able to muster, anyway.

"Are you approaching other papers? Is that it? *The Times*? *Guardian*? *The Mirror*?"

Again, I didn't answer.

"All right, here's what I propose: give us the password and we'll leave out any mention that incriminates Golden Sentinels."

Here we go. Blackmail. Roger would be pleased.

"I really don't know what you're on about," I said.

"We've had dealings with you lot before. Your boss, he's a slippery one. But this. Stolen bank documents, am I right? That's worthy of criminal prosecution, don't you think?"

Since I honestly didn't know what was on the drive, I didn't even need to fake ignorance here.

"Are you sure that's what's on it or are you just casting about here?" I asked.

"Come on. Your client's a banker. Doesn't take a genius to put it together. Why don't you take my proposal to your boss? And remember, we've got techies, too. It's only a matter of time before we crack it."

Yeah, good luck with that, sunshine.

"And you better hope it's before anyone links this with two dead bankers, maybe more, dropping like flies from the same bank within a day of each other. Interesting coincidence, innit? You've got twenty-four hours."

Mullins even winked as he walked out.

Lord Vishnu sat at a table in the corner, watching and tweeting on his phone. The more chaotic this got, the more they were going to turn up.

Great.

EIGHTEEN

It was nearly noon by the time I got to the safe house. Sandra was still in bed recovering from the cocaine Ken and Clive told me she was snorting the night before as she watched shows about buying and decorating houses and shouting at the screen.

"Arrrgh! Turn it off!" she cried when I threw open the curtains in her room to let some light in.

"It's the sun. It can't be turned off."

"Shit, what time is it?"

"Sandra, I have some bad news."

"What is it?"

"Darren's dead."

She froze.

"I'm sorry."

She sat up, face blank.

"What?"

"Darren's dead. It was made to look like an accident."

"FUCK!"

Well. Not quite the display of shock and grief I was expecting.

"Is there anyone you'd like me to call?"

"No. No one. Fuck!"

She was lost in thought. No pain, no grief, just gears churning in her head. I didn't need to be delicate or spare her feelings, then.

"There's another thing. The *Morning Post* contacted us. You made a copy of the drive and sent it to them?"

She froze again.

"Fuck," she said.

"You might have told us about that."

"I did it the day before Tim died. Darren made two, one for me and one for himself to keep us safe. I took his and sent it to the *Post*. I didn't know it needed a password then."

"Why did you send it?"

"Look, after this I can never work in finance again, yeah? I need to make money."

"Sandra, if you wanted to sell your story, we could have helped you, though we would probably have advised against it. Now the *Post* are in a position to dictate terms."

"They wanted proof! I was under pressure! I'm sorry!"

Like a kid throwing a tantrum. Textbook borderline personality disorder.

"Is there anything else you're not telling me?"

"No, that's everything."

I looked at her, unconvinced.

"I've told you everything!"

"Are you sure you don't know the password?"

"Are you calling me a liar?"

"I just need to be sure you've told us everything."

"I don't believe it! The man I loved has just been killed and you stand there and accuse me of lying! Get out! GET OUT!"

She burst into a very theatrical gust of tears. I didn't buy it, but I wasn't getting anything out of her, so I walked out.

"Don't let her leave," I told Ken and Clive before I left the safe house. "Don't let her out of your sight. And don't let her make any calls. We don't need any more surprises."

NINETEEN

The rest of the day turned up fuck-all. Fortunately, there were no more surprises. I put in a call to my mum to see how she and Dad were doing.

"He's still a bit weak, a bit groggy from the drugs, but getting along," she said.

"And how's everything else?"

"Oh, your sister and I are still arguing over the wedding arrangements. Vivek is as disturbingly compliant as ever. And Mrs. Dhewan has been very nice. She thinks so highly of you."

"Because I've been making the payments on time."

"Oh, Ravi, don't say that. It won't be that much longer."

"Hopefully the final payment will be right before Sanji's wedding."

"I'm sure we're all looking forward to that," Mum said.

Me more than everyone else.

I put the phone down and glimpsed Lord Shiva lounging in the sofa in the reception area, waiting for something, anything, to happen. For a moment I thought of Julia and wondered how she was doing, and quickly stopped thinking about her. Olivia was working on a forensics case of her own, so she wasn't bothering with trying to crack a password she knew was a waste of her time. Roger and Cheryl were in his office on a conference call, with David giving legal pointers. Benjamin was logging the videos on Sandra Rodriguez's computer just in case any of them ended up becoming used as evidence later on. As for me, I was waiting. No leads to chase up, no one to interview.

The odd, abstract feeling of limbo, with two dead bodies and a bunch of killers out there, and nothing to do. I suppose it was something the gods understood better than us. That was probably why they were hanging around more than ever. How bored they must have been to come here for this show.

I clocked off early and went to Ariel's hotel. When she opened the door to her room, I could tell she was in a post-spa state of radiance.

"Long day?" she said.

"Aren't they all?"

She took my face in her hands and kissed me.

I let the day and the case melt away in her embrace.

TWENTY

We ordered room service, left our clothes on the floor, lounged naked in bed for the rest of the evening. God, it felt good to escape from my life for bit, into this fantasy of sex and hanging out. We talked about spiritual journeys and gods. And how some people saw gods.

"I've been avoiding the gods for a long time," I said.

"Maybe they're trying to tell you something," Ariel said.

"I wish they'd come out and say it, then. The question is, are they projections, extensions of our desires and fears? Or are they really entities poking their heads in from outside Time and Space?"

Ariel studied me and arched her eyebrow. "Are you sure you're a private eye?"

"My coworkers are a bunch of brilliant fuckups with nowhere else to go. They're ex-coppers, lawyers, hackers, tech geeks. I feel underqualified next to them. I'm not sure I belong, but I have nowhere else to go, either."

"I think sir protests too much."

"What do you mean?"

"I think you really like swimming in the chaos. It makes you feel alive. I've been there."

"As a result of that, my karma's like a minefield. Worst path to enlightenment ever."

"So why did you give up the religious studies in the first place?"

"Burned out. I realized it was what my father wanted, not what

I wanted. It was all too abstract for me. What good was pondering the big moral questions about life and how we should live life from the ivory tower of academia? After that I got my teaching qualification and taught secondary school for a number of years."

"No way! You were a high school teacher?"

"That was another life ago."

"Did you like it? Was it, like, your vocation?"

"Not really. Paid the rent, kept me in the world. Maybe helped some kids, that was it."

"So why did it end?"

I didn't tell her about the scandal that had gotten me sacked.

"Cutbacks. I got made redundant. So I was cast adrift. Again."

"Ouch."

"Six months with no luck. My overdraft ballooning. Then my friend David, who's the legal counsel for the detective agency, got me an interview. They hired me, trained me, I started making decent money. The insane shit we got up to, though! It's like the gods have dropped me in this new, clichéd detective story for a laugh."

"Do you hate the job? You sound awfully ambivalent about it."

"What? No. I like it. It has long stretches of total boredom when you're just waiting for someone to show up, or when you're following someone and they're doing the most boring things ever just so you can photograph them, but the rest of it, I find out interesting things about how the world really works. And I'm in a position where I can actually help people. In some cases the police can't help, but we can."

"Holy shit!"

"What?"

"You're a knight in shining armor!" She started laughing.

"Oh, stop it!" I was laughing, too.

She thought about it for a moment, then came out with it.

"Hey, why don't you come with me?"

"To India?"

"Why not? You got one foot out the door, as it is. You're worried about the bad karma you've been racking up. Why not leave it all behind for a little while? Get away from it all?"

"And do what? Travel with you, smoking some quality drugs and seeking answers like a pair of Sramanas?"

"You're thinking about it right now. You got the image in your head."

"Thing is, India isn't an exotic escape for me like it is for you. It's my native culture as much as Britain is. I still have family there."

"But it's huge! You can still disappear."

I thought about it. The case. Dad. Mum's debt. Sanjita's wedding.

"I can't. I still have things to take care of and people depending on me."

She smiled sadly, like she knew what I would say.

"Know what you remind me of?" she said. "Hanuman the monkey god. Loyal, faithful, and selfless."

"I'm no god. I've got enough of them swimming around in my head as it is."

"I'd love to meet your gods some time."

I looked at her Kali tattoo. Maybe she had been sent by Kali, after all.

"Did you know," I said, "your name means 'Lion of God'? But what I see is a playful mischievous spirit, like the Ariel from Shakespeare's *Tempest*."

She smiled and climbed on top of me, taking my wrists in my hand, and pinned me down.

"Hi, I'm Ariel, your designated spirit for this evening."

"And how are you with the ways of the flesh, O spirit?"

"Let's find out!" she said.

We laughed, play-wrestled for another round.

TWENTY-ONE

That was a nice dream. A dream of fresh sheets and room service, safe sex, and a promise of escape that I'd never have.

But every dream ends, and I had to return to reality the next morning.

Ariel and I walked out of her hotel together to prolong the last embers of that dream, until she got into a taxi for the airport and I headed for my car to the office.

Mark was back from Mexico when I walked in.

"Que pedo güey!" he cried, Mexican slang for "What's up, dude!" or its equivalent.

"Mark, how can you spend a whole week in Mexico and still come back white as a sheet?"

"I am tan-proof, sir. My deepest mark as an Englishman."

Benjamin and Olivia were watching and logging the videos on Sandra's laptop. There was one of Darren, Powys, and six other bankers in balaclavas and tracksuits in a conference room at Holloway-Browner, shouting and laughing as they gathered around Jack Higglesworth. He was in an orange jumpsuit and on his knees.

"Is that—?" I began to ask.

"We are here to execute our brethren who has failed to live up to our code and make maximum moolah!" cried Darren in the video.

The other bankers yelled in agreement.

"Failure is a disgrace to us all! He is to be punished! He must pay!"

"OFF WITH HIS HEAD!" they cried.

"Jackie boy, your volumes lack volume! You are crap!"

Gavin began to mime sawing Jack's head off with a wooden ruler while the others clapped and laughed.

I realized that Sandra was the one behind the camera, filming on her phone.

"Well. That's fucked," deadpanned David.

"Completely off their faces on coke," Benjamin said.

"This is probably not an approved team-building exercise," Marcie said.

"I take it Roger's seen this?" I asked.

"He was well pleased," Cheryl said. "More leverage."

"Leverage for what?"

"Whatever deal he might want to make with the bank down the line."

"Oh. Of course."

Roger came out of his office in announcement mode.

"I just got off the phone with the editor of the *Morning Post*. They're leaning on us about the password. Where are we on that?"

"Nowhere," Olivia said.

"And Holloway-Browner's legal department called earlier," Cheryl said. "They were fishing about Ms. Rodriguez and, quote, 'any confidential information she might have passed onto us.'"

"How did they know about us?" I asked.

"My guess is the *Post* must have called them to fish for information and get a statement," Cheryl said.

"They're applying pressure on us from two fronts," Roger said.

"I better prepare a brief," David said. "If we're getting accused of theft of confidential papers, I want us to be prepared. Cheryl, if Holloway's lawyers call again, put them through to me."

"Ravi," Roger said, "you have my permission to do whatever it takes to get that password out of Ms. Rodriguez. If we don't know what's on that drive, we can't control the situation."

"But that affects her, not us. Why do you want the information, boss?"

"Leverage, old son. Now, be firm. Don't be her psychiatrist. Don't be her priest. You need to be teacher here. Sir is very cross. Drag it out of her."

"Why do I get the feeling you know something I don't?"

"I always know something you don't, old son. Now on your bike."

TWENTY-TWO

I was barely two blocks out of the car park from the office when a black SUV screeched up and cut me off.

I hit the breaks, narrowly avoided plowing into it. Three burly bastards got out. Casual clothes. Denim. Jeans. Boots.

Glowing eyes, canine teeth, burning red skin. The Rakshasas I'd seen twice before in my visions of the two murders. These were the ones. It was this lot all along.

I blinked. They were human now.

One of them walked right up to my side of the car. He had friendly eyes and a warm smile, but I already knew he was a monster.

He tapped on the window. I lowered it just a jot.

"How ya doin' today, brother?"

American.

"All right," I said. "Apart from just getting cut off. Who might you be?"

"Call me Jarrod. Let's talk about Sandra Rodriguez."

"What about her?"

"We need to talk to her."

"Regarding?"

"Stuff she took from her employers. And some other stuff, but that's really between her and us."

I glanced at Jarrod and his two men. They kept flicking between human and Rakshasa. It felt like a migraine. My heart was pounding, but I wasn't about to panic yet. None of the scenarios that were going through my head had a good outcome for me here.

"She's under our protection. So if you want to set a meeting, I'll run it by her and get back to you."

Jarrod laughed.

"Oh, man. You don't know the bear you're poking here, brother. We can be your worst nightmare or your new best friends."

"I don't need arseholes for friends."

Jarrod's smile didn't waver.

"You're a cool customer. I like that. Say, can I call you Mr. Chips? After the movie about the schoolteacher? Always liked that movie."

"I hate movies about teachers."

They know about my past? What else do they know?

"Look, brother, I'm approaching you here out of professional courtesy. We're going to have our talk with Ms. Rodriguez with or without your blessing. She's playing a dangerous game."

"Because an investment bank is hiring ex-military types to kill people for a cover-up?"

Jarrod's smile grew wider.

"They tell me you're smart. Let me give you some advice. One professional to another. Walk away. This isn't going to end well for your client. No dishonor in admitting you've done all you can, since you and us, we're not in the same league."

"Ah, now that you've said that, I can't very well drop her, can I? I have a duty of care to my client."

I held Jarrod's gaze and didn't blink.

"What next? Are you going to take me someplace and torture me? Bit of waterboarding? Beatings? Electrodes? Urine-soaked sack over my head?"

Given what I'd already seen they were capable of, I was well and truly fucked, but I wasn't going to beg just yet.

Jarrod backed away from my car, still smiling.

"I'll see ya around, Ravi."

He gestured to his men, and they got back into the SUV and drove off.

Slowly I unclenched my grip on the steering wheel and started to breathe again.

TWENTY-THREE

I waited till Jarrod and his goons were long gone before I phoned Roger.

"I just met the killers of Jack Higglesworth and Darren Cowley."

"What?!"

"Three men. Ex-military. Professionals. American. Wanted us to drop Sandra. They let me go."

"The bloody cheek of it!" bellowed Roger.

"They know who we are. They know all about my past. That means they must know all about us."

"Damn and blast! This is completely unacceptable!"

"They said they were approaching me out of 'professional courtesy.' What's that about?"

For the first time, I heard Roger become flustered.

"We'll talk about this later," he stammered.

"They could have grabbed me, tortured me, and killed me. Why didn't they?"

"Just thank your lucky stars they didn't. Are you coming back here?"

"No, to the safe house."

"Make sure you're not followed. Any trackers on the car?"

I got out and looked in the wheel wells, under the chassis.

"No tracking devices, thank God. Don't think they had time to hack the GPS or computer, either."

"Remember," Roger said. "You can't be paranoid enough here."

"One of them called himself Jarrod."

There was a pause on the line.

"Did you say Jarrod?" Roger asked.

"I told you they would come back to bite us in the arse one day," Cheryl said. They had me on speakerphone.

"I know, I know," Roger grumbled.

"Who are they, boss?"

"We'll talk about this when you get back here. Get to the safe house, read Ms. Rodriguez the riot act. I have some calls to make."

He hung up.

I realized my hands were still shaking.

I got back in the car and started the engine.

When you're worried someone might be following you, you take different, circuitous routes, all the while watching in your rearview mirror for a tail, even up to five cars behind you, then you try to shake them off.

I could sense Lord Ganesha towering over the city, looking down on me and all my folly as I drove my ridiculously convoluted route before I got to the safe house. The problem with elephant heads was you couldn't really read their expressions. I didn't need to look out the window to know how sage his face looked as he loomed over us all.

As I drove, I let out a long, hard shout, venting all my frustration and madness. I howled all the way to the safe house.

TWENTY-FOUR

I didn't bother ringing the bell, used my keycard, and stormed right in. Ken came out of the kitchen with a pot of tea.

"Where is she?"

Sandra was in the living fiddling with her phone while Clive was reading the *Mirror*.

"So how much longer am I going to be stuck here?"

"You want to leave?" I said. "There's the door."

I was no longer in the mood to indulge her.

"Oy!" she cried, indignant.

"I just met a pack of American paramilitary dickheads. Apparently, they want you very badly."

"Fucking what?" Clive jerked to attention.

Even Ken tensed up.

"So if you want to go out and take your chances with them, be my guest."

The look on Sandra's face changed. Her eyes darted about, gears turning trying to find another way to talk herself out of giving me a straight answer.

"Look, I—"

"We can't assess the threat to you or how to help you until we know what's really going on. We need the bloody password!"

"I told you! I don't know!"

"I don't believe you!"

"Fuck you! I hired you! You work for me!"

She looked to Ken and Clive for support, but they just stared at her.

"So do you have any expert security advice for me, then? Who are the men that are after you?"

"I don't know."

"Bollocks. They're the ones who tossed Jack off the roof. They hung Darren and tried to make it look like an accident. You saw them at the office the day Jack died, and you knew they did it, didn't you? That's why you were running scared."

"All right, all right!" she said. "They're a private military contractor. They're called Interzone."

"Fuck me!" Ken said.

"*The* Interzone?"

"Yes."

"The same Interzone that shot up that village in Afghanistan?"

"Yes!"

"We ought to charge you extra, luv," said Ken.

"Ravi," Clive said. "You sure they didn't follow you here?"

"I made sure of that."

"They don't need to follow you. They could have tracked you via the GPS on your phone."

Shit.

"They don't have my keycard," I said. "They can't get through the front door without it."

I turned back to Sandra.

"Now the password."

"I don't know," she said, voice shaky now.

"Tell me the password or you're out on your ear."

"I don't know! How many times do I have to tell you!"

"Ken, Clive, pack her shit up. We're done."

"You can't do that!" she cried.

"We'll charge your credit card for services to date and email you an itemized receipt as well as a termination letter. We can refer you to another agency, but I don't fancy your chances."

"You can't do this!"

"WHAT'S THE BLOODY PASSWORD?"

"I don't know! I don't know! I don't know!" She burst into tears.

We watched her sob for about a minute. I believed her, finally.

"You knew what was on the drive all along, didn't you?"

She nodded.

"It wasn't Jack or Darren who downloaded those files off the bank's servers. It was you."

"Yes."

"You're not as innocent as you like to make yourself out to be. You wanted payback for getting sacked. Tell me I got it wrong."

"You're right."

"We need to know what it is people are dying for. What's in those files?"

"It's the deal we worked on as a team. Jack, Darren, and I."

"What, it fell through?"

"No. It went brilliantly. We are—were the best. But the blokes got bigger bonuses than me just because they have cocks. Even though I was the one who kept everyone focused, who had her eye on the ball when they were slacking and nearly got some figures wrong. Then when I brought it up, I got sacked for not being a team player. When I was the one who held the whole thing together."

"For wanting your due."

"When they gave me my notice, I decided to copy all the files on the deal to hold it over their heads."

"Blackmail."

"Compensation. I deserved it for the years I put into that fucking place. Darren agreed if we could split the payout."

"So why was Jack killed? Was he in on it?"

"No. When he stepped out for lunch, I used his computer at the office to copy the files. So they wouldn't know it was me. Darren was in on it."

"And when they traced it to Jack's computer later, they thought he was the one who did it," I pressed.

"Took them a few days to notice, but yes. That was when they launched an internal investigation. They focused on Jack and didn't suspect me. I didn't think they'd go all Scorched Earth on us!"

"Those PMC, they were there the day Jack died, weren't they? When Powys called him in, they were there to interrogate him. Did you see them?"

"Yes. We all did. Two big fuckers in Powys's office. We thought they were security guards or investigators. We saw them lead Jack out of Powys's office, and that was the last we saw of him."

"How big is this deal? What kind of deal is it that would make them call in an American PMC to silence you lot?"

As she started to answer, we heard footsteps outside the front door, and the familiar whirl and click of a keycard being inserted into the lock and opening it. Who the fuck could it be? Only Ken, Clive, and I had a card.

We all stepped in front of Sandra by instinct, ready to face whoever it was coming in. We heard hurried, heavy footsteps down the hall, stomping towards us.

Then they stopped before the came in the living room.

It occurred to me then that if they had guns, we were well and truly fucked.

A metallic ping.

A pin being pulled.

A little black cylinder clattered in from the hallway at our feet.

"GET DOWN!" screamed Clive.

Later, Benjamin would tell me it was an M84 stun grenade.

Flash-bang.

I can tell you that it lived up to its name.

Everything exploded in white, and the bang was loud enough to feel like permanent damage. I was already on the floor, my head scrambled as I struggled to work out if I was still alive.

The explosion settled into a ringing in my ears. I tried to get up, but my inner ear was all doolally, and I fell over again. I could just about make out Sandra screaming. Colors danced all over my eyes. I sensed three, maybe four large men running into the room.

A voice above me, behind my head, close enough to my ear, above the pain and the ringing.

"Stay down, brother. You're better off that way."

Jarrod.

I'd stopped thinking by that point. I tried to shake off the blindness and deafness and stumbled out after them. I made it out to the street and saw the tires of the BMW had been slashed beforehand. I saw Jarrod and his men had put a black hood over Sandra's head and bundled her into a black SUV.

And behind the wheel of the SUV was Ariel.

And it all came crashing down on me: she was Interzone all along. It wasn't a coincidence that she had come back into my life just when Sandra hired me. They must have been watching Golden Sentinels for a while. She was there to keep tabs on me. She must have cloned my keycard while I was asleep last night. They just needed to know where the safe house was. Jarrod showed up to goad me into coming so they could track me by my phone's GPS.

I could only watch as the SUV peeled off and disappeared around the corner.

Behind me, Lord Vishnu watched and tweeted this on his phone. I felt all of them watching me now, taking photos with their phones. They were all around, scattered all over the street. I knew why they chose me now. Who else was in my position of witnessing the madness of not just my life, but my job gave them a ringside seat to the times. They wanted to watch and learn. I was their lens into this world. They were here now because they wanted to see what I would do next. They always showed up en masse when I was about to do something drastic, and they would tweet to each other about it.

#ourownpersonalholyfool

TWENTY-FIVE

It took five more minutes for my head to stop spinning before I could stand and think again.

Think.

I was fucked. I lost. They got her. Game over.

The gods patiently stood there, waiting for me to do something, anything.

No.

There was one play to make.

I pulled out my phone and dialed.

It rang. It wasn't switched off.

"Hey, Ravi."

"Ariel. You all right talking on the phone while driving?"

"I did this all the time when I was gunning a Humvee through Kabul while insurgents were firing rockets at us. No biggie."

"Just don't let the police stop you."

"Please! Hands-free set. We're cool."

"We are so not fucking cool!"

"Oh yeah. Sorry about all that Mata Hari stuff with you. We had fun, though, didn't we?"

"So I was just an assignment for you? Ever since we first met on the plane from New York."

"Yeah, but you're cool. I didn't hate any of it."

"Thanks a lot."

"So I guess I should say, no hard feelings? It wasn't personal?"

"This is where you say we're all professionals?"

"I wouldn't be that mean."

I could hear Sandra screaming under her hood in the backseat.

"Guys, could you keep her quiet? She's so annoying."

"Don't hurt her!"

"Relax."

"I've seen what you did to her boyfriend and Jack Higglesworth. You bastards relished too fucking much."

"Hey, for Jarrod, it's a job. He just does it. Me, I figure we should have some fun while we're at it. Better job satisfaction."

"You're crazy."

"Oh, honey," she laughed. "We've been over this. You like crazy. That's why you were into that Julia chick, that's why you flirt with Marcie at the office."

"Look, don't torture her. Don't hurt her."

"Why are you so hung up on saving her? She's not your personal friend. She's just a mean bitch who got her boyfriend and some dude in the office killed for a payday. You don't even like her."

"She's my client, and I'm responsible for her."

"Ah, ethics. That's so quaint. Listen, it'd be easier for all of us if she was out of everybody's hair. She's the cause of all this bullshit. She's that chaotic little butterfly that fluttered its wings in the City and causes a tsunami of mayhem all the way up the Dow Jones."

"You can't just murder her!"

"Dude, we're solving a problem. Just like you do."

"We don't kill people!"

"Really? What about Ken and Clive?"

Christ, they knew all about us. Like they'd kept dossiers on us, everyone who worked for Roger. How long had this been going on?

"How can you just, be so casual about all this? After all your talk about spirituality, finding your path?"

"Ravi, this is my path. I'm not Chaos. I'm part of the force that fights the chaos. And I get paid for it."

"What about your karma? What about your soul? Have you thought about the cost to all the killing you've done? How that—that eats away at you? How killing someone kills you, too? Have you thought about how it's going to hollow you out?"

"Yeah. And you know, I don't have a problem with it. I don't feel hollowed out at all. I'm still little ol' me. Same as how I always was. I know what you're thinking. Yes, I'm a sociopath. I have the psych evaluation to prove it."

"So everything you told me was a lie."

"Honey, I never lied to you. I really did work in a bank in Chicago. I really do want to seek my spiritual path in India. I just never told you what I did before. I was in the army, I was in Iraq and Afghanistan. I did my tour and got out, got bored, Jarrod and Collins offered me a job. Travel, medical, and benefits. My dream job."

"Don't hurt Sandra."

"Ravi, come on. You're still charging her credit card. No one will know she's dead for days, weeks, even months if we do it right. It's a win-win for everyone."

"Not her. Do you even know what was on the files she took?"

"We have an idea."

"She doesn't have the files. We do. And we've read them."

There was a pause on the line.

"Ariel?"

"I'm listening."

"I'm proposing an exchange. The drive for her. We've all had a bit of excitement today. That was very bracing. I suggest we all go back to home base, get our heads back, then talk again. But you do not touch Sandra."

"Or what?"

"You've been dropping bodies in London. The police are already investigating. We keep this on the down-low, you give us back Sandra for the drive. You even break a fingernail on her, and we will shop you to the police, give them the drive, and you and your client suddenly become very famous. That's the deal."

"Wow," she said.

And chuckled.

"I love this. Oh, Ravi, don't ever sell yourself short. You are way too interesting to ignore."

"Don't dump this phone. I will talk to you. Only you. Not that murderous nutter Jarrod."

I hung up.

My head was reeling, and not from the flash-bang. My world had just been stuck in a blender and set to "liquefy." I'd bought Sandra some time. First things first, call Benjamin. Go back inside and check that Ken and Clive were okay. Call Benjamin. Sort out the slashed tires on the car. If any of the neighbors called the police, we would have to sort that out, say it was vandals or something, hopefully Ken and Clive could smooth it over with them. Of course I remembered the license number of Jarrod's SUV. Maybe we could trace it.

We had to get back to the office, crack that fucking drive and find out what was on those files.

TWENTY-SIX

I had time to piece it all together in the taxi back to the office:

Interzone had us in their sights long before this case. I was the newbie, so they sent Ariel to feel me out. Reconnaissance. She relished doing it quite literally. When they were hired by Holloway-Browner to get the stolen files back and went through the suspects at the bank, they got wind that Sandra Rodriguez had hired me. This would mean they'd been monitoring Golden Sentinels' phones and communications. That was when they set Ariel back on me. When I was asleep last night, she must have gone through my pockets and cloned my keycard for the safe house.

What I didn't understand was why Interzone, a Private Military Contractor that handled international contracts worth tens of millions of dollars, would bother to keep tabs on Golden Sentinels, a private investigations firm with just a few international branch offices. Had Roger done something to piss them off back in the day? It wouldn't surprise me.

"Where's Roger? Hang on, where's Cheryl?"

"Urgent meeting," Benjamin said. "She made a couple of calls after you phoned earlier and the two of them were off like a shot."

"That's just great."

"So you got flash-banged in the face, yeah?"

"What of it?" I still had a headache and my ears were still ringing.

"What was it like?"

"Why are you asking me?"

"I always wanted to know the actual physical sensations of getting flash-banged. Call it research."

I really was not in the mood, but Benjamin was not going to let this go until he got the data he wanted.

"Blinding light, big bang. Inner ear fucked. Eyes stop working. Brain feels scrambled. Nausea. Wanted to fall over. Took ages for the senses to work again."

"Wish I'd been there," Benjamin said wistfully.

"Next time I'm going to get flash-banged, I'll give you a call."

I walked over to Marcie.

"You okay, dude? Sure you don't wanna go to the hospital?"

"What kind of relationship does Roger have with Interzone that they would pay us this much attention?"

"What makes you think—"

"Marcie, I'm sick of the evasions and the allusions to spook bullshit. We are up to our necks in it. Ken, Clive, and I could have been killed. What the fuck's going on? What has Roger gotten us into?"

The room fell silent.

"Benjamin," Marcie said. "You swept the whole office this morning, right?"

"Every morning, per the boss's orders."

"Okay," Marcie turned back to me. "Here's the deal. Laird Collins, the head of Interzone, is the most dangerous motherfucker on the planet—"

"I know that. I already read the editorials."

"—but he's *our* dangerous motherfucker."

"By 'our' you mean the CIA's."

She didn't answer. We were getting to the point where a nonanswer from Marcie was as good as a yes. And each time she didn't answer only deepened the pit in my stomach.

"Technically," she finally said, "that means they're on the same side as us."

"Bullshit. We don't murder people."

We sat nursing our wounds. Ken and Clive were pissed off that they'd been wrong-footed. They hated to have the rug pulled from under them.

Finally, Roger and Cheryl strolled back in from their errand.

"Gather around, children," Roger said. "And hear the tale I have to tell."

Oh, this ought to be good.

TWENTY-SEVEN

WHAT FUCKERY IS THIS?"

We all stopped to look at Roger. His Majesty demanded an audience for his latest performance.

"That's right," he said. "I said, 'What fuckery is this?' to the high-and-mighty Laird-fucking-Collins. How dare he come into my town and pull this malarkey on my people."

"Is this true?" I asked Cheryl.

"More or less," she said with a shrug.

"That's where we were," continued Roger. "I wasn't neglecting you, my children. I look after my people. I tracked down—"

"Actually, I tracked him down," Cheryl said.

"Yes." Roger flinched. "Cheryl found the hotel where His Murderousness was staying while in town for the arms fair. She even got his itinerary and knew when he had a gap in his meetings with warlords and despots so we could ambush him."

"So where did you pull said ambush?" Mark asked lazily, knowing he was feeding the rhythm of Roger's showmanship. He just had to put on a show, even to us, his employees.

"Would it surprise you that the bastard was staying at the Chesterfield Mayfair? Nothing but the best for his poxy, born-again arse. We knew he booked up the whole tearoom for afternoon tea, one of his few weaknesses. With other bigwigs, it's sex or dominatrices and whips and dog cages. With him, it's his love for a civilized English tea with crumpets and champagne. That I might make him choke on his champers gave me great pleasure."

I glanced at Cheryl, who rolled her eyes.

"He always has two armed bodyguards with him," she said.

"Didn't matter. It was just Cheryl and I, alone and unarmed, demanding he call off his fucking dogs."

"Bit late for that, isn't it?" I said. "Two people are already dead and they have our client."

"Well, I impressed upon him that we are in England, the First World, not some village in Mosul where they could just bump people off willy-nilly."

"Not to mention that we're supposed to be on the same side," Cheryl said.

"What 'same side' is that supposed to be?" I asked.

"Why, Western Democracy, of course," Roger said. "Western values. Market capitalism."

"The CIA," Cheryl said.

"And we now have a conflict of interest," Roger said. "Interzone have been tasked with recovering the stolen files and hush up anyone threatening to blow the whistle, and we have been hired by one of those people who are in their sights."

"So what are the chances," I asked, "that any of us here might end up one day mysteriously and 'accidentally' dead? Car accident. Mugging. Drug overdose. Slashed wrists in the tub. Stepping off a rooftop. Faked autoerotic asphyxiation like poor Darren Cowley."

"Blimey, you *have* been keeping score," muttered Ken.

"Never say never," Roger said without batting an eyelash. I guess he'd thought about all this, too. "But what's keeping that from happening is that technically, we're on the same side as Interzone."

"We don't kill people," I said. "Not in our brief, anyway."

"We're at the service of our clients," Cheryl said. "And at the end of the day, the biggest client we have is the same one they have."

"The CIA," I said.

"We call 'em the Company," Mark said.

"Why should the CIA care?" I asked.

"Daddy doesn't like to see the kids fight," Olivia said. "Makes everyone look bad."

"I might as well see this to the end," I said. "I'm fucked anyway."

"That's the spirit!" Roger smiled. "Now back to work!"

TWENTY-EIGHT

Cheryl, what's all this between Roger and Collins, anyway?" I asked.

"Roger and I know Laird Collins from back in the day," Cheryl said. "The CIA recruited him out of the military, and he was born again then, too."

"So he actually believes he's doing God's work?" I asked. "All that stuff he says in interviews about bringing about the Apocalypse and the Rapture?"

"Absolutely sincere," she said. "That means everyone he kills, everyone he sells out, is all perfectly justified in the name of the Greater Good. He truly believes he'll be welcomed by God into the Kingdom of Heaven when his Time comes, that his accounts will be balanced."

"But he had a soft spot for you didn't he, Cheryl love?" boomed Roger from his office. "Still does, I reckon."

Cheryl stared daggers at Roger from her desk.

"Collins's nickname for her was Cheryl the Wild."

She knew from my look that I would ask, so she preempted me.

"All because I stole a car so that the three of us could escape a riot in Brixton."

"Riot—? How long ago was that?"

"This firm was barely a thought then," Roger said. "We were practically still kids. I was just getting an inkling there was money to be made from private eye work. Cheryl sort of fell in with me."

"Roger was hired to find some posh girl who'd run off with her Jamaican musician–drug dealer boyfriend. I knew who he was. We ran into Collins because he'd been sent after him for some black bag work he did back in Jamaica. He was on a reconnaissance mission and was green as us then."

"And it was more than you nickin' that motor, Cheryl. There was the Molotov cocktail you chucked, that drug den you blew up with the gas explosion, and that toerag you kicked several shades of shit out of. That's right, Ravi. Our Cheryl wasn't always the prim office manager you see before you. She was a full-on punk with a Mohawk and rough leather jacket and all, one of the few half-English, half-black punks we had in London."

Cheryl continued to glare at Roger as he wistfully recounted their salad days.

"That was when Collins took a shine to her. He wanted to 'save' her. I think he really wanted to save her marvelous bum as encased in those leather trousers. But she was mine. And she wasn't havin' none of that."

"Collins left the CIA around 2000 and set up InterZone. After September 11, the War on Terror was a boom time for him. He has contracts worth hundreds of millions of dollars, all from the CIA, various governments and corporations."

"That's why you don't ever want to end up on his radar, Ravi lad," Roger said, bitterness rising in his voice. "That bastard's fucked me over on more jobs than I can count in the last ten years. One day I'm going to fucking destroy him. And I'm going to enjoy every second of rubbing that into his sanctimonious mug, and show him what useless bollocks his beliefs are. The Torah trumps his born-again fantasy bullshit."

"Damn you, Ravi," Cheryl muttered. "For dredging all that up today."

She turned away, the topic closed, and went back to typing up their meeting with Collins. I was about to protest that I wasn't the one who brought it up when it all came flooding into my head: the sad, failed love story of Roger and Cheryl. For a long time, she loved him. He might have loved her, too, but his lust for power and prestige proved stronger. All that was over now, with his trophy wife and their relationship now strictly business but filled with the disappointments of their shared history. How much and how often he must have let her down over decades. All they had now was this firm.

Looking back, I should be grateful now that Marcie took me by the arm and led me back to my desk.

"You still need to crack Sandra's drive," she said.

Olivia was still sulking at her desk.

"Any luck cracking the password?" I asked.

"What do you bloody think?"

"You didn't even try, did you?"

"Why bother? It's finding the right haystack before we can even look for the bloody needle."

"Can't you feed it through a program to run the combinations?"

"You're talking about trillions upon trillions of numbers, letters, and special character combinations, never mind words. If it's a string of two or three randomly combined words, that's even more infinite. I'm better off doing sod-all than to try to guess or run it through any program."

"Look, Darren Cowley wasn't a genius. He had a punter's grasp of security. At best he might have been slightly above average when it came to encrypting that drive with a password."

"Then this is on you, Ravi. You're the one who talked to him. Didn't he leave you some sort of clue?"

"I barely heard ten sentences to Darren before they killed him."

"Did Sandra say anything? Something about the two of them or their relationship that might have stood out? He would have chosen something simple and personal for him as a password. Perhaps something unique that brings her to his mind? One word? Two words? Perhaps three, tops?"

I thought back to everything I heard Darren say. We only had the two conversations, not enough to get any real insights beyond his resentment at Sandra and fear for his life. Nothing the last time I spoke to him on the phone. That left the first time I met him, outside Sandra's door. Again he was all gak-fueled rage and panic. Didn't really say anything memorable except . . .

except . . .

"Try 'manicpixiebitch,'" I said.

Olivia's fingers finished typing that before I even finished the sentence. Presto.

"Huh, no special characters, not even numbers. Typical," Olivia said.

And the contents of the drive opened themselves up to us. Her fingers typed faster than we could follow as she opened up file after file of emails, account details, transactions, charts, proposals, prospectuses. Figures danced down the screen, currencies shifted from pounds to euros to dollars and back again.

"Interesting," Olivia said. "We're looking at a self-sustaining investment portfolio, driven by bots to generate a self-driven and growing income pool."

"So what is it, exactly?" I asked. "Some kind of slush fund? Whose accounts are these?"

"It belongs to one client." Marcie said. "All these companies listed as the account holders? If you run a trace on them, you're going to find they're all dummy corporations with letterheads, a couple of offices and PO boxes but hardly any staff."

"So who is it?"

"Do I have to spell it out, Ravi?" sighed Marcie. "There's only one client that could possibly have the funds and resources to set all this up in this much secrecy."

That sinking feeling, back again.

"The CIA."

"You win the prize."

"Did you know about this slush fund?" I asked Marcie.

She didn't answer.

"I see the elegance of this," Olivia said. "Take some black funds, set up a large, rotating investment portfolio that accrued interest to create a fund to pay for various outsourced, off-books operations, and take the burden off the American taxpayer. Conscientious, in their own way."

"That fund," Roger said, suddenly appearing behind us every time a result was met. "Would be the coffers that would pay us, if the Company should hire us to do some freelance intelligence gathering, and pay Interzone for a security operation, an extraordinary rendition, or eliminating certain problems."

"The Company can't be seen anywhere near this fund, since it's not supposed to exist," Marcie said. "So of course they outsource it to a favored contractor to get the leaked documents back."

"Yeah, I can see people getting killed to keep this secret," I said. "And professional courtesy is what's keeping them from knocking us off? That's what Jarrod meant earlier?"

Roger laughed.

"Don't you get it yet, old son? We're expected to cooperate. And you've given me—er, us—a nice bit of leverage over them. We know the details of these accounts, more than they do."

"And that's how we'll get Sandra back in one piece," I said.

"What? Oh yeah," Roger said absently. "That, too."

TWENTY-NINE

I still had Mullins to take care of. I phoned him and said we had the password for the drive. We arranged to meet down the pub.

"You brought your PR tottie with the tits," Mullins leered. "All this for little old me?"

"I'm just here to vet anything that might adversely affect our client," Marcie said.

"And Benjamin here is our IT," I said. "He's got the password and will talk you through the steps."

Benjamin opened his laptop on the table and booted it up.

"First round's on me," I said. "Vodka tonic, right?"

"Good memory," Mullins said. "You're not totally useless after all."

I walked over to the bar and ordered Mullins's drink, the vial I got from Mark hidden in my hand. As the barkeep handed over the vodka tonic, I tipped the liquid into it and slipped the vial back into my pocket.

I brought the drink over to Mullins, and he practically grabbed it out of my hand.

"Cheers! You lot not having anything?"

"Too early for us, dude."

"Chin-chin!' Mullins said, and downed it with one gulp.

He took Sandra's thumb drive out of his pocket and brandished it like a wand. He was the cat that ate the canary, a bottom-feeder who thought he had the winning lottery ticket.

He plugged the drive into Benjamin's laptop and waited for it to show up on the screen.

"Come on, then. What's the password?"

"fuckface123," Benjamin said.

Mullins dutifully typed it in with two fingers.

The drive didn't open up its files.

"Or what?" Mullins muttered.

"Type it again," Benjamin said. "fuckface123."

Again, no change.

"Come on," Benjamin said. "fuckface123."

Mullins typed it again, stopped, and finally realized what Benjamin had been calling him.

"Are you taking the piss?" He glared.

"You must be typing it wrong," Benjamin said. "fuckface123."

Mullins's face went red with rage.

Benjamin and Marcie burst out laughing.

"Right! That's it!"

Mullins pulled the drive out of the laptop and got up to leave.

"Come on, mate," I said. "Sit down."

"I don't know what game you think you're running here, but you just proved to me this is a big fucking deal. And you are going to regret fucking with me."

He started to storm off. Benjamin and I got up after him.

Mullins barely took two steps before Mark's drug kicked in. His eyes rolled back in his head and his legs went wobbly. Benjamin and I caught him by the arms before he went down in a heap. As we guided him back to his seat, I reached into his jacket and took the thumb drive.

We left him unconscious at the table and walked out, nice and smooth. To all eyes in that pub, this was not the first time Mullins had passed out drunk at his table.

"Not the first time we drugged a journalist," Benjamin said with a shrug. "Won't be the last."

Another first for me, though, and a totally shitty one.

THIRTY

Olivia confirmed the drive was identical to the first one we had gotten from Sandra. That included the password that unlocked it.

"Good," Roger said as he took the second drive and put it in his safe. "Nobody knows there's a second drive, so let's keep it that way."

"Why are you keeping it?" I asked.

"Always useful to have some extra leverage on tap," Roger chirped.

"Now that we know what's on the drive," Cheryl said, "there's no way we can give it to the *Post*."

"So sod 'em," Ken said. "They tried to blackmail us. Now they've got nothing."

"Nah, we should give them something," Mark said. "Just not exactly what they were expecting. We might need them on our side in the future. Best not to burn any bridges if we can help it."

"So we still want to keep the bed warm with the *Post*?" I asked, disgust in my voice.

"Ever heard of the term 'useful idiot'?" Marcie said. "That's somebody of influence who helps out with your agenda without even knowing it."

"You're saying we turn journos like Mullin, Vankin, and whoever we have in our address book into our useful idiots?" I asked.

"Sure. They're assholes. Might as well make 'em our assholes. Spokespeople, celebrities who drink the Kool-Aid champagne. Anyone who's going to publish. It's all PR in the end. In principle any journalist can be a useful idiot."

"Always handy to have some on our speed dial. The more the merrier," Roger said.

Marcie was still grooming me. I realized that now. She'd been quietly teaching me these tools since I got this job. And I hadn't resisted, because the lessons had been useful.

"It's an old-school spook term," she said, knowing I couldn't stop being curious. "The Soviets were using it all the way back to the 1940s. Since the Cold War was in swing, it's been a definitive term ever since. I like it a lot better than 'fellow traveler.' It has a better layer of insult to it."

"So what are we going to give the *Post*?" I asked.

"Leave that to us," Benjamin said. "Olivia and I have a brilliant idea."

THIRTY-ONE

David spent nearly an hour on the phone with the lawyers from Holloway-Browner, who were making threatening noises, but since they couldn't in fact prove we had their stolen documents, they couldn't do more than that. He fulfilled his brief of shielding Sandra from them, and managed to coax from them the name of the man who set them after her, namely Stuart Powys, her former boss.

"Did you ever think it would come to this?" I asked.

"Christ, no!" David said, shitting bricks. "If I knew we'd end up dealing with black-ops killers, I would never have gotten you this job!"

"For what it's worth, I don't blame you." I said.

"Ah, cheers, mate. You have to believe me, I thought it'd be a cushy enough job that kept you from going off your nut with boredom."

"Why would you be concerned about me getting bored?"

"Are you joking? You become a moody sod when you get bored. And we had the maddest times back in uni. When you dropped the religious studies, you became a right lump, with the breakdown and the visions of gods and all that. It broke my heart, mate."

"I didn't know you felt that way."

"Of course not. You were too busy being depressed and weird, talking about gods. So when you lost the teaching job, I was afraid you'd go into that rut again and never come back."

"So you thought I should become a private detective?"

"To be honest, I wasn't sure Roger would hire you, but he saw something in you like I thought he would, and here we are. I thought it'd be good to have us watching each other's backs at this firm. In case you haven't noticed, our colleagues are stark raving mad."

"What makes you think I'm not?"

"You're *my* mad friend."

"Yeah, fair enough."

When David got nervous, he would talk a lot and spill his guts. It was one thing to feel pressure from his family of high-flying Nigerian immigrants who expected him to go far; it was quite another to come within kissing distance of trained paramilitary killers, which was the type of social interaction David was ill-bred and ill-prepared for. All he ever really wanted was to be a lawyer who helped structure business plans and helped stave off lawsuits. Like the rest of us, Roger had seduced him into working for Golden Sentinels with his plans for global expansion and domination. David treated the company like it was a start-up and Roger had been very pleased with his work. Roger wanted to tap David's family connections in international banking and business, and the work kept David's parents off his back. Eventually, David planned to run for political office after he'd shored away all his contacts and important friends in his work as a lawyer.

As far as David was concerned, meeting up with Interzone was beyond his brief. Apart from fearing for his own skin, he was feeling genuinely bad for me.

"Don't worry," I said. "They're not going to kill us. Yet."

And with that, I headed off to my meeting.

THIRTY-TWO

I arranged to meet Ariel in Green Park, the most public place I could think of so nothing violent could happen without loads of witnesses. A goose was all set to attack an American tourist who was trying to feed it some bread.

"Hi, babe," she said.

For a life-and-death meeting, Ariel was her usual chipper self. She looked like an American tourist in London who saw everything as fun and interesting. She even smiled when she saw me, and she didn't seem to be faking her cheerfulness. Context was everything. I now saw her as someone utterly without boundaries.

"Are you seeing any gods right now?"

"Did you know about that all along?"

"We saw your medical records, so yeah, we know about your breakdown back in college," said Ariel. "When you gave up the religious studies."

I didn't answer her.

"What if you're not crazy? What if you're a shaman?"

"Funny. My father brought up that idea a few months ago," I said. "But I don't buy it. Shamans don't really fit in cities, especially not in the twenty-first century."

"Don't sell yourself short, babe. You get to see things I would kill to see. People usually have to take drugs to see what you see."

"Or take drugs so they don't."

"Like I said, you are too interesting to ignore," she said. "Even when our guys were grabbing Samir Langhani months ago, they noticed you trying to chase them down at the hotel."

"That was your lot that snatched Samir Langhani?"

"Don't be so shocked," Ariel said. "The Company stopped sending their own guys on extraordinary renditions a while ago. They outsource to guys like us so they can have deniability."

"So you've been in our faces all this time, and I didn't even know."

"We're just that good." Ariel shrugged.

There were no gods around. No, Kali was there. The tattoo on Ariel's arm. Signs and portents. Death and rebirth.

"Here's the deal," I said. "You get the thumb drive, and we get Sandra Rodriguez back, breathing."

"That could be a deal breaker," she said. "The Holloway-Browner side's been too much of a leaky boat, and our job is to plug the holes."

"Right now, your boss and my boss are negotiating with each other to play nice. I suggested a compromise that your boss might be open to."

"What's that?"

"Call your safe house and get let me talk to Sandra."

Ariel called Jarrod and asked him to put Sandra on. She handed the phone to me.

"Sandra," I said. "Are you all right?"

"S-so far," she stammered. "They haven't laid a finger on me, but I think they're waiting for the order. What's going on?"

"We're going to get you out of there, but you need to listen to me. I'm getting you a new job."

"Doing what?"

"What you do best," I said. "Investment banking, managing a hedge fund."

"Why are you bringing that up now?"

"Because you're going to work for Interzone."

"What?!"

"As an employee, you're bound by confidentiality. The contracts are getting drawn up now."

"What if I don't want to work for these fuckers?"

"Then you're going to meet up with Jack and Darren and talk about how you all ended up."

"How is this supposed to work?"

"It plugs the hole you opened up when you nicked those files. If you're Interzone's investment manager, you're entitled to know about and have access to those files. And think about it. Interzone has over a hundred million dollars distributed worldwide that they need someone to look after. You said you were the best at that, and thanks to Powys, you're not going to get hired by any other bank out there."

"I suppose I could make this work."

"I know you can. So it's a yes?"

"Shit. Yes. Yes!"

"David will sort out your contract and smooth over any rough spots with Holloway-Browner. The main thing is you agree not to leak the files you took."

"All right."

"When they took you, you were as good as dead. Think of this as being reborn."

I handed the phone back to Ariel and took out my own to set up the exchange.

Half an hour later, Marcie showed up with the thumb drive and Jarrod brought Sandra. Ken and Clive eyed Jarrod's men murderously while Mark took Sandra to the car, and Ariel plugged the drive into a computer. I gave her the password, and she opened the files to verify they were the real thing.

"Very smooth," Jarrod said.

"If you'd just given us a call in the first place," Marcie said. "We could have saved a lot of time."

"And lives," I said.

"He's not letting that go," Ariel said.

"There's one last loose end," I said.

"Shoot."

"Stuart Powys was your point man at Holloway-Browner and has been acting like he's the boss of this whole operation," Marcie said. "He's not. The Company is."

"We let him think so to save time," Jarrod said. "Alpha wannabe."

"He was getting paid a bonus from the Company to supervise the establishment of that account," I said. "He was supposed to share that bonus with the team that put that account together. That included Jack Higglesworth, Darren Cowley, Sandra Rodriguez, and the three other investment bankers whose names I'm sure you have as well. Do you see where I'm going with this?"

"Son of a bitch," Jarrod grunted as he put the pieces together.

"He used you to commit murder so he could keep some extra cash. Nothing to do with keeping the world safe. He's put you lot in the frame for two murder charges."

"This is fun," Ariel said, grinning.

"As I see it, someone needs to be the face of this whole mess so the CIA can keep themselves out of it," I said. "You lot have become a potentially embarrassing loose end if the police find out what you've been up to the last few days, and the CIA will deny anything to do with you, so I'm offering a solution to your problem, as well. Sandra Rodriguez only stole the files because Powys was a sexist prick who had her sacked, so this whole mess was his fault to start with. She never thought anyone would die. So why not lay the blame on the one arsehole who escalated the situation in order to game the system?"

"You have a bit of Old Testament in you, honey," Ariel said, still grinning.

"Bastards like him like to give orders without getting their hands dirty," I said. "He ordered the murder of three people. He's the type who never thinks about how the sausage is made as long as he gets his fat salary and club membership. It never occurred to him that one day, it'll be his turn to *be* the sausage. That day has come."

THIRTY-THREE

It was after eleven p.m. when Julia opened the door of the suite and let me in. She was wearing a tasteful but slinky black cocktail dress and the most crimson lipstick imaginable.

"Are you all right?" I said.

"Of course. Why wouldn't I be? He's in here."

She led us to the bedroom where Powys was laid out like a baby.

"He's all yours," she said.

Jarrod and his men came in for him.

"You'd been working the whole time?" I asked.

"Of course. The money's good. I told Roger and Cheryl we'd broken up, and they worked out my schedule so I didn't have to come in the office when you were around. I'm a freelancer, after all. They could just phone me when they needed me."

"How many cases did you work in the last three months?"

"Let's see." She made a mental count. "Twelve."

"Twelve?!"

"They were mainly meet and greets, arm candy, soft honeytraps. I was working with Marcie a lot, and Mark. And then Olivia used me a few times to expose a couple of Buddhist monks of sexual impropriety."

"Bloody hell! Did—did you have to have sex with any of the marks you were watching?"

"Of course not. Roger never insisted on that. He trusted me to find ways around that. I wasn't going to give in to my addiction."

"Oh, thank God for that."

"Don't worry, Ravi. I drugged his whiskey with a muscle relaxant. He can't move."

Considering that Julia was drugging a man to have sex with him when I first met her, drugging a man to avoid having sex with him now was a distinct improvement. And considering I'd just drugged a tabloid reporter the day before, I was in no position to judge.

"How long had you been working Powys?"

"Two days," Julia said. "Marcie gave me his schedule. He'd been living large in town after office hours, spending his bonus money. It was easy to pick him up from his favorite bar."

I looked over to Powys. He looked up from the bed at Jarrod and his men. If it were up to me, I'd have handed him over to the police, let him face the humiliation of a trial and jail term, but Marcie kept pointing out to me that if there was any chance of Powys singing to try to save his own skin, all would be exposed and everything would fall apart.

"Know how we got Jack Higglesworth to jump off the roof?" Jarrod said. "We told him that if he did it willingly, we would leave his wife and kids alone. We're making you the same offer."

Powys went pale. A wet spot appeared on the front of his trousers and expanded. He was fucked and he knew it. Live by the faked suicide and cover-up, die by the faked suicide and cover-up.

I didn't want to hear anymore. I took Julia out of there, leaving Powys to the three Rakshasas he'd unleashed. I drove Julia home.

"I'll call you. Is that okay?"

"I'd like that," she said, and kissed me on the cheek before she got out of the car.

THIRTY-FOUR

Powys's wife found his body in their garage the next day. Jarrod had Powys drug the dinner so his wife and the kids wouldn't wake up during the night when he went into the garage to meet with Jarrod. He was in his Jaguar with a hose attached to the exhaust pipe that ran into the closed window of the driver's seat. He even left a note about the shame the scandal had brought to his family and his responsibility for driving Joe Higglesworth and Darren Cowley to their deaths. Nice to see Jarrod and company could follow direction.

We contacted Mullins and let him rant about drugging him and stealing the thumb drive.

"Come on, mate. You were the one chasing the hair of the dog before lunchtime."

"I know how much I have to drink before I pass out," he grunted. "And one drink wouldn't have done it."

"You passed out right there in the pub," I said. "It wouldn't have been safe to leave the drive there with you like that. You can come pick it up from our office or we can meet and give it back to you."

He insisted I bring the drive to him at his office, with his editor and coworkers as witnesses. That was fine with me. I went in and gave him the drive, told him the new password we'd created for this drive. What he and his editor saw gave them orgasms and warmed their shriveled little tabloid hearts.

Olivia had taken a fresh drive and loaded it with the videos from Sandra Rodriguez's computer, the ones of her and her colleagues coked out of their faces and misbehaving. Not a single mention of the black-ops slush-fund portfolio. The *Post* ran the videos on their website and got their best clickbait for years. The videos went viral and stayed in the zeitgeist for months. Everyone hated bankers these days. The *Morning Post* was more than happy to fan those flames for more hits.

Mullins was well pleased. The story ran and ran and put his name in the game. Powys's death was the perfect punch line to his story about corrupt and misbehaving bankers, a boss who let power get to his head and let his underlings run amok, only for everyone to come crashing down in the most awful way, a sordid story of decadence and cocaine-fueled hubris. Shame, guilt, and depression, the sheer pressure of it all got to him at the end. This confirmed everything Sandra said in an interview that we arranged, after we briefed her on what to tell him. The paper would be milking this for weeks, letting its readers tut-tut over how low humanity had sunk and so on and so forth until the next big news story hit and everyone would forget this one.

Roger was so pleased with how all this had turned out that he gave me another bonus. I sent the bonus to Mrs. Dhewan to cover the last installments of my mother's debt. Glad to be rid of that blood money. I made up the last of the debt by depleting the savings I'd amassed since I started working at Golden Sentinels. I preferred the peace of mind of not owing any more money to the Asian Housewife Mafia, and anyway, Roger reassured me that we would be earning mint for the foreseeable future. If Mrs. Dhewan needed my services as an investigator, we could work out a new deal.

Even Laird Collins was pleased with the spirit of cooperation both our firms displayed, and sent a Fortnum & Mason Gift Basket to Golden Sentinels. After Benjamin checked that none of it was poisoned, which took about half an hour, everyone in the office polished it off by end of day. I didn't eat any of it, because I didn't want anything of Interzone's. Ken and Clive also refused, though I thought I saw Ken sneak the jar of Strawberry & Champagne Preserve into his pocket.

As for Sandra Rodriguez, her career in London was over. She said good-bye to friends and family and packed her bags for a plush office in New York City to manage Interzone's private hedge fund. She got what she wanted in the end: a big pay rise, more power and status, even if it was largely in the shadows. Not bad for someone who got a few people killed. We never heard from her again. Frankly, we didn't miss her.

Was I all right with all of this? What do you think? No amount of spiritual enlightenment would ever make me believe I was clean in my complicity. My karmic debt would have to be settled in due course, I'm sure. For now, I had to settle for managing to protect my client and getting something that passed for justice for the victims, but I was under no illusion it was real justice. Interzone, the gun that was used by Powys, would still be out there being aimed and fired by other powerful clients.

With their work done, Collins's people got on the first plane out of London; no doubt there were more people to do a security detail for, more poor bastards to extraordinarily render, or put down.

That left Ariel.

"Come see me off," she said on the phone that morning, like a cat playing with her food. "It's just polite, as one liaison to another."

When I showed up at her hotel to pick her up, I was greeted with the sight of her and Julia together in the lobby, all chummy and giggling like schoolgirls.

What. The. Fuck.

"The look on your face," Julia laughed.

THIRTY-FIVE

Ariel and Julia sat in the backseat while I drove us to Heathrow. I had resolved to say as little as possible to Ariel when I agreed to drive her to the airport, and Julia made that easier for me to keep my mouth shut while she flirted with Ariel in the backseat.

Julia met Ariel for a drink the night before when I begged off. She spent the night with her. Was she out to punish me? She knew how dangerous Ariel was. I didn't even have room to feel jealous or turned on at the image of them doing it. I was more preoccupied with the thought that Ariel would cheerfully murder us if she was ordered to.

Their schoolgirl flirting continued all the way to the departure terminal.

"Hey, Ravi." Ariel smiled. "You never told me about this firecracker you got."

"We had broken up at the time."

"So I was your rebound? Guess what? I was her rebound as well."

"The thing about rebounds," I said, controlling myself, "is they're temporary."

"You realize I'm bound to you now," she said, as she kissed me full on the lips. "Both of you."

She kissed Julia as well, a bit longer or was it my imagination? Was this to torture or titillate me or both?

"Till next time," Ariel said, picking up her carry-on.

"I sincerely hope not," I said.

"Babe, you know there's going to be a next time."

"Let me at least fantasize there won't."

"Hey, why don't you come with me to India? Offer's still open. Julia's open to the idea. You could use a vacation, too."

"Once again, I have to decline. Besides, life is even cheaper in India, and my chances of getting murdered there are much higher than if I stayed here."

"I'll protect you," she said jokingly.

"And who will protect us from you?"

"See?" said Julia. "I told you he'd say that."

"I'm going to miss you kids," said Ariel. "Julia, look after him, will you?"

We watched her go through the gate. She turned back one last time and waved like this was the end of a lovely holiday.

"Oh, one more thing." She seemed to remember something. "Watch your ass with that Marcie Holder, or whatever her name is. She'll sell you out in the end. Goddamn spooks always do."

Then she was gone.

"Right, then." Julia took my arm. "Shall we be off?"

She seemed awfully cheerful as we got in the car and drove down the M4 back to London.

"I suppose I should be glad I didn't have to slit her throat last night," she said.

"You what?"

"I was going to kill her. During sex. I brought a blade and everything."

That feeling of the world dropping away from my feet again.

"You're not joking," I said, rather weakly, because there was nothing else I could think to say even as my mouth was already moving, so the bleeding obvious became the only option.

"Marcie told me what had happened. That you were worried she might be a danger to you and your family."

"And to you."

"That's why I arranged to meet her for a drink. Suss her out, right?"

"I never wanted you anywhere near her."

"I wanted to see if she really was a threat. What I saw was that she has even fewer boundaries than me. Anything really does go with her. Once I saw that she was up for it, we went to her room and had it off. I didn't like her, so it fed my addiction something fierce. At least it was for a purpose. I made sure she wasn't going to forget it, even if she might be dead shortly after."

"You were going to murder her."

"If she was a threat to you. I decided she wasn't. For now."

This fucking job!

"She's a trained professional. She could have killed you instead."

"I got her right and proper drunk and tied her wrists to the bedpost with the sheets. I knew not to take chances. She was well into it. If she somehow got loose and killed me, I would have made sure I took her with me."

"Did you think about how you were going to get away with it if you survived?"

"Oh, Ken and Clive gave me a few pointers. Like taking a shower afterwards to wash all the blood away and scrubbing my prints off everything. If the law caught up with me, I would have said she attacked me and it was a sex game gone wrong. Why are you looking at me like that?"

"You could have gone to jail."

"But you would be safe from her. That's what matters in the end."

I felt the impact then, of how far she was willing to go for me, a gift I didn't deserve.

"I brought you into this job, and now it's warped you like it did me."

"Stop it, Ravi. I chose to work at Golden Sentinels. I always had it in me. The abuse I suffered, then the years of protecting Louise, I was perfectly prepared to kill to keep her safe."

"Well, I'm really glad my girlfriend hasn't committed murder. Or been murdered."

"Did you just call me your girlfriend?"

"Well, breaking up didn't exactly work, did it? Neither of us really wanted it."

"I told you. I don't need someone to protect me. I want someone to share my crazy life with."

"And I have the same crazy life."

"So we're stuck with each other, then?"

What was I going to say? I felt whole being with her, with her generosity, her seemingly infinite capacity to forgive, and her refusal to be less than an equal.

"Aren't you going to ask me for details?" she asked.

"About what?"

"About how she was in bed."

"I already know what she's like in bed."

"Well, it might be different with a woman."

"Unless there are real academic benefits to that, I'll keep it to my imagination."

"Don't you want a threesome? She would have well been up for it."

"No, thank you. I draw the line at sex with murderous sociopaths."

"Bit late for that, my love."

"That was before I found out what she really was."

"Semantics. Randiness knows no bounds."

"Might I suggest you talk about this at your next therapy session?"

"I'll leave out the murder part," she said, happy.

"I've never had a girlfriend willing to kill for me before."

"Ravi, do you want to quit Golden Sentinels? I'll leave with you if you decide that."

"I still need the money. And, well, sod it. There are people who are in real trouble that I can help."

"That's a far cry from all the times you were talking about getting out if it gets too horrible."

"I don't think Marcie will really let me truly quit, anyway. To her, I'm an asset she finds useful. So even if I were screaming and kicking, I'm well in it. I'm all in. Might as well accept it."

Ariel may have gone, but Kali was still there with me. She had probably been there all along, never leaving me.

EPILOGUE: A WEDDING, AN OFFER, AND A VOW

Weeks, months of preparation, rehearsals, and we were all gathered under the *mandap* for Sanjita and Vivek's big day.

Sanjita, dragged kicking and screaming (on the inside), and me with her. As her brother, I had my part to play in the rituals, of course, so we were in it together. We both vowed not to complain or snark and to play nice for the whole day.

This was what Mrs. Dhewan's twenty grand–plus loan had bought us: a full-on ceremony at a hotel with a large reception room to accommodate about three hundred guests in from India. Sanji and I probably recognized about fifty of the relatives from Delhi and Mumbai. We left it to Mum and Dad to greet and chat with them all while we smiled and nodded politely. We even hired a priest so seasoned that he didn't need to have a copy of the script in his hand as he conducted the ceremony.

The ceremony took place in the garden of the hotel on a slightly cloudy day. Some of my aunties complained that it was as bright and sunny as Mumbai, as we expected they would. We were lucky it didn't rain.

Sanji in a red sari and Vivek in a gold *kafni*. His family in from Delhi and Manchester. I could see on Vivek's face he was well into it. He was a bit more traditional than Sanji, after all.

We watched Vivek approach my mother so she could dab *kumkum* on his forehead. He bowed to Mum and passed her the coconut he was holding. Then she and Dad escorted him to the tent. Once he was in place, Sanjita came out with his garland in her hand, me and some flower girls following behind. Now it was on.

The priest began his speech to begin the wedding, invoking the Earth, the sacred fire and the radiant sun as the foundation of the marriage. The chorus sang the invocations to Lord Ganesh, to Saraswati, and a prayer for harmony.

Now the garlands for the bride and groom. Mum and Dad washing Sanji's and Vivek's feet, applying the kumkum, and giving them the flowers. Mum and Dad formally declaring their approval of Sanjita's marriage to Vivek. Sanji and Vivek declaring their commitment to each other.

I saw the curve of a smile in the corner of Sanji's mouth as she sat down first. As he presented me with his gift, Vivek exchanged a smile with me: we knew this would happen. Was there any doubt that Sanji was going to be the boss of this marriage?

Now the priest directed Sanji and Vivek through the seven steps: the blessing for an abundance of food, for wife and husband to be strong and complement each other, for prosperity, for eternal happiness, for children, for harmony, for friendship and trust in the marriage.

I glanced into the audience and caught Julia's eye. She wore a bright green evening gown and was getting on with my relatives. I knew there would be whispers about me dating an English girl even as the aunties would tease and gossip about when I would finally tie the knot. Of course some of them would talk loudly to my mother about getting a matchmaker to find me a proper Hindu girl. My father had a fixed smile as he went through the day tolerating the busybodies and the gossip.

Though it all, I felt a bit wistful. Here was my sister, my confidante and partner in crime in our childhoods and teenage years, a unit we formed to protect us from the high-strung craziness of our parents, now going off to form her own unit with Vivek. We would still have that bond of secrets and language, but she would be separate from me now, with her own husband and, eventually, children to get busy with. I was forming my own unit with Julia, with its own set of secrets and bonds. I glanced at my parents, and my father's eyes met mine, and I knew he was feeling the same mix of melancholy and happiness.

As the bride's brother, and the one who pretty much paid for the whole shindig, I was responsible for doing the rounds to make sure everything went smoothly while my parents got to be the doting in-laws giving away their daughter and holding court. My teenage cousins Francis and his sisters Priya and Anya were in charge of the guest list, the visitors' book, and greeting the guests.

The main rituals were over, and we settled down to eat at last. I went to join Julia and the smattering of Sanjita and Vivek's non-Indian friends.

"I'm so turned on by your outfit," Julia whispered to me.

My phone buzzed. Who the hell would be calling me? They knew I wasn't available.

I looked at the text message, and the blood drained from my head. Julia saw the text and asked if I was all right. I had to excuse myself to walk out to the waiting limousine at the front of the hotel.

Of course it had to be a Lincoln Continental, one of the few American limos in the UK. Even had tinted windows. I noticed the bulge under the jacket of the big, burly Rakashaka in the chauffeur's uniform to know he wasn't just a driver but an armed bodyguard. He opened the door for me as I stepped in.

"Forgive me for the intrusion, Ravi," Laird Collins said. "We've never formally met, and I thought I'd correct that. I'm on my way to the airport, and this was the only time I could squeeze in a meeting."

"You shouldn't have gone to the trouble. What's this about?"

"I have a proposition for you. An offer, if you will."

"What kind of offer?"

"Well, I'd like you to come work for me."

"Me?! What brought this on?"

"Don't be so surprised. We've been looking at you, and everyone at Golden Sentinels, but you were their newest addition. I read Ariel's After Action Report on the Holloway-Browner job. She was especially impressed with how you handled it. You could have cracked under pressure, completely caved in to Jarrod when he came after you."

"That wasn't just me. That was a team effort."

"Not according to Ariel. You were on your own when you seized the situation and negotiated terms with her just minutes after my people snatched Ms. Rodriguez. You changed the game from that moment on, all the way to turning the tide and having my people take out Stuart Powys, and tied it all up in a neat little bow. You saved our company's mutual boss a lot of trouble. That showed some serious strategic and lateral thinking."

"I wasn't thinking in terms of strategy. I was trying to keep my client and myself alive. Then I was thinking in terms of getting the bastard who set the whole mess in motion. Don't forget I still blame your men for being the weapons Powys used to murder two men. They still have to pay the piper."

"And they will. Eventually. Everyone has to account to God at the end."

"I prefer them to do it in this lifetime."

"Moral conviction. That's the other rare thing. Simply put, I like the cut of your jib."

"I really don't see what I could bring to your company, Mr. Collins. I'm strictly small-time. Street level. I'm not a trained soldier and certainly not a trained killer who can switch it on and off at will."

"Don't sell yourself short. You want to do good. I can see it in you. Ariel saw it in you, and she's very hard to impress."

"And what would I be working towards if I was with you? Perpetuating the global state of war? All to bring things to a head so we can bring about the Rapture?"

"The Kingdom of Heaven is a good thing, Ravi. It's the pinnacle of everything we as men can strive for. Once we succeed, there would be no more suffering, no more war. It'll be paradise, and no one will ever kill or hurt or die ever again."

"But what about the moral cost?" I asked. "All the people who die, all the suffering you're going to cause along the way?"

"They'll all be accounted for when they reach heaven."

"But you don't believe everyone will get to heaven. Only the born again will. As a Hindu, I don't get to go your heaven. So what's in it for me to work for you? I would be bringing about an apocalypse where I'll be screwed at the end if you succeed."

"I think you know the answer to that, Ravi."

"What, convert?"

He smiled. Paternally.

"Is that a prerequisite for joining your little shop?"

"It's not necessary, but it hurts less morally and psychologically if you believe. If not, just enjoy the money you make, and what it can buy."

"I see."

"Now, I know Roger brings in decent money with his diversified portfolio and services to his clients, but we're in a completely different league. Our contracts are worth tens of millions at a pop. We have a wider global reach with higher payoffs. You come work for us, you'll make your first million in a year. You'll be worth ten million dollars in just five years."

I looked at Collins, so sure in his fanaticism. His belief was so absolute that he was almost Zen about it. I'd thought I was a dead man when I came in here. Now I was feeling something completely different.

"So how about it?" Collins said. "You can bring Julia along if you want. I'm sure she'll stick with you. We'll offer her opportunities as well."

"You've read my medical records, so you do know I'm mentally unstable, don't you?"

"You're selling yourself short again, Ravi. From everything we've seen, you're perfectly functional. You're not schizophrenic. You don't act schizophrenic. If anything, I suspect your visions are what gives you an edge."

I could see it now. Laird Collins was a collector. He amassed resources, tools, and weapons, and he had no qualms about where they came from or if they went against his personal beliefs. He was practical in that respect.

"Mr. Collins, I'm Hindu. We believe in lots of gods. But even our gods are accountable to the cosmos. I've read the Bible. Your God declared, 'Thou shalt worship no other gods but me.' That implies that even the biblical god is aware there are other gods other than Him."

"Well, that's an interesting way of looking at it."

"So forgive me if I'm don't really think of the Supreme God as a white guy in the sky with a beard. The one in the Old Testament always struck me as a narcissist and a psychopath. If He was the same one in the New Testament, then it feels like He went into rehab and has learned to temper his nastiness with talk of love, but he was still the same abusive arsehole. Now, I'm not saying this to get into a pissing contest and how my gods can beat up your god. Why would they even want to? I think they have better things to do with their time, like watching us mere mortals make complete idiots of ourselves. My gods seem to enjoy watching me in particular act like a prat as I try to get through life in one piece. Praise the Lord and Hallelujah!"

"Are you mocking me?" Collins raised an eyebrow.

"I'm British. Our default mode is 'snark.'"

I watched his face for any anger or contempt, maybe even hatred, but aside from a momentary twitch of irritation in his eyebrow, he stayed unflappable. It was that air of absolute moral certainty that makes him the most dangerous man I've ever met. At least I knew where I stood with Roger: he was shifty and egotistical, but he wasn't rigid and he wasn't batshit-crazy.

"Mr. Collins, I'm going to let you in on a little secret," I said. "I'm an atheist."

For the first time, I saw his eyes widen in surprise.

"Yes, I was raised Hindu and I was a religious scholar, but at the end of the day, I don't believe there's a god who's a guy in the sky with a beard who's going to bring down divine retribution. Heaven or hell isn't in the afterlife, it's here, depending on which we decide to make. That's right. I don't believe in God. And at the same time, I think the gods are real."

"How can you think that?"

"They're in our heads. That's where they really live. Not out there waiting for us to end the world. We created them. They talk to me just like yours talks to you. We make them up as we go, and I don't like yours very much."

He looked at me and blinked a few times. He was trying to decide if I was taking the piss or if I was genuinely mad. For the first time, I saw uncertainty in his eyes, maybe even a little fear. Not fear of me. That would be ridiculous. He could kill me with his bare hands, and very quickly, if he wanted to, but fear of the unknown, of the utter chaos of the contradictory notions I carried, where the binary collapsed and everything was both true and false, and gods of everything snuck in and out of the nothingness.

"Mr. Collins, are you familiar with the expression 'Try anything once except incest and Morris dancing'? If you ever saw actual Morris dancing, you would understand why. I'm going to add 'working for a private military contractor' to that list. Now if you'll excuse me, I have a wedding to finish overseeing, and you have a flight to catch."

I got out of the limo and walked back to the hotel. *Back straight, look ahead, don't show how much you're shitting yourself.* I tried not to imagine a red laser dot on my back and a shot ringing out or poison in my food. Ridiculous paranoia. *Hold it together.*

Julia was waiting at the hotel entrance and sighed in relief when I got out of the limo and reached her. She'd watched the area surrounding the limo and said there wasn't anyone milling around who could be Collins's backup or muscle. She put her arms around me and hugged me tight. I nearly sagged into her arms. She had been as terrified as I was when I went into the limo.

We made it back to the banquet and sat down. I checked my phone and saw the recording of my conversation with Collins was intact. On Monday, I would be playing it to Roger and Cheryl at the office. Ken and Clive would grunt. Mark and Benjamin would applaud. Marcie would shake her head in amusement. David would be stoical. Roger would laugh heartily and go on a rant about Collins trying to poach his "best people," the greed of the man, and he would praise me for my loyalty. He would ask if my sister received his wedding gift, the £1,000 check he sent to the wedding. Yes, she did. She and Vivek were gobsmacked as Roger expected they would be. My mother was suitably impressed and my father harrumphed, but they were basking in the glow of their daughter's wedding to kick up too much of a fuss.

Even in the crowded hall, the gods found a way to sit behind me and join in the celebrations, even if I was the only one who saw them. I looked at them now, and they at me. They seemed pleased and raised their glasses to me.

"Over the last year since I started this job, I've destroyed a politician's career, destroyed an author's career, caused a man's abduction by the CIA, been directly or indirectly party to at least one murder. I'm now on the radar of a private military contractor. I'm being groomed as an asset by a CIA officer. Once you're in this, they don't let you leave. This becomes your life. You don't get to just quit. And all my own choices."

"You also helped a bunch of people."

"It's going to take me a long time to suss how much that balances things out," I said.

"We could try to leg it," Julia said. "We know how to get new papers. Just disappear, go somewhere, and start over."

"No. We both have family we care about. We have people who depend on us. It wouldn't do to just drop out of their lives suddenly. The grief and uncertainty isn't worth it. I'm owning this."

"Are you sure?"

"I'm going to see this to the end, and try to balance my karma."

"Whatever you decide, I'm with you," she said. "You and I are better together, since it won't make me any safer if we're apart."

She took my hand.

"So yeah," I said. "I'm all in."

And the gods applauded my decision.

Julia and I went into work together on Monday, the gods following eagerly behind.

ACKNOWLEDGMENTS

Much of Ravi's story was informed by the conversations I've had with various people over the last few years. It's a work of fiction trying to keep up with the craziness of the world without becoming a complete fantasy. Real life is already weirder, crazier, and more unpredictable than we realize.

Michael Wilson and Minh-Hang Nguyen's insights on politics, finance, power, recent history, and espionage were the biggest influence on my thoughts about genre storytelling and Ravi's story. They often told me about the real story behind the ones we hear about and reminded me to be suspicious of every official account.

Thanks to Alan Moore for the conversations about gods and our relationships with them, which came to inform Ravi's beliefs, and for reassuring me that I did not inadvertently rip him off. It was Alan who also understood instinctively the inherent, unspoken theme of Britishness in the figure of Ravi from the moment he heard this story, that it was about how many Indian-British people can be more British than the British in their embrace of the culture without losing their own.

Thanks to Roz Kaveney for playing sounding board and listening to my flights of fancy as I planned out the books, and to Richard Markstein for the perspective and reminders of the structures and workings of London that still course through the city's veins, that Ravi exists as part of the legacy left behind by his father George Markstein, who created The Prisoner TV series that has warped our perception of reality ever since.

Thanks to Leopoldo Gout for working tirelessly to get Ravi published, and for pushing for the magical realist layer that resulted in Ravi seeing the gods as part of his journey.

Thanks to James Handel for volunteering his time to help address some narrative issues and grounding some of the story where needed.

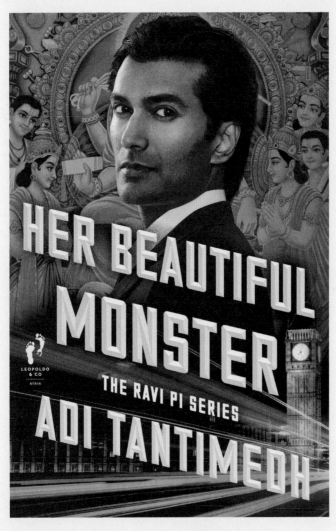